Published by:

Boss Status Publishing
304 S. Jones Blvd
Suite 2222
Las Vegas, NV 89107

Books published by Boss Status Publishing are available at special discounts for bulk purchase by corporations, institutions, individuals and other organizations.

Edited by: Pitta-Gay Powell

Cover design: M. Pirro

Author: Demetria 'Mimi' Harrison

ISBN: 978-0-996-94072-6

YURI'S VENGEANCE

DEDICATION

This book is dedicated to my big brother, Greg Mitchell. I've always looked up to him, but was too stubborn to listen when he told me to do the right thing; instead, I rebelled, ending up in federal prison. I learned my lesson and now I take feedback well. I will never put myself nor my family in that type of situation again, if I can help it.

I love you, Greg. May your soul rest well in Heaven. Every book that I write, from this point forward, is to make you and the rest of the family proud of me.

This book is also dedicated to my sister, Megan Jackson. Rest well, sis.

ACKNOWLEDGEMENTS

First and foremost, I would like to thank my Heavenly Father for giving me the breath, strength and creativity to come up with the concepts to write these books and let my imagination run wild!

Bringing a book to fruition takes more than one person. I would like to acknowledge everyone who had a part in bringing 'Yuri's Vengeance' to life. If I happen to accidentally leave a name or two out, please forgive me, know that you are appreciated, and that I am only human.

To my beautiful mother and my stepfather, Cathy and John Tate: words can't express how much gratitude I feel for you two. No matter how things turned out, you guys were still there for me. I'm home now, and I'll make up for the time we lost, God willing. Thanks for believing in me, no matter the situation.

My father, Charles Harrison: I haven't seen you in a few years, but you come through for me, like you always have and a real man is supposed to do for his child. I love you, Daddy! You guys raised me well.

My children, Benjamin, Shamika, and Sharoni'a: I thank God for my respectful and loving children. Even though I was in a place that children would never want to see a parent, especially their mother. You all showed me the respect and love that any child should show their mother. I thank you for understanding that no one is perfect, but God. No matter what, you all know that I'm still The Boss! Now I'm home and we're complete. I love you guys, with all my heart! God won't put more weight on us than we can bear. Like you always say, Sharoni'a, "We have to keep the Faith!"

My G. Babies, Ziah, Bryana, Nevaeh, Khaaliq, Akeem Jr., Khloe and Royal: I get to spoil you guys! G. Momma loves her angels!

My sister in law, Sheila, and my brother's siblings: even though you were grieving, you were right there for me! God will take care of all of us.

My sister, Charleszette: "Mimi" doesn't sound right without your name before or after it; that's how close we are! I love you, and your children and G. Babies. My sisters, Dorthy and Reenita. I love you ladies, more than you could know and my nieces and nephews. We're all in this together, blood in, blood out.

Special shout out to my nephew, Leon Nash: you made it home! Stay out of trouble, and stay focused on knowing there's a better life than behind those concrete walls!

My cousins, Zeb Lawson III and Kenneth Harrison: You guys always made sure I had commissary. Thanks for the support! I can take you guys out for dinner now.

To my cousins, aunts, uncles, and good friends: I love you all!

Team BSP; Alicia Mills: Thanks for all the help! I'm like Popeye with no spinach without you! Our time is here. Also, Kre, I love you all!

To my readers: Thank you all for your support, whether you like my work or not, without you all, I have no critics to help me improve.

Sherice Sr., Melanie, Charleszette, Devon, Adrial, Mardae, Carla, Tracy, Nicky, Anika, Victoria and Alvin. I LOVE YOU GUYS!

My cousin Val: thanks for being here for me when I needed it most, your mail made me smile, and kept me positive, and motivated.

Jacki Harris and Livingston Nelson, thanks for your mentorship.

To my little sister, Latess Hill: You always smiled and were encouraging while I was trying to accomplish this book. I'm standing on it, just like you better stand on your word about getting out there and laying those tracks down! Boss Up, Sis! We can do this! 1-Love!

My other little sister, Lia Hopkins, my P/R: thanks for helping me come up with ideas and for teaching me how to make cards for my family and friends. You are an inspiration. You're very talented! Now we're free and we can show the world.

To all my FPC Coleman and Greenville women: Yo-yo, Kim, Toya, TT. I am grateful to all of you who may have given me a punch line, or told me I wasn't just going to be a good author, but a great author. For the ones that are still on lockdown, God bless you!

Special salutes to Francine Sweet aka Gangster Granny, for helping me bring this book alive. I'm praying you come home soon.

My final super shout out goes out to my Boss Status, Bossy COO/ Best friend, Sherice Sr. Thank you for believing in my vision and always being willing to jump on board. Thank you for holding down our company when I was unable to do certain things. I couldn't have had a better business partner than you. Each endeavor gets better and better for us. Let's keep making it happen, Captain. It's 1:11 pm. 2017 is our year and every year after.

To my readers: Thanks again, for all the support. I do this for you!

I have so much love and admiration for you all.

Demetria 'Mimi' Harrison
Boss Status Publishing

MUTUAL RESPECT

On my journey through Federal Prison, at FCC Coleman Camp, I have met some of the strongest, most beautiful, intelligent women I have ever known! Most of them, including myself, did not deserve the sentences we were given. Whereas I did wrong, getting more time than murderers or sex offenders makes absolutely no sense! Michelle Alexander really puts it out there in her New York Times Bestseller, 'The New Jim Crow'. Everyone who is incarcerated and anyone facing incarceration should read it.

Many of the women in the Camps are there for very petty offenses. I have love for all of you! We all have bright futures ahead, if we believe! Some of my special Coleman ladies include Mrs. Betty Strickland, Tamaya Jenkins, and Ms. Sue from Miami Over town. We all will get home, just keep the faith!

To all the men I know who have, or had long sentences, or life in prison. Some have been blessed to make it home. Kevin and Joe Page who got a murderer's time, but never took a life; the ones like my two brothers, Dale Willis and Chad 'J-Bo' Brown; as well as Brian Thompson, Dave Throw 'Bezzy' Walker, Big Meech Flenory, Tom Tom Riley, Cortez Stacker, Ike Mc Cloud and my nephew, Seneca Harrison, I have respect and love for all of you. When will slavery end? Unfortunately, we are still living it! I hope change is coming. I love and respect you, strong men!

This section is mainly aimed at all the people who said, "Good, she went to prison. She didn't succeed, she failed." It's a small thing to a giant! I have already succeeded, with God's permission. I needed no one else's consent, but His. If nobody else believed in me, I believed in myself! Some people lack confidence and have self-esteem issues, I don't. For the ones who laugh at what a person is trying to achieve, the joke will be on you. We can do all things through Christ who strengthens us! I will not let anyone, nor the temporary detour stop my dreams. Some people think that when they come to jail, their life is over. Mine has just begun again! I'm FREE!

If you have a dream, never give up on it! It can become a reality with dedication and perseverance. Don't allow those who speak negativity to you keep you from reaching your goals! They are called dream and destiny killers. I will remain Boss Status all the days of my life, so if you can't beat me, join me! There's enough love out here for everyone. Don't envy the next person. I won't let anyone steal my joy: you shouldn't, either! God has given me a gift and I'm using it; not for fortune, nor fame, but because it has become a part of my life. God makes no mistakes. "And no weapons formed against me shall prosper." -Isaiah 54:17

Before I end, let me say a few words about prejudice, hate, respect and love. My editor and close friend, Francine Sweet, is a fifty-two-year-old, silver-haired, white, Jewish Grandma, turned 'Gangsta', through her partnership with me, in these writings. She is talented, smart and kind, and doesn't see the differences between us, because she can see people from the inside. We clicked. She 'got me' and could finish my sentences, leaving her 'whiteness' aside, and sharing my voice. We look, speak, and worship God differently, but we have so much love and respect for each other that none of those things matter. People tried coming in between our friendship by saying she was racist, but I know her better than that. We were a very powerful team and our differences, through our mutual respect, only made us stronger. Ignore the haters, and see with your heart. The world will be a much better place, when everyone thinks that way! Free Ms. Sweet

Boss Status forever!

CHAPTER 1

As Yuri laid in the bed heavily sedated, the psychiatrist from ward five, Doctor Snider, entered the room, staring at her for several minutes. He admired her beauty, and her body, with lust in his eyes. He walked over to the bed, lifting her gown, and began kissing all over her body. He heard someone walking down the hallway which startled him, making him jump because he knew what he was about to do was against the policies that the mental hospital stood for. He knew that he could lose his license and his career. He pulled down the gown acting as if he was checking her vital signs.

After he heard the footsteps walk past the room, he walked over to the door, opened it, looking both ways down the hall. Once the coast was clear, he closed the door and locked it.

He turned around to gaze at Yuri, once again, admiring her sexy figure, instantly causing all his blood to rush to his penis. On days that he knew he would get a chance to fuck Yuri, he made sure to pop two Viagra pills before he left home.

Doctor Snider was a very tall, skinny man, weighing only around a hundred and sixty-pounds. He was sixty years old, but didn't look a day over forty-five. He wasn't a good-looking man, but he was doable. Once he opened his mouth, his breath smelled like someone had taken a bad shit down his throat. Because of the daily coffee, cigarettes, and all off the ass that he licked around the ward, his breath was deadly. One of his craziest patients, Mary McClain, told him about his breath. She had even told a few of the nurses in the ward how his breath smelled every time he would kiss her; yet, no one would believe anything that the crazy women had to say. Doctor Snider knew that they would just laugh at her.

No one would believe any of the patients, giving him permission to get away with raping any he deemed worthy to have sex with or sodomize. Doctor Snider had a short, skinny, pink pecker. As he slivered towards Yuri, jerking it off, ready to take care of his favorite patient in the best way that he knew how. He licked his lips, moaning "umm," as he proceeded, pulling up her gown, and admiring her perky, 36B breast as he caressed and sucked on one then the other.

Doctor Snider was so infatuated with Yuri that he noticed she always stared at an ad in the newspaper for Marc Jacob's Decadence perfume, prompting him to go to Macy's and purchase it for her.

He sprayed her with the perfume, took in the aroma. He noted mentally how the smell went so well with her natural body odor. He started kissing her all over, from her head to her toes. He opened her legs, fastening them with the harness straps that were on the end of the bed then proceeded to crawl up her, moving like the snake that he was. Once he reached her midsection, he smelled her pussy and took a long deep breath inhaling and savoring the scent, taking his fingers, spreading her lips apart, putting his tongue inside of her, all the way down her hole. He licked and sucked on her as if she enjoyed it. He had violated her in every way possible while she helplessly laid there, sedated.

After he ate her pussy, he walked around to the head of the bed, touching himself, making sure that he was as erect as he could get, he stepped onto the stool that he kept by her bed and rubbed his dick across her lips, closed his eyes, pushing himself in her mouth. After he felt his dick dripping with pre-cum, he put on a condom, climbed up and positioned himself on top of Yuri, spreading her lips opened once again, so he could admire how perfect and pink it looked on the inside. Slowly, he slid inside of her, starting to fuck her as hard and as fast as he could, like a jack rabbit, not wanting to get caught but making sure that he would get off. He talked nasty in her ear, licking inside of it with his wet sticky stank breath as he continued raping her. The Viagra made it hard for him to release. After twenty minutes of pounding inside of Yuri, he knew he would have to hurry up and finish. He knew what to do to make himself cum quicker. He bit down on Yuri's bruised nipple, sucking hard on it, drinking her milk that never dried up. He had been sucking on her breast from the time she arrived at the ward, not allowing her milk to dry up since losing her baby. As he sucked harder, on her nipple, Doctor Snider filled his condom with his warm cum.

Once he finished, he carefully slid off the condom and the non-latex gloves that he had on his hands. He placed them in the sandwich bag that he always brought to work so that he could get rid of all the evidence - that could destroy him entirely. Finally, taking the face towel that he made sure to bring with him from home every time, he wiped Yuri's body down, straightened her gown, making sure that everything was right and back in place, before resuming his day of normal duties.

CHAPTER 2

Tuesday morning had finally arrived; it became the day that Yuri liked most because the male nurse was kind and treated her with respect. His hours were 7:00 a.m. to 7:00 p.m., Tuesday through Saturday. She had charmed Dexter over the past several months.

He entered the room to give her the daily dose of Effexor for her depression, and Zyprexa to treat her psychotic bipolar episodes.

Yuri wasn't near as crazy as everyone at the hospital thought, and Dexter knew it. She was a totally different person when Dexter was in her room. She would get naked and dance trying to arouse him. He realized that Yuri could move her body like a stripper, wondering what had made her go off the deep end.

A man maybe? He thought. Only the doctors knew why she was there and what had happened to bring her. Yuri would beg him to have sex with her. Dexter liked his job and never would he jeopardize his career for Yuri or anyone else, sane or insane. Though he thought Yuri was not as crazy as everyone believed, he was wary because she still managed to wind up on the mental ward.

Unlike Doctor Snider's nasty ass, he cared for her. He adored her body and the way she looked at him, but would never touch her, or take advantage of her. Dexter got a kick out of Yuri's flirting with him. As he observed Yuri, he knew that she wasn't like the other nuts that were there. She was smart, charming, and outspoken. She always wanted to read the daily newspaper and magazines, keeping up with latest style, and fashion. He noticed that she became very excited every time she looked at designer clothes, he could tell had she not been a little looney, she would be a fly girl.

Dexter was way more comfortable with Yuri than anyone else in the psych unit. He wouldn't even enter some of the other patients' rooms without backup. Other patients would throw shit at him and even spit on him if they had the opportunity. Dexter had worked the fifth floor, with some of the wildest and craziest patients for six years. He couldn't understand how Yuri even made it to the fifth floor, but he was kind of glad she was there; it was good to see someone half way normal.

When Yuri was admitted to the psych ward, Doctor Snider had given her a mixture of pills that was guaranteed to make her act out and appear crazier than she really was, knowing that she would automatically be assigned to his unit, the fifth floor.

Dexter thought once again at least he had one room he could go to without being attacked or tormented. He walked over to the chair where Yuri always sat, noticing that she was reading and staring at a picture, for the last two months. Dexter had brought her the paper she read this article at the same time every day. It was 2:15 p.m. as she read page A-14 from the Atlanta Journal of Constitution. The section read, "Engagement Announcements." He started reading it with her.

It read:

" *Brian and Yvette announces the upcoming marriage of their daughter, Ms. Chanel Denise Brown to Mr. Shane Deshaun Mitchell, the son of Clarence and Jamille Mitchell.*

The beautiful couple have been engaged for one year and are planning their wedding six months from today. The wedding will be in sunny Maui, Hawaii. Mr. Mitchell is a well-known real-estate broker. He also helps fund several homeless charities. Ms. Brown is an accounting analyst with National Bank and Trust in, GA. They are the proud parents of one son, Chandler D. Mitchell and plan to have several more children. Congratulations to the both of you."

Dexter had asked Yuri several times if she knew or remembered the people in the photo, because he noticed her expression changed from anger to frustration every time she read it. She told him it was a terrific story, and she wanted a fairy tale ending like theirs. But he knew otherwise, he could feel that something bothered her. She asked Dexter if he wanted to marry her.

He laughed, saying, "I'm taken, Yuri, but I know that you will find someone to make you very happy one day, and you must make him happy as well."

Yuri figured that she had been in the crazy hospital for over a year now, from the newspapers that she kept and counted. She looked at all the small burns that ran up her legs to her shoulder, relieved that her pretty face had not been marked up, and felt that she was still beautiful. If she wasn't reading the article she would be rubbing cocoa butter lotion that Dexter snuck in for her, all over her scars and bruises. He saw that she cared about her body and wanted to help her heal the wounds. They were almost gone, thanks to Dexter. She was only able to care for her scars when Dexter was on duty, because when Doctor Snider was around, he made sure she was always heavily sedated with the crushed Ambien that he made her take daily.

Yuri's hair had grown almost to her butt. It was already long; now, it was even longer, more beautiful and healthier than ever. Her hair usually stayed plaited in two cornrows, but today she took it down. Her hair was jet black, and silky. She showered, washed her hair and waited for Dexter to arrive. As he entered the room, he had his head down writing her room number on his board. He looked up and noticed Yuri standing there, looking beautiful.

"Wow, Yuri" he said with genuine admiration. "Look at you! You look great!"

Yuri blushed, trying to act shy, grateful that she was being admired by such a handsome young nurse.

"I feel great Dexter!" Yuri said, showing her perfect smile. He couldn't take his eyes away from her.

He sat his coffee down and pulled her pills out of his apron. Yuri asked Dexter to get her some tissue because her nose was running. Dexter didn't have a problem with that, but he told her she would have to promise to take the pills with no argument. He knew Yuri didn't like taking the pills.

She said the same thing every time: "I'm not crazy, Dex. These people are crazy."

He would shake his head and laugh, "I believe you, Yuri."

She smiled and promised she would take her pills without a fight. Dexter went and got her tissue and came back to the room smiling, He was hoping she would keep her promise and take her medicine. He handed Yuri the tissue and told her to take her pills.

Yuri pouted and folded her arms like a child, "I don't want to take anymore medicine."

Dexter couldn't help but smile at her childish ways. "But you promised Yuri."

Yuri responded, "People break promises all the time. Sit down and talk to me, just for a few minutes."

He chuckled, "Yuri, I have six more patients to give out meds to, I can't sit here with you right now."

Yuri pouted, "Please?"

Yuri always got what she wanted, even when she wasn't totally in her right mind.

"Okay, Just for a minute.

Dexter sat down and grabbed his coffee, "So, what's up?"

Yuri couldn't help but smile,

She started talking about what her wedding would be like, and the kind of man that she dreamed about - one who would make all of her dreams come true and wife her. After ten minutes, had passed, Dexter was sitting back in the chair listening, totally relaxed. He smiled at Yuri as she chatted away. Yuri watched his eyes open and shut. Her subject totally changed, he could hear every word she said. He just couldn't move.

"Dexter, I'm sorry that I had to do this to you, but you will be okay. They will find you in a little while and pump your stomach from the pills I gave you. Now do you see why I don't like this medicine? It has me sleep within twenty minutes and I'm useless on it. I can hear when they call me crazy, I feel when Doctor Snider plays in my pussy and fucks me, then stick his long pencil dick in my mouth. Yuck!"

She leaned over and kissed him on his lips sorrowful for what she had just done to him.

"I don't like feeling helpless, oh, and for the record, he better watch his motherfucking back because not only did he violate me, he violated me with his skinny little pencil dick! I hate little ass dicks Dexter!"

Yuri was flipping out.

She repeated, "I hate little ass dicks!"

As Yuri reached into Dexter's pockets for his keys, she kissed him once again.

"Thank you Dex, for always respecting me and not taking advantage of me while I was defenseless."

She grabbed her only three possessions: her comb, brush, and the article from the newspaper she couldn't stop reading. With those items in hand, she unlocked the door, peeked out, and waited for the other nurse on duty to enter another patient's room so she could make her move. She walked out of the room, locking the door behind her like they always did to her, and escaped with vengeance in her eyes.

CHAPTER 3

As Yuri walked out of the crazy hospital, she inhaled the fresh air. She had not been outside in over six months, which made her skin pale. She concluded that places like this one that she had been held captive in made people crazy, if they were not already. She felt bad for all the patients because she knew all the medications they gave them would make the sanest person incapable, helpless and disillusioned.

Yuri had no money, not even to make one phone call. She walked quickly until she was far away from the hospital. Her outfit wasn't the best, but it wasn't the gown that all of the patients wore. She tried remembering who had given her the dress. She knew it was after she had been admitted to the hospital. It helped her blend in with the everyday crowd; not confirming her status as an escaped patient. As she hurried down the busy street, she now remembered where the dress came from.

When Yuri had arrived at the Henry County Psychiatric Facility, one of the doctors would come in wearing a pretty blue dress. Yuri always stared at it and touched it when she made her rounds. Before Doctor Lozada retired, she brought the dress in for Yuri, along with a cute pair of flats to match. She had definitely made Yuri's day. Some days when Yuri wasn't drugged up, she would get dressed and dance all around her room.

Today had been the perfect day to wear the dress and shoes because she walked out of the nut house without raising any suspicion. She looked just like a visitor. She walked as fast as she could, knowing soon they would go into the room, find Dexter and realize that she had escaped.

Once she was well over a mile away, a guy driving a truck slowed down, checking her out.

He called out to her, "Hey sexy."

She kept walking until she remembered she was broke, carless and needed a lift.

"You need a ride?" he asked.

She played like she was close to home saying, "My apartment is not far, but thank you."

He still tried to talk as she kept walking. Yuri looked out of place, although still beautiful.

He continued, "What's yo name?"

She smiled, thinking about how Georgia people never said whole words. "I'm Angel, and yours?"

"Tony," he replied. Even though he was a little too homely to be her type, she had to play along.

"Nice to meet you, Tony." He wouldn't let up.

"Do you have a number where I can call you?"

With a quick attitude, she replied, "No."

He ignored her tone and kept trying, "Do you have a man because I'm trying to get up with you?"

Yuri smiled as she thought to herself, *I still got it.*

She realized she needed a place-to stay so she did what she did best and went into her act. She started crying uncontrollably.

"What's wrong?" he asked.

"I had a fight with my boyfriend and he put me out," she managed between sobs. "He wouldn't even let me take my bag or my cell phone!" She could have won an Oscar for her performance.

He yelled, "That is so cruel!"

She cried harder. After driving as slow as he could while Yuri walked, Tony pulled over finding a parking spot. He got out, catching up as she walked.

"There's a little diner up the road, can I walk with you up there and buy you a cup of coffee?"

Yuri wiped her fake tears. "I guess that would be fine."

As they walked down the street, he asked, "So how long have you been with him?"

She started to say with who forgetting her story, but remembered she had to keep up with her lies. Yuri had now become Angel.

"Over a year, I moved in with him six months ago, but he puts me out every three weeks. I'm so tired of this shit!" She cried some more. "He is mentally and physically abusive. I don't know what I'm going to do."

She whimpered softly. He fell for it.

They walked into the diner and were seated immediately. There weren't many people, which made Yuri feel a little more comfortable.

The waitress asked, "Can I get you guys anything to drink before you order?"

"I'll take a sweet tea," Tony said, looking at Yuri. "And for the lady?"

Yuri asked for a lemonade. Her stomach immediately started growling when the aroma from the food hit her nose.

Tony heard it and asked, "Damn, is he starving you too?"

Embarrassed by his comment, Yuri responded, "Well, he put me out last night and I had nowhere to go. The only friend I had in this city, I stopped talking to her when I got with him. He never wanted me to talk or hang out with anyone. So now I'm all alone." A tear ran down her face.

When the waitress made it over to their table, she cheerfully asked, "What are you guys having?" Tony ordered a BLT sandwich and Yuri ordered a bacon cheeseburger, fries, and onion rings. Tony couldn't help but smile, thinking, *damn she can eat.*

Once the waitress came with their food, Yuri was quick to grab Tony's hand and pray over their meal. They started eating, and for every one bite of food Tony had, Yuri managed to shove three bites in her mouth.

Tony laughed, "Hold on, sweetie. You have to chew, before you choke."

She slowed down. Yuri had not eaten food so good in so long that she acted like a kid that hadn't had anything to eat in days. The food that she ate at the ward was tasteless.

She wiped her mouth and apologized, "Sorry, I was hungrier than I thought."

He chuckled, watching the beautiful, distraught woman enjoy her meal.

Tony asked, "So where you going to go, if he won't let you come back?"

Yuri had not thought about that, yet. She did not know how but she needed to get out of these clothes and figure it out. Yuri didn't know anyone she could call in Atlanta. She had double-crossed everyone. The only numbers she knew by heart were her mother's and father's. She knew Barb still hated her and wouldn't help her do anything.

"Tony, may I please use your phone to call my father? He'll help me."

Tony was relieved that she had someone to help her, handing Yuri the phone. "Sure, take your time."

She called Mike, who was still living in Florida with his wife, and Yuri's half-sister, Janie.

The phone rang a few times, Mike finally answered, "Dr. Jones, how may I help you?"

Yuri couldn't help but cry; this time real tears.

She managed to whisper between sobs, "Daddy?"

Mike was so relieved to hear his baby girl's voice. "Yuri, baby, how are you? Where are you?"

Yuri could hear the pain in his voice. She turned and noticed Tony staring at her, so she asked if she could step outside to talk to her father.

He assented, "Sure, I'll be here when you get back, Angel."

"Hello! 'Angel' now are you?" Yuri's father asked painfully.

Yuri managed to stop crying, "I'm okay, Daddy."

"You don't sound okay. What's going on? I've been trying to locate you for over a year and a half. No one knew where you were. I called your Mom over and over and that woman has a vendetta against the world. I've even put out a missing person report on you. Thank God you're okay."

Yuri didn't even think twice about telling her father the truth, "Daddy, I've been in a relationship with this guy that was abusive. Today I walked away with nothing but the clothes on my back, and I have no money and nowhere to go. "

Mike was getting angry.

"Bastard! He growled. I can arrange for a car to pick you up and take you to the airport. I'll get you a plane ticket to come to Miami."

Yuri was quick to cut him off, "No, Daddy! I don't want to intrude on, you like that…"

"Yuri, don't be ridiculous. You're my daughter, you could never intrude on us. Please, don't hesitate to come if you have to."

"Daddy, I just need a little cash to get me on my feet and, I'll start fresh, get a job, and be okay."

Mike didn't like the idea of leaving his first born by herself, but she always got her way

"Alright, Angel, I'll Western Union you $2,500 and I hope that will help. I hope you don't plan on going back to that son of a bitch."

Yuri smiled to herself, "Don't worry Daddy, I'm never going back there. Daddy, I don't have my ID to pick up the money and they only let you receive up to a thousand without identification."

She remembered anything and everything about money.

"Well, look, I was about to call my buddy, Larry Harper. He works at Atlanta Medical. Are you still in Atlanta because that's where you were the last time that we spoke?" Yuri responded "Yes daddy, that's where I'm at." "I will have him meet up with you and give you the cash. What area are you in?"

"Hold on, Daddy, let me see," Yuri rushed back inside towards Tony. "Tony, where are we?"

Tony was puzzled, "Down the street from your house."

Yuri looked frustrated, "I just can't think straight right now. I meant, is there somewhere you can take me to meet my Dad's friend so I can get some money for a room?"

Tony suspected she was up to something, but decided to help her out anyway, "Sure, I don't have to go back to work, tell him we are in Henry County. Where do you want to meet him?"

"Daddy, I can meet him wherever is convenient for him, but Daddy, I can't even rent a room because he kept my purse."

Mike sighed, "Don't worry, Angel. I'll call the Hilton Downtown. I know the manager very well so head down there and by the time you get there everything will be taken care of. Larry will bring the money there, also."

"Thank you, Daddy! I love you!"

"You're welcome, Baby. I love you, too! It's good to hear your voice, but you have to at least come to Miami to visit. Your sister keeps a picture of you in the little purse that she carries around always talking about her big sister."

Yuri thought, *I hope she doesn't carry on like me.* But she only said out loud, "I will soon, Daddy. Thank you again."

She hung up and told Tony to go to the Hilton Downtown. He paid for the food and was on the move. Tony jumped on the freeway headed towards 75 North. He popped in a Jeezy CD, and the first thought that came to Yuri's mind was Candice. She laid back in the truck, closed her eyes, taking in what must have been

Jeezy's newest release. She started thinking. She began to remember it all.

Everything that had happened flashed right before her eyes. She remembered Candice at the hospital talking crazy as hell. Candice was there with Passion, a stripper that worked at a club. She remembered seeing the hate in Candice's eyes. She also remembered seeing Shane in the hospital bed, and how he looked at her with pure hatred in his eyes, and how he looked at Chanel. She was the only one there for him while he was on his death bed. After that, her thoughts became a nightmare. She closed her eyes tighter...

As she laid on the basement floor, she clearly saw Chanel slap her around. While she was drugged. Chanel burned her perfect skin with a cigarette. She moved around in her seat, but she couldn't wake up. Chanel took a broomstick and started ramming it up her ass while she screamed about how Yuri had fucked her brother, Chance.

Out of nowhere, there stood Chance in her dream, butt-naked. He walked over toward her and stood on a chair. He started jacking himself off. He worked his dick as hard as he could to bust a nut. He tugged and tugged and before he came, he jumped off the chair and hung himself.

Yuri let out a loud scream almost causing Tony to wreck.

"Angel," he tried to wake her by shaking her leg. "Wake up, sweetie."

She jumped up, looking around, with her guard up and moving closer to the car door.

"Are you okay? I think you were dreaming?"

Yuri wiped the sweat off her head. "Sorry, I'm fine."

When they pulled off the exit, Yuri looked over the freeway and noticed the club where she first met Uno. It only brought back more memories. She remembered the day she followed Uno, trying to set him up for Shane, only to witness the mafia-style shootout that took place. She remembered the call that Detective Wallace had received, that one man was found dead on University Avenue. Her past was all but flashing right before her eyes.

Pulling up to the Hilton, Tony interrupted her thoughts. "Angel, we're here."

The Hilton would be paradise compared to the crazy house that Yuri had lived in over the past year. Before she climbed out of Tony's truck, he asked if he could see her again if she didn't go back to her boyfriend. Yuri assured him that he would see her again, asking for his phone number. Tony wasn't good looking in any shape, form or fashion, but, with all of the memories that came to mind, she figured that he could come in handy later.

She leaned over and kissed him on the cheek, thanking him. "You'll hear from me soon T. Is it ok if I call you T?"

"You can call me anything you want, and I'll come a-runnin'," he said.

Yuri knew right then that she could manipulate Tony into doing things for her just by the way he looked at her. She also knew that men would do anything for a piece of new pussy.

Yuri checked into the hotel with clout from her rich doctor daddy. He had already paid for the room for two weeks, with a sixty dollar a night room service limit. The suite had a living room separate from the bedroom. The bathroom featured a Jacuzzi, sunk into the middle of the floor. This was how Yuri was used to living and things were about to change.

CHAPTER 4

Yuri knew that it was time to start getting money flowing again in some kind of way. When her dad's friend delivered her daddy's money, his mouth dropped at the sight of her. She had just showered, and answered the door wearing only a towel.

Larry could not believe his eyes, "Wow, you're Mike's daughter?"

Yuri smiled seductively "Yes, sir."

She let him in and strutted over to the couch with her wet ponytail hanging down her back.

As he counted the money, his hands shook. Larry didn't know what had come over him, but he felt some kind of strange attraction towards Yuri. He had to recount the bills several times because every time he got to one thousand, he had to start over. Yuri finally nicely took the money out of his hand counting it herself, her soft touch sent sparks through his entire body, making him red-faced. She teased him, every time she reached one thousand dollars, she would lick her finger to flick the next hundred. After she counted it, he asked how old she was.

"I'm 23, but don't you know that you should never ask a woman her age?" Yuri winked at him.

That was his cue to get the hell out of there. He knew that he had to leave that instant because he found himself getting a hard on, and Yuri was enjoying every minute of getting him aroused.

"And how old are you handsome?"

Yuri's flirtatiousness was infectious.

"I'm 46," he replied.

"I like older men."

Larry tried to appear unaffected.

Yuri knew that Larry had money, because he was an anesthesiologist, easily grossing $350,000 a year. Larry had a wedding band on, but Yuri could tell that he wasn't sexually satisfied. She could read men better than she read books. Yuri knew that if she seduced Larry, she could get what she wanted and he would never tell her dad. She knew he wouldn't ruin their longtime friendship.

After Yuri counted and put away the money, Larry told her that he hoped she would be fine and not to go back to the scumbag that had put her out like only a coward would. Before he made it to the door, Yuri was standing in front of him.

She grabbed hold of his tie and asked, "How would you treat me? Would you treat me any better?"

Larry tried to back up, but his back was against the wall. "Yuri, I... I..."

He couldn't even get it out.

He closed his eyes, concentrated hard, was finally able to speak. "I'm going now."

Yuri noticed the bulge in his pants.

"Why? Your dick is hard and it looks like it wants to go somewhere else." She dropped the towel and grabbed his hands, putting them on her titties.

Larry snatched his hand back, "Yuri, I can't do this. Your father would kill…"

Before he could get the rest of what he wanted to say out, Yuri grabbed his crotch and started rubbing it hard. "Please don't go, I don't want to be left alone." She started kissing his neck, rubbing her hard nipples against his chest. Larry tried fighting the feeling that was taking over him, but Yuri won. Once he couldn't take it anymore, he picked her up and carried her to the bedroom. Yuri laid on the bed, opened her legs and played with her pussy. Larry watched as he undressed. Larry was a very attractive older man, he turned Yuri on. Finally, she would have sex willingly after being raped and sodomized by Doctor Snider over a years' time. Larry crawled on the bed, trying to get inside Yuri. She stopped him, grabbed the condom that she had found in Tony's truck.

She told Larry, "Before we fuck, I have a special treat for you."

She pulled him off the bed, and dropped to her knees. She studied Larry's hard dick as if it was a new science project, which had him anxious to see what she had in mind.

She looked up at him with lust in her eyes, saying, "I like the size of your dick."

She spat on it, taking him into her mouth. She sucked on the tip seductively, making Larry almost stumble back. She then took him all the way in her mouth, pulling him back towards her like a vacuum cleaner. Larry grabbed the back of her ponytail, and stroked her mouth. It was exactly what she wanted him to do: let go.

"Oh shit! I shouldn't be doing this," he whispered, moaning with pleasure as she sucked harder.

She said, "Well, take your dick out of my mouth and walk away, sexy."

Larry knew there was no way he could stop, there was no turning back. He wanted her as bad as he felt she wanted him. As she sucked his dick, she reached over to the table, pulled a piece of ice out of the cup without once letting his dick come out of her mouth. She knew that he was intoxicated by what she was doing to him, she had the effect on so many other men in the past, as she thought of the old saying: a tiger never loses its stripes.

She put the cube in her mouth, continuously sucking. Yuri made the freezing ice cube melt around his dick, taking both the cube and him to the back of her throat where his whole dick disappeared. Larry pulled out of her mouth, and fell back onto the bed. Yuri had buckled him, making him almost lose consciousness. Larry thought he saw the moon and stars, but had not even cum. He could barely breathe, but when he saw her climb on the bed on her knees with her ass up, he got it together, grabbed the condom that she had set on the night stand, put it on and fucked Yuri like he would fuck girls back in his college days. Since he was married now, sex wasn't the same: good, but nothing like what he was experiencing at this moment. Yuri changed that, she made him feel impulsive and optimistic, making him positive that he still had what it took to please a woman.

For the next two hours, they pleasured one another - Yuri fucked Larry and sucked on his dick like no one had ever done before. Once again, she could work her magic, and gain control over another victim. Within that first week, Larry had come back twice and Yuri pleased him each time with a different tactic.

He promised her that he would provide whatever she needed, but never wanted it to get back to her father. She assured him that she would never tell her dad; not only would it destroy their friendship, she would never want her father to know how she seduced men, especially his good friend. He also explained to her that he was married and how much he loved his wife, and would never do anything to hurt her.

Yuri thought, *He's been eating my pussy and fucking me all week, but doesn't want to hurt her. What does he think he's doing?*

Yuri did not once think that she was the reason; she played the victim.

Yuri still had $1,100. She had yet to ask Larry for anything, but when she did, she knew that she would hit him hard every time. Yuri had spent $1,200 on her new wardrobe and eating out. She had gotten tired of room-service and started eating at restaurants every day. Her clothes weren't Gucci like before, but she still wore nice things. Instead of Juicy Couture sweat suits, she had downgraded to Victoria Secret's Pink Collection, which looked even better on her.

Yuri had one week left at the hotel. She had gotten her Social Security card and ID back, but she knew that she couldn't use her name because she didn't want the people from the nut house to find her - or anyone for that matter. She meant what she said; she wasn't going back.

Three days before it would be time for Yuri to leave the Hilton, she called Larry. She asked him to stop by after work.

Earlier that day, she had gone to Victoria Secret, and bought the sexiest outfit that she could find. She purchased a bottle of Bond #9, spending two more hundred dollars and leaving her with ninety-three dollars. She knew she had to make tonight count.

Larry knocked. As Yuri opened the door, he was already turned on, ready to rip off his clothes. Her hair, which she always wore pulled up into a pony tail since the day they met, now hung loose, allowing her fine, silky jet black curls to bounce around, just like her fat ass. She turned and walked towards the couch. Larry was completely aroused as he watched her hair damn near touch her ass cheeks. Her fat ass ate the string of her thong. Her body was perfect. Except a small scar that crossed her stomach, which Larry had never paid attention to until now. It didn't matter. Yuri had the best pussy and gave the best head that he had ever had in is life! Larry immediately started taking off his clothes.

Once he reached the couch, he said, "Damn girl, what have I got myself into that I can't get enough of you?"

He reached to grab Yuri's breast, but she stopped him, holding his hands in her own. "How much do you like me, Daddy?"

Larry frowned, "Don't call me Daddy, it reminds me that I'm fucking my buddy's daughter.

She grabbed his dick, not caring about what he had just said, asking him once again, "Daddy, how much do you like me?"

Larry smiled mischievously.

"I like you a lot, baby," he said, while yearning to touch her skin, and longing to be inside of her, but she wouldn't let him.

She bent down, kissed his dick, making his veins pop out.

"I don't want to go back to my boyfriend and I don't want to ask Daddy for any more money."

She put his dick all the way in her mouth this time, wetting and warming it with her tongue, looking up at him with her seductive big brown eyes, putting him straight into fuck mode.

Larry closed his eyes and said, "As long as you keep making me feel the way you do, you can have whatever you like."

Yuri knew she had him right where she wanted him. She really liked sexing him. After being raped while she was unconscious by Doctor Snider for a whole year, it felt good to be in control. It really helped, to know that he was packing for a forty-six-year-old man, which wasn't all that old, but made things a whole lot better.

Once Yuri heard those magical words, 'You can have whatever you like,' She fell down on her knees and sucked his dick like a porn star. She licked all around his balls, sucking on them gently, then licking the crack of his ass making him shiver. Yuri was doing things to Larry that he had never experienced. He felt like he was about to explode. She stopped sucking, climbed on top of him and rode his dick like the stallion he was. Yuri did everything that he had not received for so very long.

As she rode him, she looked into his eyes and took charge, like she used to.

She wrapped her hands around his neck and asked, "Whose dick is this, Daddy?"

He screamed out like a bitch, "Yours, baby, yours!"

She lay totally flat on to him making every thrust count winding and grinding her body into his.

She asked, "How do I feel, Daddy?"

He could barely breathe, "Damn Yuri, it's so wet! You're going to make me cum."

Yuri smiled, "Where do you want to cum, Daddy?"

Larry was quick to respond, "Inside of your pussy, baby! Oh, oh, oh."

Yuri knew she didn't want a baby, so she jumped off Larry's dick just before he came. She put it in her mouth and sucked all his cum down like water going into a drain.

Larry was amazed at how Yuri could swallow like she did. Her sex was so good that it brought tears to his eyes.

As they both lay there breathing heavily, Larry asked, "Baby why don't you ever let me cum inside of you?"

Yuri ran her fingers through his hair, "Because we started with using condoms; now we're practicing unsafe sex; and what would you say to your wife or my father if you got me pregnant?"

She had a point; and the way Yuri swallowed cum, who really cared about anything else?

Yuri climbed on top of Larry and started asking for everything she ever wanted.

CHAPTER 5

One month had passed by and Yuri was staying in Larry's downtown apartment. Larry's wife didn't have a clue about the apartment, because Larry used it when she pissed him off and he needed to get away from her. He went to an auction in town and bought Yuri a 2013 Lexus, which was only five years old. Yuri didn't care what year it was, she just needed to get around.

Yuri started getting back into her usual wardrobe. Larry had very good taste, and a Black American Express card that wifey didn't know anything about.

Yuri had seen pictures of Larry's wife. She was an Asian and black mixed woman who worked as a pediatrician. She was thirty-five years old, yet she had the body of a 24-year old model. Yuri could tell she stayed in the gym. She stood around 5' 2" and weighed 125 pounds. Yuri thought her height would never have allowed her to become a model. Yuri was amazed how he could cheat on someone so smart and beautiful. Yuri noticed the bag in the picture that his wife was carrying, she knew that a python bag like that would easily have cost at least five thousand dollars or more. She made a vow that she would fuck and suck his dick so good that she would be laced up like wifey, or even better.

The week that Yuri received her car, she called Tony to thank him for giving her a ride downtown, and also for helping her when she needed him most. Tony was surprised to hear from her. He told her that it was his pleasure and he would like to take her out sometimes. She told him that she would like that, but first, if he wasn't busy at the moment, that she wanted to treat him to lunch, maybe to the same place that they had eaten lunch the day that they had met. Tony was all in, he decided he was going to take the rest of the day off from work. She asked him which exit was the restaurant off. Tony was kind of puzzled.

"The same exit you lived on with your ex-boyfriend," he responded.

Yuri had been so drugged up that day, and days before meeting Tony that she didn't know where it was nor how to get there. Everything was a blur, before, during, and after - all she knew was that she woke up in the crazy hospital. She couldn't even remember how she ended up in the nut house to begin with, but as weeks went by, her memory resurfaced.

She realized she needed to rephrase her question, "What street is the restaurant actually on?"

He told her that it was off Eagles Landing, and that he would meet her there.

"Okay," Yuri responded, "see you there."

She knew she would be able to find her way from there. She could have cared less about the restaurant, what she was really looking for was the hospital, which she knew was about a mile and a half away from the restaurant. Her top priority was finding Doctor Snider, and making him pay for everything that he had done to her.

When Tony saw Yuri at the restaurant, he was in awe. It was a total transformation from when he had met her she had been wearing an unflattering, homely sundress. Her hair was long and curly, but a little too greasy. Now her hair was straight, flowing with body down her back. The jeans she had on looked as if they were painted on her body. She smelled and looked fabulous. It was as if she had stepped out of some type of fashion magazine. Tony's mouth just hung open. He was speechless.

Yuri smiled, "Hey, T."

Tony said nothing so Yuri asked, "Are you okay?" He still just stood there staring at her.

He finally responded, "Wow, if it took for you to leave ya man ta look like that, you should have never been with him, and you should never go back!"

Yuri and Tony laughed.

Tony was lighter than Yuri remembered and uglier as well, but he was kind. His eyes were too pushed together, making him look cock-eyed. Yuri thought he looked better the first time, or maybe it had been the drugs.

Tony was short, around 5'5", with a stomach that looked as if he would deliver a baby at any moment. He had a couple of teeth missing on the left back side of his mouth, making his jaw cave in, giving him the look of an old man. His grammar was terrible, bringing memories back of Uno. Tony's jeans fit way too tight. His high-top Nike sneakers leaned to the middle, because he was pigeon-toed – but none of that mattered, because he was going to be Yuri's friend. After all she didn't have any.

Once they were seated, Yuri ordered a ginger ale. She told the waitress to take Tony's order, as well as his drink, stating to him that he could order whatever he wanted. Tony ordered his food, while hoping he could spend the rest of the day with Yuri. That thought didn't last long. Yuri told him that after they ate, she would have to go on a job interview, but she wanted to return the favor. Tony was a little disappointed, but he was glad that he was blessed to have had such a stunning woman in his presence and call him back to repay a favor.

It was a first for a woman to do something like this, and he prayed it wouldn't be her last.

Yuri asked, "So, Tony are you single?" he smiled,

"Ye, very single. Why, you lookin' for a new man?"

Yuri couldn't help but smile as he flirted. "No, not quite yet, I was just wondering."

Tony replied, "Well, I was tryin' to get with dis lil' shawtee, but she wanted way more than I was able to give her. Turn out she was usin' me. I work at the water company durin' da day, and to make some extra money, I started workin' at Quik Trip, in Jonesboro that's where I met La'Quenishia…"

Before Tony could continue, Yuri interrupted, "LaQu-what?!"

Tony laughed.

"Her name is a lil' complicated, it's La-Que-nishi-a."

Yuri just about fell over laughing, saying, "Sorry to say, her name isn't complicated, it's ghetto as hell!"

Tony knew this to be true because his boys and everyone else said the same thing.

He went on telling his story.

"So, we started talkin' and she would always come to the sto' to buy blunts and cigarettes. I liked her style. She was younger than me, and her clothes was always tight. She had a nice figure and it showed in her apple bottom jeans."

Yuri thought, *Chicks still wear apple bottoms?*

Tony went on with his story, "So, I was tryna charm her so I started just givin' her boxes of blunts and six packs of Colt 45 beer. I would even see her fill her purse up with all kinds of shit, and I would jus' turn a blind eye, and pay her no mind. After a month or so of this goin on, she slipped me her numba and I called. We started hangin' out, but every time I went to see her, she expected me to bring blunts and buy her sacks of weed. I didn't mind buyin' her weed at first, because if she didn't have no weed to smoke, she would flip out. Damn shawtee could be mean as hell. So buyin her da weed made hu sweet as pie."

Yuri wanted to laugh because she knew he was being played. But she kept it in listening to him vent about La'Q-Ghetto.

"Anyway, after a few more months, the water department started workin the hell out of me. I was pulling fifty hour there, then going to the sto' so, I quit the Quik Trip gig, and that's when everything went left."

"Like what?" Yuri asked.

Tony answered as if he was looking in his thoughts, rather than at Yuri. "Well, instead of buyin her a twenty sack of weed, I was only able to afford dime sacks. Then I wasn't at the sore no mo' giving her beer and blunts. She couldn't go in the store and grab all the stuff she wanted like when I was there, so she left me alone."

Yuri tried to act like she cared, "Man, do you miss her?"

Tony felt a little embarrassed about what he was about to reveal. "Yeah, but since I didn't get in her pants, I guess it wasn't that hard to get over hu."

Yuri almost choked.

"You mean to tell me that didn't fuck her! All the blunts and the weed you bought her country ghetto ass, and you still didn't get to fuck!?"

Tony was talking so low that it was almost a whisper. "No, she keep tellin' me when da time was right dat she would gimme some."

Yuri tried not to laugh but could no longer hold it in, thinking, *this nigga has got to be slow.*

"Well T., I'm sure you'll find the right woman that will treat you right," she said.

Tony smiled.

"I wish the right one could be you."

Yuri thought, after what he described about La'Qu-whatever her name was, with the apple bottom jeans, drinking malt liquor, and smoking dime sacks of weed, that was his lane. And maybe he should stick with his kind.

She thought, *keep wishing ugly.*

Tony's wish would never come true. They ate their food, and as they talked, Tony told Yuri more than any man had told her in a lifetime in just one day. Tony must have had no friends and needed one. Yuri learned and remembered as much as she could, finding, out everything about Tony and how green he was. He would work just fine for her plan that was about to take place.

The check came. Yuri took her wallet out, paying for the food and leaving a generous tip for the frail waitress, who looked as if she could use an extra burger and fries in her life.

"Well, I wish we could talk more, but I have a job interview at 2:30. I had to let you know how grateful I was. We'll hang out again soon."

"Promise?" Tony responded desperately.

"Of course, Tony. We'll even make it a date."

Tony smiled, showing the naked side of his mouth which made him look even worse. That would be even better for her plot. No one who had Yuri dealt with in the past would ever think that she would be dealing with someone like Tony. As they departed, Yuri looked back and saw how Tony watched her with his tongue hanging out of his mouth like a stray dog, Yuri thought, *yuck, he looks like someone who would get used.*

CHAPTER 6

Yuri had been sitting in the hospital employees' parking lot since 2:30 in the afternoon. It was starting to get dark. She got low in her seat when she saw Doctor Lozada walk to her convertible Ford Mustang. Even though she retired she still checked in from time to time. I guess today was one of those days. She looked like the type that would let her hair blow in the wind. She was a Spanish woman with long, wavy hair. Yuri wished she could thank her for the dress that helped her make her escape. The doctor climbed into her car, dropped her top and sped out of the lot.

Finally, Doctor Snider pulled up at 6:15pm. Yuri remembered that his shift was from 7:00 p.m. until 7:00 a.m. He ran around all night raping female patients and probably even the men - she wouldn't put it passed him. He was a pervert and probably a pedophile as well.

He got out of his white 2016 7 series 750i BMW. Doctor Sider was pushing a $113,000 car. Once she looked at the car, she hated him even more.

He made a lot of money, and all he did was walk around the ward drugging and raping women. His Beamer also brought back memories of Spida. He had the exact same car, except Spida's car was a black 2015 model.

As she watched him walk inside of the building, things began to surface to her memory. She remembered everything now. She remembered exactly how she had even ended up at that crazy ass hospital.

Once Doctor Snider walked inside the building, Yuri walked over to his car and attached the tracking device that she had purchased online. It tracked movement for up to one week; that's all she needed to find out where he lived, or where he was going. She wanted to take her key and write "rapist" right on the hood, but she had something better in store for the crooked ass creep.

Yuri made her way back to the luxury condo. After watching for Doctor Snider all day, she was tired, she knew that

Larry was stuck working at the hospital and was glad that she could relax by herself.

The next morning, Yuri got on the internet she pulled out the article that she had kept about Shane and Chanel's engagement. She Googled both their names. Chanel popped right up but there was nothing really on Shane.

It showed Chanel's job address and how she counseled people about their finances. Chanel was doing very well. Yuri tried putting her name in, looking for a home address, but nothing came up. She knew that they would be smarter than that, after learning that Shane was not just the real estate business man that he had claimed to be, but a kingpin drug dealer. Yuri wondered where their child went to daycare while they were working - or did they have a nanny? She was determined to find all of this out.

Within four days of Yuri tracking Doctor Snider, she found out his home address. He lived in a million dollar-plus subdivision in Love Joy, Georgia. His home was incredible. Something out of a dream home magazine. She also found out that he had four children; ranging from eleven years old to thirty-five.

She thought, *This old bastard is in his late 50's making babies. So, that means his nasty pink semen was potent and still working when he was fucking me. That's why he always wears a condom when he fucks the patients.*

She learned, too, that his second wife was thirty-five years old, the same age as his oldest son. She was the mother of his eleven-year-old, and had been with her rapist husband for thirteen years. Yuri could tell that she had had several surgeries: her face had already been lifted, plus the Botox showed; her lips had been injected with collagen, and her boobs were too big for her petite frame. She couldn't have weighed more than 110 Pounds. It looked as if she would fall over on her face, with such big breasts. Yuri thought how sometimes money made you look good and sometimes, if you overdid things, it could fuck you up. Doctor Snider's wife was a prime example of surgery gone wrong. She looked like a young Joan Rivers: a total mess.

Yuri started following Doctor Snider on a regular basis. She had his daily routine packed. She had even met the young hooker that he stopped and paid for sex and blow jobs right off the freeway at the Eagles Landing exit.

Her name was Sasha, a short light-skinned black girl who was 19 years old. She was cute, and petite, but needed to be cleaned up.

Yuri thought, *I'll give her a makeover.*

Sasha had gotten addicted to meth with her family disowning her. Yuri saw her eating at the Waffle House next to the motel that Doctor Snider would meet her at on a regular basis. Yuri sat in a booth behind her, watching her eat two waffles, six strips of bacon and a plate of scrambled eggs that looked to be a half dozen. For a person that looked like she only weighed one hundred pounds wet, she could eat like a line-backer football player. Yuri had already done research on Sasha and had learned that Sasha ate like this when she was coming off one her high escapades. Yuri felt sorry for her, because in a way, something about Sasha reminded her about herself.

Yuri finally laughed, saying, "Dang, girl, your real hungry today!"

Sasha looked back at Yuri, rolled her tired red eyes, and kept eating as if Yuri didn't exist. Yuri got up and sat at her table.

"Hey."

Sasha gave a nod while still devouring her food.

"Where do I know you from?" Yuri asked, trying to make conversation with her. Sasha looked up, trying to talk with a full mouth, but food spilled out on to the table. Yuri felt as if she might puke.

"I don't know and really don't care," was Sasha's reply.

Yuri paid her sarcastic remark no mind, but was disgusted by the way Sasha spoke out with food in her mouth. She didn't let it show on her face. "You look really familiar."

Yuri had already looked Sasha's information up, learning that she came from a middle-class family with both parents in the home. She graduated from high school with honors and had done one year in college. From what Yuri had read about her, Sasha had a bright future before she started partying and getting turned out on meth and a host of other recreational drugs. She dropped out of college and started selling her body and stealing anything she could to supply her bad habit. Eventually, she was on her own.

That's when she started whoring for cash and a place to live. Doctor Snider paid for her to live at the motel; therefore, he was the only one allowed in the room with her. Any other tricks that she had, she would have to take somewhere else. Yuri also found out that her name wasn't Sasha - it was Sarah Ann Smith.

Sasha must have had something good between her legs, because it seemed as though Doctor Snider was hooked, making frequent stops before and after work, and sometimes even on break, when the ward was too busy for him to be mannish.

Yuri got back to the conversation, "Did you go to Clark last year?"

Sasha nodded, "Yeah, why?"

Yuri smiled, "That's where I think I know you from. I went to Spellman, and maybe we bumped into each other on campus. I never forget a face even though you look a tad bit different, thinner maybe."

Yuri did go to Spellman, so she wasn't lying.

Sasha finally smiled, looking at Yuri.

"What's your name?" asked Sasha.

Yuri was relieved to see her smile.

"I'm Angel," Yuri said, "and you are?"

"My name is Sasha."

"Nice meeting you Sasha". Yuri replied. "Do you live around here?"

Sasha looked at Yuri and asked, "What's with the 21 questions?"

Yuri chuckled. "I was just wondering. It's just a coincidence that I see you way out here.

Sasha asked her with a bit of attitude, "I wouldn't see it like that, um what's your name? Oh, Angel. People live all around the United States that goes to college. We're still in Georgia. Do you live around here?"

Yuri ignored the sarcasm once again, "Well, I live in a condo downtown, but one of my sponsors lives around here."

Sasha asked, "What's a sponsor?"

As if her hoeing ass didn't know.

"A sponsor is one of my many clients who I might sleep with from time to time, and have them breaking bread. They give me thousands of dollars for things that I want." This sounded good to Sasha - she was a nickel and dime hoe fucking for a motel room and drugs. Yuri looked like a high-class whore, who had top notch men, sponsors, or whatever she called them, breaking her off generously.

Sasha thought, *Angel just might be someone that could help her get back on her feet.*

She studied Yuri, thinking, *This Angel chick is pretty but something looks off about her, like she's missing a couple of cans in her six pack.* She couldn't put her hand on it, but something wasn't registering. What she didn't know was, Yuri was trying to get her on her team - and now she was interested.

Sasha asked, "So how many sponsors do you have, Angel?"

Yuri used Sasha's sarcasm back on her. "Is this an interrogation Sasha? 21 questions?"

Sasha knew that she was trying to be funny, repeating her question. Yuri responded, counting off her fingers, "Well I have a doctor, an attorney, a couple of city workers, and I've been working on the manager at the Hilton Hotel Downtown that I was staying at a while ago."

Yuri had been fucking the manager at the Hilton, to the point that he had fallen in lust and wanted it to be more than it was between the two. Yuri could have stayed there for long as she wanted to, but he had gotten in his feelings when he saw Larry coming in and out of the hotel room as he stalked Yuri. Yuri knew that the sixty-dollar a day room service limit wasn't enough per day, so she seduced the manager, putting him under her spell, giving him what he wanted, good sex, and just a little attention. She ate and drank whatever she wanted. She popped a bottle of Rose' champagne daily, but once she asked him for cash that he couldn't provide, she dismissed him then moved out moving in to Larry's condo downtown.

Sasha smiled, asking, "Why do you want to know about my sponsors?"

"It's a long story, and I don't want to bore you with my troubles," Yuri responded.

"Girl, I have nothing to do right now, I have plenty of time to listen, if you have nothing to do shoot, I'm all ears, I'm a pretty good listener."

The waitress came with their meals. Yuri thanked her then prayed for their food. They ate their food, not really talking to each other, but trying to figure one another out more than anything. Once they were finished, Yuri paid the waitress, thanking her once again for being a good server. Yuri only had thirty dollars on her and their bill had come up to twenty-one dollars. She left the rest for the waitress, Sasha, paying close attention to this, decided she liked Yuri's kindness. She thought that too was generous, because people at this Waffle House never really left tips for the waitresses, herself being included. She didn't because her money was for her to eat, and supply her drug habit.

Yuri told Sasha, "Let's take a ride and you can tell me your story."

They got in to Yuri's car, jumped on the freeway going 75 North, with no destination in mind.

Sasha rattled on, "So, like a year and a half ago, I was staying in an apartment on the west end, right around the corner from the campus. I would drink every now and then but that was it, maybe a strawberry daiquiri or a sex on the beach, nothing that would get me drunk, just a nice buzz to take to edge off from my daily studies, I only drank in the evening. I didn't do any drugs, and hated the way weed smelled.

"My grades were mostly A's and nothing worse than a B- with a 3.8 GPA. My mom and dad paid half of the rent at the apartments where I lived, because I was doing so well. My roommate, Josh, paid the other half. He was gay, and wild as hell! Josh had a good job, and a full scholarship at Morehouse, and girl I mean, he was fly as that thang!"

"What thang?" Yuri cut her off.

Sasha laughed, saying, "Girl I don't know what that 'thang' is, that's something that my friend at Clark, from St. Louis used to always say. It's whatever you think is good or bad I guess. Sometimes I find myself saying it a little too much. Anyway, Josh was intelligent, but he did a lot of drugs, I mean everything. You name it, he was doing it, and had no problem getting it.

"From opiates, to coke, shrooms, weed, ecstasy, to meth. Oh, and can't forget about that syrup we use to sip on. One day he'd be on uppers, the next he'd be down, or both some days. Josh was a walking pharmacy. I started hanging out with him, tested a few of the drugs then I tried the meth and got hooked."

Yuri interrupted her, "Not to offend you, but meth? Why meth? I've never known anyone black to do meth."

Sasha said, "Well, actually, there's not a lot of black people that do meth. Josh is white."

Yuri was a little shocked that a smart white guy would attend an HBCU. It was as if Sasha was reading her mind, saying, "I told you that Josh was gay; well, the first guy that he said he slept with was a big-dick black guy."

She made a big 'O' with her fingers to emphasize her statement.

She continued, "He fell in love with him and as the saying goes, once you go black you never go back. Josh never went back to dating his race. I guess he had, had so much black dick up in him that he thought he was black, so he went to a black school with a full ride." They broke into giggles together.

Yuri asked, "What the hell is meth anyway?"

Sasha explained, "It's some man-made shit, like a stimulant or something, they cook it – it makes everything go so much harder and faster.

Yuri still couldn't quite understand. "But what *is* it?"

Sasha tried to explain further "It's over-the-counter meds mixed with a bunch of stuff - shit like brake fluid, antifreeze, battery acid, or even liquid plumber to cook it."

"Damn," Yuri replied. "They cook it? That sounds nasty – how do you even use it? Does it even feel good?"

"When I started, it was just smoking, like weed and oh my God- it was like this rush of euphoria, straight to my head just a feeling of being on top of the world and full of energy and like I could take on anything and I felt like I was the shit. And it's different every time. One day I might want to have sex all day and it keeps me wet and freaky; other days, I'm sluggish and just crave for more, and will do anything to get it."

Sasha felt relived getting this out, it felt therapeutic to talk to someone about it, she went on, "…So once I wasn't getting high on smoking it and feeling the same, I started snorting it. One day, I was so high that it felt like something was crawling on me. That shit had me all out of my element. Do you see these scars on my neck?"

Sasha said this while pulling up her shirt, showing Yuri the scars on her side just below her under arm.

"Wow, what happened?" Yuri asked, sickened by what she saw.

"I was so high that I picked at my skin until it started bleeding and it started looking like this. Then it became a spot that I would pick at all the time because no one could see the pain that I was inflicting on myself."

Yuri became nauseated just looking at the scars. "Damn Sasha, that looks bad."

Sasha started to feel embarrassed and self-conscious. She continued anyway. "I know Angel, and to make matters worse, my mom started noticing the changes in me. She told me that if I didn't stop doing whatever I was doing, she was going to stop paying my rent and helping me out. So about eight months ago, she noticed my grades had dropped to D's because I wasn't showing up for my classes. That's all it took for her and my father to pull back. They stopped making my car payment, my half of the rent, and everything else. My mother told me when I was ready to admit that I have a drug addiction, that they would start helping me again. I didn't feel like it was a problem then, but now that I've been trying to stay away from meth, I see what it has done to me. Now I'm stuck here alone turning tricks at a dirty ass motel."

Yuri asked, "if you've been out here and you say you're no longer around your roommate, how do you or how were you still getting meth?"

Sasha answered without hesitation, "Well, I started messing around with the guy who sold the meth to Josh, and man that was all she wrote. He kept me high as hell…"

She smiled as she thought about the dangerous drug.

"…and once I started using a lot more, not only did he want to fuck me all day, but he started letting his dirty ass friends fuck me as well."

Her eyes watered.

"…When I say dirty ass white boys, I mean it Angel, it makes me sick to my stomach. I love me a white boy, but these were the ones that I would have never let touch me. That's when I knew that I was really fucked up in the head."

Yuri was thunderstruck at what she was hearing.

"Wow," Yuri thought.

Sasha was just as fucked up as she was, just in a different way. She remembered being on ecstasy with Uno; she could totally relate to Sasha's experience with men using and abusing her body. That's how she had ended up sleeping with Spida; Uno had sold her to his little dick ass, to pay off his debt.

Sasha continued her story like it was the first in a long time since she had someone to really talk to.

"The last straw came like six months ago, I was driving back to my apartment, paranoid as hell, and hallucinating at the same damn time. I thought someone was chasing me, so I began to speed. That's when the police got behind me. I kept going so he started following me. I took him on a high-speed chase. After what seemed to be thirty minutes of damn near killing others and myself, about ten more police cars had joined in, chasing me down. They put out the spike strips, they popped my tires, and I crashed and hit a pole, totaling my car. They had to use the jaws of life to pull me out. Once they pulled me out of what was left of my vehicle, they found meth and liquor. My blood alcohol level was way over the 1imit at point 24. Plus, I had all types of drugs in my system."

"That's messed up," Yuri said.

Sasha smirked, smacking her lips. "No, what was really messed up was after the accident, I had to stay in the hospital overnight, then I was arrested and taken straight to jail. My parents never tried to help me get out of jail, which was probably good. Four months ago, I was released. The guy that I was messing with paid my bond. He wouldn't give me anymore drugs for free, or give me a place to stay since I'm on an honest path. Just keeping it real with you, I live right next door to the Waffle House that we just left from in that motel. I turn tricks for a living, and from time to time, I still snort a little meth to make me deal with some of the men that I sleep with."

Sasha felt good finally being able to talk about her problems, she felt as a weight had been lifted from her chest. Yuri felt sorry for Sasha, especially the part that her parents had written her off because of drugs. Yuri knew, had her problem been with drugs instead of sleeping with her mother's husband, Barbra would have never written her off and disowned her.

Yuri asked Sasha, "So you're turning tricks, giving up your goods and all you have to show for it is a broke down motel room?"

Sasha responded, "Yeah, a woman got to do what a woman's got to do."

Yuri didn't hide her disappointment. She frowned as she pried some more, "How old are you, Sasha?"

"I'm nineteen."

Yuri replied, "Girl you have to get it together. What's your normal weight?"

Sasha was a little embarrassed by the question.

"My normal weight is about one hundred twenty-five pounds."

Yuri choked out in shock, "Damn, you can't weigh any more than 90 pounds right now."

"Maybe, I haven't weighed myself lately, but I would say one-o-five."

"Girl, you're way too pretty to be out here like you are. The niggas I trick off with wouldn't even want to fuck me in a motel. What kind of customers are you dealing with? Bums?"

"No, I have one guy that works for Purina Dog Chow, he makes a nice buck. Then there's one who is a veterinarian. Oh, and I even have a psychiatrist."

Yuri stopped her right there and asked "So you're telling me that you have a vet and a shrink and you are still living like that, boo? You need some schooling and I am the right one for the job."

Sasha felt foolish but she was happy that she had met Angel, as she knew her. After they rode around for the next few hours, Sasha felt like she had known Yuri for years. They talked about everything. Yuri was like the big sister that she never had. Sasha had a younger brother, but never knew what it was like to have a sister. She knew that Yuri was a tad bit older than her. Now she hoped Yuri would stay around and maybe give her guidance.

Yuri pulled back up to the motel she parked finishing up their conversation.

She turned to Sasha, asking, "How many of your tricks do you mess with here?"

"I only mess with one here because he pays the monthly bill. They charge him like four hundred dollars a month."

"Which one is that?" Yuri asked.

"The psychiatrist, his name is Doctor Snider."

Yuri wasn't surprised.

She exploded, "Fuck that, it's not worth it! He may as well pay for you to live in an apartment. I'll tell you what, you don't mention that you met me to any of your tricks, but I'm going to help you get out of this dive. This shit is not even fit for a damn dog, and that rich ass piece of shit has you living in this slum ass motel and using your youth up."

Sasha saw the anger is Yuri's eyes and knew that she wanted to help her, yet she was kind of scared about how upset that this had made her.

Yuri smiled. "When this Doctor Snider, or whatever his name is, comes around, treat his ass bad! You must get your life back because if you're going to be kicking it with me, you must straighten up your act. You must make it count! Your pussy is priceless, and girl, your mouth is a jewel. I'm going to pick you up tomorrow around six thirty if you're free."

Sasha quickly nodded, "I'll be free."

"So be around by the Waffle House. Do you have a number that I can reach you at, Sasha?"

"Only the motel phone."

Yuri had been locked in the crazy house but thought, *Shit, she could have taken my place.*

Yuri raised an eyebrow and asked "You don't even have a cell phone, Sasha?"

Sasha felt awkward once again.

"No, I don't have one Angel.

"Well, just make sure that you're outside of the Waffle House at six thirty and I'll scoop you up, okay?"

Sasha smiled as she opened the car door and alighted from Yuri's car.

She eagerly assented, "Okay Angel, thank you! I'll be waiting."

Yuri smiled back at Sasha, "Oh, and take you a good shower because we are going to hang out for a while.

"Okay Angel, I guess I'll be seeing you tomorrow."

Sasha waved as she watched Yuri drive away. Yuri knew since it would be Friday, Doctor Snider would be at work at seven p.m. She had big plans for Doctor Snider, with Sasha's help.

CHAPTER 7

Yuri had slept well after all of the information that she had learned from Sasha. She thought about how she could help the lost little chick. She would make Sasha her little sister and her accomplice to get next to Doctor Snider. She remembered how Candice had taken her under her wing and put her up on street game. Candice had once told Yuri that men in Atlanta gave way more than what she was charging. At that time, Yuri was around the same age as Sasha, sleeping with men for a little bit if not nothing. She had been through so much in so little time. She had everything that she wanted and lost it all within a couple years. She mused, easy come, easy go. Yuri took no responsibility for anything that had happened to her. She was determined to get her life back on track, and if that meant fighting, stealing or killing someone, that was just what it would be. After what she had learned, her maxim was, "Fuck the world, and everyone in it."

Larry stopped by his condo bright and early. It had been raining all morning. He thought there was no better time than making love on a dark, cloudy, rainy morning with the young freak that rocked his world anytime they sexed each other. He walked in, totally aroused. Yuri was all ready for him. Seeing the eager look in his eyes made her put on her sexy game face.

She had invited him over for breakfast and when he saw her laying in the bed butt-naked, with her legs spread apart, playing in her pussy. He already knew what time it was.

"So, this is breakfast?" Larry asked, pulling on his goatee with one hand, and using the other to unbuckle his pants.

Yuri winked, responding, "It sure is," while pleasuring herself with two fingers inside of her wet nest, then taking them out, sucking her own sweet juices off. "Now it's your turn, Daddy. Come and eat your breakfast."

With a mischievous smile, licking his lips, he walked over to the bed, finished getting undressed, and wasted no time going straight in-between her thighs, lapping at Yuri's sweet treat. Yuri let him feast while talking dirty and nasty to him, just the way he liked it. She liked the way Larry ate her pussy; no matter how wet she got, he never wiped his lips or face off. She enjoyed seeing her thick slimy cum all over his face; it turned her on when he licked around his lips, savoring her juices, making them flow even more. But her goal this morning was to please him in every single way she knew how, not only because she was horny, but because she needed extra cash as well. She grabbed his head, pulling his face up out of her butt crack, looking him in his eyes, grabbing his mouth, putting her tongue down his throat, tasting all her own juices. Larry loved Yuri's freakiness. She flipped him over on his back, getting herself positioned to suck his dick just the way he liked. She knew that in the morning his testosterone was at its peak, allowing her to take advantage of his vulnerability. She firmly grabbed his shaft and started sucking with an alternating slow pulsation, running her tongue around the ridge where the head of his dick connected. She was extra cautious because she knew how sensitive the head of a man's dick was.

She continued, blowing warm air from her breath around his wet tip. He shook like he had cold shivers. Then, with her soft, wet, flattened tongue, she licked the underside of his dick like a chocolate ice pop, continuing down, sucking all around his balls, making every vein that he had from his head to his toes pop out. Once she got back down to the tip, she slid into her mouth, taking it all the way down the back of her throat, sucking in and out at rapid pace, almost in tandem with the beat of his racing heart. Yuri was nasty and straight pornstarish.

Larry grabbed the back of Yuri's head screaming out, "Oh yes baby, don't stop!"

Yuri realized he was completely aroused.

"You don't want me to stop, Daddy?" She asked, with a full mouth, and her tongue swirling all around his dick.

"No, baby! Please don't stop. Oh Yuri," he panted. "I…I… I can't take this, what are you doing to me?"

Yuri liked that she still had the power to make men feel so vulnerable. She would teach her new friend the skills that she claimed God had blessed her with. Sasha would learn everything she knew, and they would explore new things together.

Larry was trying to keep it together but he could not have been prepared for her next move. Yuri deep throated him, spitting all over his dick like a wild animal. Pulling his dick in and out of her mouth, licking it all around, then making it disappear. She pulled it out of her mouth, continuing to slide her tongue down his shaft licking straight down, through the crack of his ass.

Larry was right to the point of cumming.

Yuri increased pressure with her hands, putting him back inside of her mouth while jacking him off, making Larry screech like a pig, "It feels so damn good! I'm about to cum, baby! I can't aww…aww... oh... aww shit! Jesus!" Larry yelled out helplessly, and came.

He collapsed with one last moan like a wounded dog. They both laid there while Larry tried to catch his breath. He was sweating like he had just run a 5k marathon. Yuri crawled on top of his wet chest, putting her tongue in is ear, sucking on his earlobe. Larry told her give him a second. She didn't listen, as usual, continuing her mission, kissing on his neck. She knew it was his pay day so it was hers as well.

She whispered in his ear, "Daddy, I want to shop today. I think I deserve a better bag than this last season Michael Kors bag. My ex kept all my bags but even then, I wasn't carrying this kind, plus, your wife…"

Immediately cutting her of, Larry said, "Hold it right there. I told you not to bring my wife in to this, ever!"

He was irritated that Yuri had brought up his wife once again. Yuri pouted. "Fine, I just want to go shopping."

He gave her an enraged look, but as she pouted, looking innocent, and sexy necked, he softened up, rolled over and reached for his wallet pulling out a nice wad of cash. He counted the hundreds out and gave Yuri fifteen hundred dollars. Yuri wondered what he expected her to do with that. They had pillow talked on a few occasions with Larry revealing to Yuri about all his investments and the salary that he made. She knew Larry was rolling in dough, and she wasn't settling for less anymore like she used to do.

As she sat on him, she grabbed his dick, rubbing it against her sticky wet pussy. Larry was instantly hard, tired, but ready for round two. For the first time, finally she rammed his dick inside her warm, tight pussy without a condom. Larry's eyes rolled to that back of his head. Yuri sat back up on her feet and bounced on his rock-hard pickle. She kept riding while telling him, "This pussy is worth much more than what you gave me. I want a new bag, Daddy."

Larry's eyes were closed while he tried to concentrate. Yuri rode him even harder, but not too hard that she would hurt him, making her wet pussy fart and squirt all around his dick. He had been waiting for this day, he could do what he had been wanting to do to Yuri since the day that they started messing around; he came inside of her. Larry saw fireworks, damn near wanting to cry. Yuri's pussy was so good that he felt that he wanted to call his wife at this moment and tell her that he was in love and never coming back home again.

Yuri's first stop was by Lennox Square. Walking through it brought back so many memories. She hadn't been in Lenox over a year and a half. She thought about how Shane would take her on endless shopping sprees at Lennox and Phipps Plaza with credit cards that had no limit. She smiled, thinking about how fly and sexy Shane was and how she had messed up a perfect relationship with him. She headed to Neiman Marcus to see what her money could buy. Once in the store, Yuri went in every department, the only difference was now she was a window shopper. She decided that she no longer wanted the Gucci bag. She decided on rocking the new Louis Vuitton from their cruise collection, wondering what had happened to all the designer handbags that were in her townhouse.

What had even happened to her house? It was in her name and that was something not even Shane could take back. That would be on her priority list to check on. She hoped Chanel didn't have any of her belongings; it would be another reason to carry out the plan that she had for Chanel.

After spending eleven hundred dollars on her new bag, she felt that she was finally getting her swag back.

Yuri went into Macy's and headed straight for the sale rack, something that she had never had to do. While looking through the shirts, she noticed two women in the corner. One was handing clothes to the other, so that she could remove the sensors with a device just like the sales assistants used.

Yuri thought to herself, *Damn, not only were they stealing these people's shit, they done stole their machine from off the counter, too.*

They were moving fast as a team - while one popped the buzzard, the other filled clothes up into a bag that was lined with what seemed to be aluminum foil, just in case they missed a buzzard.

That was exactly what Yuri needed. She made her way over toward the women.

Once she got close enough, she whispered looking around, "Hey ladies."

They both jumped and looked at her like she was crazy.

Yuri stepped back, "I'm sorry, I didn't mean to get at you like this but I'm trying to do some business with you. When you guys leave out of here, why don't you stop by the Starbucks to discuss some things, please. I'm not security, but if I was, ya'll asses would be caught."

Both women looked at each other, the light skinned one looked annoyed, but the darker one nodded and got right back to their mission.

Yuri put down the items that she was going to purchase and left the store headed for Starbucks. She ordered a strawberry Frappuccino. She hadn't tasted one in so long that she had forgotten how they tasted. She closed her eyes, savoring the taste, enjoying herself just the way she was used to doing. She was slightly startled when she felt a tap on her shoulder. She opened her eyes looking at the two women from Macy's. They had come out of Macy's loaded with bags fast. Yuri was fascinated at how they pulled it off. They sat down.

The short dark skinned chick, said, "What's up? You said you wanted to spend some money."

She was short and plain while the lighter woman, was unnervingly tall and beautiful, though not strikingly so. The tall light skinned chick never spoke. She only sat there, observing her surroundings.

Yuri smiled at both, "Yes, I'm trying to spend two hundred dollars right now."

Brown skin asked, "You want two hundred dollars' worth of merchandise for one hundred, or you want four hundred dollars' worth for two hundred?"

Yuri laughed, "I want four hundred worth for two hundred."

She wasted no time getting down to business, "Where do you want them from?"

Yuri thought for a minute, "Well for me, I like Nordstrom, Saks Fifth Avenue, and those kinds of stores; however, for now I am shopping for my little sister. So, Macy's will be just fine."

Brown skin asked Yuri, "What kind of look does your sister rock?"

"From the looks of the way that you guys are dressed, I think I can trust your judgment. It looks like you ladies have good taste. So just find her things that she can wear to a formal dinner or to a cool or classy club."

The red boned finally spoke up, "I got you. What size does she wear?" Yuri turned to look at her and smiled, "So, you do speak? She's a size two."

Both girls said, "Damn," brown skin continued. "Well, that's going to be easy. We'll get it all now. We'll get you some from Macy's and Express."

Yuri nodded her head for approval.

She women stood up to leave, "Stick around here for about an hour and we'll be back. Give us your number and we'll get at you in a few."

Yuri wrote down her number, handed it to her, winking at her.

She was about to leave but decided to introduce herself, "My name is Bliss, by the way. That's Red, we'll call you within the hour.

Yuri stopped the girls before they left, "Can you girls also get shoes?"

Bliss and Red looked at each other.

Red spoke first, "We sure can. What kind do you like and where would you want them from?"

"I need a pair of size seven heels. It doesn't matter, as long as they're leather. I also need a nice clutch to go with it. I have another hundred if you can supply that."

Both girls smiled and waved, walking out of the door.

Yuri was beyond thrilled. She knew she was going to buy Sasha clothes and had planned on spending at least three hundred dollars and would probably be walking out with nothing. Now that she met her new friends, she would be spending three hundred, for six hundred dollars' worth of merchandise.

Now with an hour to spare, she could splurge on herself. She went through all the designer shops looking at bags as she walked around. She picked up different bags, taking in the scent of the fine Italian leather. She thought of all her bags that she left at her house once again, but decided not to get caught up thinking about the past. Today was a new day, so it didn't matter. She realized that she had been able to accomplish it all once, she would damn sure get it back again, and then some.

Larry had already tricked off on a shopping spree for her the week before, so her wardrobe was coming together. Yuri decided the best way to kill the rest of the time was by going and getting a manicure, with gel polish.

The Asians put her in the chair right away, getting her nails right with a pretty wet looking purple polish, with one nail on each finger stoned out. They begged her to spend more cash by telling her that her feet looked bad, which was totally a lie. They were money-hungry, and wanted her to stick around so they could be all up in her business. As soon as she was finished, her phone rang.

She answered the unfamiliar number, already knowing who it was. "Hello."

"Hey, this is Bliss. I never got your name."

Yuri didn't miss a beat. Lying came so easily. "Oh, my name is Angel."

"Okay Angel, we're ready to hook back up with you but we left the mall. There's a gas station across the 85 freeway. We can meet in the parking lot. I'm in a blue Range Rover. I'll be parked at the end of the lot by Publix."

"Okay, I'm on my way. I'm in a white Lexus, give me fifteen minutes."

Yuri pulled up on the side of the gas station next to the Range Rover, thinking *damn she's riding clean to be a booster.* Once they all got out of their cars, Red popped the trunk to show Yuri the items that they had lifted for her. Yuri's eyes lit up. They had so many bags of clothes, shoes, and perfumes. They showed her all the items that she was about to purchase. The clothes were fly, even the Aldo bag and shoes were cute. She handed Bliss three hundred dollars. Yuri thanked them, telling them that they would be hearing a lot from her.

Before Red had a chance to close the trunk, Yuri noticed one last thing she had to buy for Sasha.

"Wait, how much do you want for that bottle of D&G perfume?"

Red grabbed it and gave it to her for twenty dollars. Yuri was very pleased.

After they went their separate ways, Yuri pulled out of the gas station, remembering that Candice lived in the condos right across the street. At least she used to, Yuri thought. She was sure by now to be living somewhere in Alpharetta or Sandy Springs in a mansion.

"I am going to see you one day, Bitch, and it'll be hell to tell the captain!" Yuri said aloud, as if Candice could hear her.

CHAPTER 8

Yuri pulled up to the Waffle House at 6:20 p.m. Sasha was already outside waiting for her.

When Sasha saw Yuri's, Lexus drive up, she ran over to her smiling, "Hey Angel! I've been waiting for you. I'm ready to get the hell out of here."

Yuri noticed that Sasha was clean, she had her hair done, looking nothing like the same person from yesterday. Yuri smiled at her, reaching behind the seat, handing Sasha a bag. Sasha looked in the bag seeing her new outfit, clutch, and shoes.

Her eyes lit up. "All of this is for me? Wow, Angel! Thank you so much!"

Yuri said, "Take your new clothes up to your room and get dressed."

Sasha jumped out, literally running to her room. Yuri had made sure she had only given her one outfit. She knew how she wanted to play the whole thing out, and tonight would set it off.

She came back looking sexy. Even though she was a size two, she was cute with it. She had a very small waist and a nice ass that filled out her Levi jeans nicely. Yuri noticed that Sasha's walk had changed. She was strutting in her heels. Sasha walked around the front of the car and modeled for Yuri.

Yuri was smiling at her, "Come on girl, get in the damn car. I know you're looking good. Now let's get out of here."

As they drove away, Sasha said, "Thank you again, Angel. I don't know how I can repay you."

Yuri thought, *don't worry, I know exactly how you can repay me.* But she turned to Sasha and said nonchalantly, "Don't sweat it. It's all good, plus I came up on a pretty good deal."

Yuri turned up the music, playing Atlanta's finest, Young Jeezy.

Sasha started dancing in her seat screaming, "This is my song!" as Jeezy and Trey Songz sang their classic hit in her eyes.

Yuri turned up the radio as "Taking It There" blasted through her speakers.

She said, "This is a throwback, but a straight banger."

They pulled up to Billiard's Sports Bar in downtown Atlanta. She knew there would be a selection of men there. She knew that Sasha liked dealing with white men. She felt that she had bad luck with black guys. They parked the car, walking up to the door ready to slay. Yuri walked in bossy. She was on the prowl for her, a nice-looking companion that would pay the tab, or maybe come up on a few quick hundreds. They sat down and ordered drinks. Yuri had not had Grey Goose with a splash of pineapple juice in quite some time so she ordered Sasha and herself one each.

Tonight, the Atlanta Hawks were playing the Cleveland Cavaliers at Philips Arena, making the city turn up. The bar was packed with potential candidates, and the strip clubs would be just as full if not fuller later.

Yuri thought cracking her own self up, *Shit I may just get lucky with Lebron or Kyrie tonight.*

As they ate their hot wings and enjoyed their drinks, Yuri noticed a nice-looking white guy who was maybe in his mid-thirties looking their way. Yuri whispered to Sasha, "Don't look just yet, but to your right, I think you have a fan."

Sasha kept her head down for a couple of minutes, then she looked his way. He was still looking, she waved and smiled.

Once the waitress came over to collect their trays, she placed two drinks on the table, "These are from the gentleman over there. He told me to get you two whatever you guys were already drinking. Take it easy. He's a big spender around here, and he tips nicely, so when you're ready for another, just let me know." The waitress winked at them walking off.

Sasha lifted her drink, tilting it towards the white guy, saying thank you, nodding from her head and smiling seductively at the gentleman. He smiled back, winking at her. He started back talking and watching the game with his buddies. Sasha thought that he was nice looking, with a sexy smile. A nice looking, young black guy in his early twenties, walked over to the table and asked Yuri if he could buy her a drink.

She blushed saying "Not tonight, but thank you anyway."

He looked her up and down, licking his lips, as if he was licking on a lollipop.

"Will you marry me?" was the next dumb question that came out of his mouth.

Yuri laughed, almost spitting her drink out of her mouth.

"Sure, I will," she replied, never asking him his name. He smiled, "So, what's your name sexy?"

Yuri winked at Sasha, answering him, "Tasha." Sasha shook her head giggling at Yuri's lies. Little did she know, he was getting lied to just like she was.

He asked if he could get Yuri's number so he could take her out. Yuri asked him for his instead and promised that she'd call. One thing that Yuri couldn't stand was a thirsty ass nigga. He fit the description: mouth hanging open, almost drooling like a dog, and getting at any chick in the bar that might bite his bait. He was lame, and so was his game. His number would be thrown away on the tray once the next round of drinks came.

After a couple of more complimentary drinks from the white guy that was checking for Sasha, it was time to leave. As they made their way to the door, the guy that had them feeling nice and tipsy caught up, stopping Sasha. She kept moving, leaving him no time to introduce himself. He gave her his business card, telling her to please call him anytime. She told him that he would be hearing from her soon. She knew that he was watching her walk away, so she walked away with a sexy sway, knowing that she was looking luscious. Thanks to Angel she was getting her motivation and swagger back.

The next stop was the Pink Pony strip club, off highway 85 and North Druid Hills. Yuri knew that it was mostly white men who hit up the club, and not many of the people that she once hung around came to. The dancers were a selection of all nationalities, all shapes, sizes and flavors. Yuri and Sasha walked in, owning the club with their heads held high. Men were choosing them before they could even get to their seats.

Yuri strutted through, encouraging Sasha to put her best foot forward. Yuri smiled, looking back at her protégé as she swayed her hips from side to side. *That's right girl. It's on. Let's party.* They found seats right in front of the stage while waiting on the waitress to take their order.

Yuri was up dancing and tipping the first bad, big butt chick that she found worthy of her cash. The men who sat across from them watched with curiosity; they wondered who these sexy brown skinned young women were who moved like celebrities. Yuri tipped the dancer, feeling blissful. Sasha enjoyed this, and the way that Yuri interacted with the dancers, and the men who watched her. Sasha felt that Yuri was a natural at it. All the dancers saw that all the men were watching Yuri, making them dance over her way, causing all eyes to be on them.

Yuri had given Sasha money so that they could both pay for lap dances. Once the song was over, Yuri told the ladies that they were good for now, ready to work on her prey.

Once all the dancers left, the white guy that had the rest of the women dancing for him walked over to her, saying, "Hello, Ladies."

Yuri and Sasha nodded, smiling up at the stranger.

He continued, saying, "I see that you ladies are having a lot of fun."

Yuri was first to speak up, "Yes, we are, and it looks like you are as well."

"I'm Walter, and you are?"

Smirking, Yuri replied, "I'm Sassy."

Sasha thought to herself, *this chick has a different name for every damn club we go to. I hope she remembers the different names she uses in case we cross paths with some of these men again.*

Sasha piggybacked off Yuri's lie. "I'm Tasty."

Yuri looked at Sasha, pleased by her quick response thinking, *she's a fast learner.*

Walter licked his lips, "Tasty, huh, you don't say?"

Sasha licked her lips also, folding her arms, "Yes I do say."

Walter liked how playful she was being. He could sense the vulnerability that lurked beneath the sweet-looking young woman.

He proceeded to try and get to know her.

"Tasty, um… how tasty, are you?" he asked, feigning and tilting his head, pulling on his freshly cut beard.

Sasha bit her bottom lip, looking him straight in his eyes. "I'm a sweet treat."

Walter was now having a hard time concentrating. He responded, "I love treats and I do mean a treat as in both of you."

This made Yuri laugh out loud.

"Baby, you can't handle the both of us."

Walter looked at Yuri, confused, replying, "How do you know, unless you try me out?"

Yuri looked Walter up and down, "I just don't think you can, plus you look like the police."

Walter didn't look like a cop, but Yuri just wanted to be cautious.

This made him laugh, "Just because I'm white, makes me look like a pig?" He asked.

Knowing that she was putting him to the test, Yuri nodded, replying, "If that's how you want to put it."

He took the small vial out of the inside pocket of his tailor-made suit coat jacket, opened it up, took something out with his fingernail, and proceeded to snort at least a gram of powdered cocaine.

He rolled his head around to feel the sensation that the coke was giving him, looked Yuri's way, winked and asked, "Does a cop do that?"

Yuri was now more than convinced he was a professional junkie with money.

"Okay, you win," she conceded, making a mental note to keep him distant.

He offered them some of the coke, Yuri quickly declined. Yuri had let Uno turn her out on ecstasy before, and regretted it. She knew how the cocaine made women do anything for what they wanted when times get rough. She also remembered Candice's many lectures of how drugs were any persons' main downfall, making her stand clear of it. She had been promiscuous enough without drugs. She looked over, realizing how tense

Sasha was. Yuri knew that if she snorted meth, she would most definitely like cocaine. She figured Sasha needed something to help her relax.

Yuri gave her permission like a benevolent sister, "Go ahead and try it. Just know that you won't be doing this often. I mean it!"

Walter opened and handed her the small vial. She pulled a finger nail full out snorting it like a professional, without anyone noticing. First up her right nostril then the left, sprinkling some on her finger running it across her gums. Within ten minutes the drug kicked in, Sasha had transformed entirely into a completely different person. Jumping up, dancing with the strippers, singing Fetty Wap's "Trap Queen." Yuri stared at her, smiling at her transformation.

Walter called Sasha over to him. She backed her ass up, and started grinding on him. He was enjoying every minute of this. Whispering in her ear, "I want to fuck you and your friend."

Sasha turned to face him, wrapped her arms around his neck, licked in side of his ear, whispering back, "She's my sister."

Just the thought of fucking sisters turned Walter on, automatically giving him a hard on.

Lightly stroking her breasts, he said, "Well then, I want to fuck you and your sister."

Sasha smiled at the thought of this. "You're going to have to talk to Sassy about that."

He locked eyes with Yuri across the room and motioned for her to come to him.

Yuri slowly danced her way over, licking her glossed lips, "What's up, boo?" She asked.

He wrapped his arm around Yuri's small waist, pulling her close to him, "I was just telling your little sister that I wouldn't mind putting my big cock inside of you and her. What do you say?"

Yuri thought he was corny as hell, but responded, "Do you think you can afford me and my sister?"

He said, "Name the price."

First, Yuri had a game for him.

She said, "Let me take a hit of that good stuff in your vial."

He quickly took it and handed it to her, she played like she took a hit. She was good at faking it because she had plenty of practice with her medication at the ward.

She handed it back to him smiling, "Now it's your turn."

Rick took it and taking a super sniff. He closed his eyes and tilted his head back once again.

When he opened his eyes, he looked at both girls and asked, "Are you girls ready to party?"

Yuri put her hand on her hip and said, "We're ready, but I want a stack."

He looked confused asking, "What is that?"

Yuri rolled her eyes, "It's one thousand dollars."

He didn't seem fazed by the amount, "So what do I get for my thousand bucks? And for how long?"

With a smirk on her face, she replied, "You've got three hours for whatever you'd like us to do to you." Walter interrupted, "Do to me? I want her to eat your pussy while you suck my cock. And then, I want you to eat her pussy while I fuck you doggie-style.

Yuri raised her voice, annoyed at how sick men could be. "We're sisters! We don't eat each other's pussy!" She reminded him.

Walter took a sip of his drink and looked away, "Well, it's no deal, walking off."

Yuri thought about the thousand dollars, she hesitated before continuing, "What if we both suck your dick and you fuck us both for eight hundred?"

He kept looking around the room, "Umm. I wanted to see you sisters fuck each other."

Yuri sighed, "Okay, give us a thousand dollars a- piece and you got a show."

He didn't have to think twice about it. "Let's go."

His perverted ass stood, and wrapped his arms around their waists and led them to the parking lot. "I have to stop at the ATM first to get a little more cash."

Once they were following him, Sasha finally spoke up. "Sorry Angel, but I have never been with a female. I turn tricks with men, but I'm not a dyke."

Yuri laughed. "Just go along with me. Follow my lead, we're going to get his money and bounce."

After stopping at the ATM, they ended up at the Quality Inn Hotel off 85 Hwy. Once he paid for the room, they followed behind him.

When they entered the room, he finally admitted that his name was William, but his friends called him Bill. He told them that he thought of them as his new friends and if their pussy was good, and they ate one another good enough, that he would be patronizing them often. Yuri was just ready to get the hell out of there.

He took the vial out of his jacket saying, "I need another line, then I want you to suck on my cock for the next hour until it's hard and I can cum in your mouth. Let's party!"

He opened the vial snorting more, once again. Yuri thought, *damn, he snorts that shit like Al Pacino did in Scarface.*

He had another thing coming if he thought she would ever suck anybody's dick for an hour. Yuri could suck a man's dick and make any of them cum in ten minutes, tops.

This coke snorting cracker has me fucked up, she thought. As much as she liked to swallow, Walter, Bill or whatever his name was, would never get that satisfaction. He handed the vial to Sasha. Yuri realized that she wasn't playing with the coke either. After taking a big hit herself, Sasha handed it to Yuri. Once again, she played like she snorted it.

Whatever his name told them to get undressed.

Yuri sucked her teeth. "We are not doing anything until we see our money."

64

He laughed. "No problem." He took out the two thousand dollars and counted it.

Sasha's eyes lit up. No man had ever paid her over two hundred dollars for sex. Doctor Snider paid her rent for a month at a time, and that only added up to thirty dollars a day. Now she was about to get broke off like she was supposed to be. Yuri had been used to that kind of money. She snatched the money out of Walter's hand and started undressing. Sasha followed Yuri's lead, undressing as well. Once they were both naked, he turned on the small radio that sat on the night stand. He told them to dance. While they shook their asses, he started taking off his clothes, getting completely naked. He started playing with himself trying to make his small 'cock', as he called it, hard.

He motioned for Sasha. "Tasty, come and suck my big cock."

Sasha grabbed the condoms out of her purse, put it on him, and went to work sucking his limp dick. While Sasha sucked his dick, he sucked on Yuri's titties. Yuri was beyond irritated, but she knew that making Walter snort all that coke, he would never be able to get it up. Sasha was going to work on him. Yuri watched for a minute, knowing that this was about to come to an end. She could tell Sasha hadn't seen money like this before because she was going way too hard - or maybe the drugs had made her horny. Walter told Sasha to stop pulling her head back. He told her that he had to use the bathroom, and when he came back he wanted them on the bed, kissing on each other. Yuri almost laughed, thinking this is about to be too easy.

Bill got up and went into the bathroom.

As soon as he shut the door behind him, Yuri whispered to Sasha, "Grab your clothes, let's go!"

Sasha looked at Yuri like she had lost her damn mind, "But I'm naked."

Yuri grabbed her hand, "So, let's get the hell out here! Come on!"

They made sure to grab all the money and all of Walter's clothes as well.

By the time, they were at their car, Walter was running out of the hotel with a thin towel wrapped around his waist. Yuri laughed as they got into her car and sped off.

Sasha kept looking back and said, "That was crazy! My heart is beating so, fast!"

Yuri turned to Sasha and laughed, "Mine's too! Fuck his pink, limp-dick ass! You sucked on it for almost ten minutes and nothing happened. He wasn't going to be able to get it up anyway!"

They both laughed.

Yuri continued, "Trust me, I had it all planned. He's lucky that he went to the bathroom because shit was about to get bad for his ass."

Both girls looked at one another and could not stop laughing.

Yuri took out the money and told her, "I'm going to give you six hundred dollars of what he gave me.

Sasha knew how much Yuri had because she had just seen Walter count it out. It didn't matter to her because she had never been paid six hundred dollars at once from a trick.

Sasha reached over and hugged Yuri, "Thank you, Big Sis!"

Yuri smiled, saying, "That's nothing for a boss chick. There's more to come. Now that you see how easy it is to get money, you must stop settling for less."

Sasha nodded her head.

"I guess as long as I'm with you, that's how it's going to be from now on, and believe me I'm taking notes."

Yuri continued, "And you have to get out of that motel. If that Doctor can't give you more, leave him the hell alone."

Sasha agreed.

"He's going to pop up in the morning he gets off at 7 a.m. He comes by every Saturday morning wanting to fuck, and get his yucky cock sucked."

Yuri knew his perverted ass liked to fuck. "Do you like to fuck him, Sasha?"

Sasha didn't have to think about the answer to this question. "Hell no! His dick is small and skinny and his breath smells like an outhouse, I do it so I won't have to live on the street."

Yuri understood where Sasha was coming from. "Well, when he comes in the morning, you need to tell him that you have a guy friend that is willing to take care of you and get you out of that motel. Tell him that if he can't help you get a real spot, it's over. Hell, a one bedroom apartment rents for five hundred dollars. That way, you'll see how much he is feeling you. Right now, he's only paying for your room, and you still fuck other men to eat? That makes no sense."

Sasha didn't know how to respond.

"Okay, I'll tell him. But he's aggressive sometimes."

Yuri interrupted her. "He puts his hands on you?" Sasha nodded her head.

Yuri was hot just thinking about it.

They pulled up to Sasha's room. She thanked Yuri again and was about to get out of the car.

Yuri stopped her.

"One more thing, here's a gift for my little sister. Wear it for the asshole and don't forget what I told you: Don't tell him or any of your other tricks about me."

Sasha smiled, accepting the bag.

Yuri continued, "Here's my number. Go get you a phone tomorrow, call me, and tell me how things went." Sasha smiled. "Okay. Bye Angel."

Yuri corrected her, "No, Sasha, we say, 'See you later,' okay?"

"Okay sis, see you later."

Yuri thought as she drove off, *she is going to be easy to train.*

CHAPTER 9

Yuri slept in, not waking up until Saturday afternoon. Larry did family time on the weekends, so she knew that he wouldn't be coming around. His apartment was elegantly decorated, with expensive furniture and paintings but Yuri was ready for her own place. She had made fourteen hundred dollars the night before. She also had eleven hundred dollars saved up from all the money Larry dished out. She loved to shop, but she also knew how to save money. She had not asked her dad for any more money since the day he helped her when she escaped the ward. She knew it was time to hit him, and Larry, up for more cash.

Yuri had hooked back up with her booster friends, Bliss and Red, who just so happened not only to be boosters, but they had a hook up on getting people in apartments, among other things. Bliss told her that if she gave them the one-time fee of five hundred dollars in addition to first and last month's rent, plus security deposit, they could get her in just about any spot she wanted. She decided to start looking Monday.

Yuri got up and had a craving for some good sushi. She remembered how she used to go with Chanel to the Twelve Hotel's Sushi Bar in Centennial Park. She figured she would get dressed and head over there. Before she had a chance to walk out the door, her phone rang. She looked at the number and didn't recognize it.

"Hello?"

"Hey Angel, are you busy?" Yuri quickly realized that it was Sasha.

"Oh, hey Sasha. No, I'm not busy. I was just about to step out and grab a bite to eat. What's up?"

Sasha sounded panicky. "So, I woke up this morning, showered, and fell asleep waiting for Gary to stop by…"

Cutting her off, Yuri asked, "Who's Gary?"

Sasha apologized, "Oh sorry, Doctor Snider's first name is Gary. Anyway, I put on the perfume like you told me to and he must have loved it because I woke up to him licking and biting all over me. I jumped up and screamed, because I got scared. He asked me where I got the perfume."

Yuri interrupted her again, this time almost screaming through the phone in a fury, "What did you tell him?"

Sasha started stuttering, "Well, um, since he knows I have other men that do a little bit for me, I told him that I went to the mall with the veterinarian and he bought it for me. I told him that while smelling all different kinds of fragrances, I recognized the smell. His clothes used to smell like that same Marc Jacobs sometimes when he stopped by. So, I bought it, I felt that he must have liked it because his wife maybe wore it."

Yuri agreed with her, "Yeah, you're probably right."

Sasha continued, "Not to get off subject, but what's crazy is when I sleep with the vet, Gary likes to fuck me while I still smell like the animal hospital. He got mad and asked me why I showered knowing that he liked to smell the animals while we fucked, that's how sick he is. Anyway, back to what I was saying about the perfume, he asked me what would make me think that he wanted me to smell like someone special to him. Then, he started fucking and choking me, hard and crazy, pounding like he was on some type of drug and couldn't reach his climax. Angel, he almost choked me to death! He even called me someone else's name, I can't remember what it is because I thought I was going to die."

Yuri stopped her. "Wow Sasha, are you okay?"

"My neck is messed up but I'll be okay. So, I never got to ask him about putting me in a new spot. He was in a rage, Angel. I was scared. I have never seen him act so crazy. Before he left, he yelled at me and told me that since the vet is buying me new clothes and perfume that I should have him pay for the dump I live in. So, I may be on the streets anyway, sooner than I thought."

Yuri thought for a moment that Sasha was crying. "No, you won't because I'm going to help you get a spot. You'll have to sell some pussy; your body will pay for it. Sorry for talking like this, but you've been selling yourself short. Fuck Dr. Snider! He'll be back and when he does come back, you're going to make him pay for what he did to you. Look Sasha, I'm going to grab a bite to eat, be ready around eight and I'll pick you up. Shower and do your hair like you had it last night."

"Okay, should I put on the same outfit I had on yesterday, the one you bought me? I don't have any other clean clothes." Sasha asked.

Yuri felt like she was talking to a kid. "Sasha, you made six hundred dollars last night, the least you could have done was go to the laundromat in the hotel and wash your clothes"

Sasha felt ashamed, responding, "I know I should have."

Yuri decided to let it go. "Well, at least you were smart enough to get yourself a cell phone."

"Yep, and it feels good having one too. Thank you, Angel. I really appreciate you."

"Okay, I'll see you later, Sasha."

"Okay, see you later."

As Yuri drove, she thought about what Sasha had just told her about Doctor Snider. She wondered what he meant by asking Sasha, about wanting to smell like someone special to him. It played in her head.

Repeatedly, she wondered, *how could this funky-breath motherfucker say that I was special to him when he raped me on a regular basis?*

She felt sick to her stomach. She could now even smell his breath, which resulted in her losing her appetite and going back to her condo. All she could think about was how she would pay him back, and it wouldn't be nice. Yuri decided just to lay around and chill in her apartment until it was time to pick Sasha up. She got dressed in a pair of tight-fitting Levi jeggings that showed off her camel toe, and every curve of her body, a tank top exposing as much cleavage as possible, and a pair of five-inch Jimmy Choo heels that were in the back of Larry's closet; they must have been his wife's. She put on her accessories, bringing her whole outfit together. Before getting into her car, she looked in her trunk and chose one of the outfits that she had for Sasha.

Once she picked Sasha up, she drove around trying to decide what to do. Yuri knew that they couldn't go back near the Pink Pony where they had stolen the man's money. She wished that she could go to the new strip club, V Live. The radio stations were promoting it heavily. She knew she was bound to run into someone that she knew there. She needed time before she could see Candice, Shane, or anyone from her past. She wanted to go somewhere with only white men and she knew just the place. Yuri jumped on 75 North and headed to Cobb County. There was a club that she had gone to once or twice before, Club Mardi Gras.

She knew that Sasha could make a quick buck there. She might even make some quick money herself if the price was right. They arrived at the club, and Yuri handed her keys to the valet.

Yuri didn't have to show ID; however, Sasha was carded by the bouncer. She flashed her fake ID and they walked right in. The club was nice, and the dancers were all different races. They noticed more white girls than anything. Three of the white girls had black girl shapes.

Sasha asked Yuri, "Do you think that white girl's ass over there is fake?"

Yuri noticed the white girl she was asking about – she had the biggest ass in the club.

"Real fake," Yuri answered. "That shit is tight and sitting on her back like balloons. I think she could have used a little less. Now, hers over there, is perfect. It's fake, but perfect."

Sasha nodded. "Angel, do you think I could use a little more ass?"

Yuri laughed, "Sasha, you can use a lot more weight. You have a nice ass now, so when you gain weight it will make that ass plump out. I've heard that when strippers need to gain weight, they drink Ensure. Maybe that's what you need."

Sasha agreed, "What I want is an ass like yours, you got a fat ass."

They both laughed.

Yuri thought about how since losing her baby, her ass had become more voluptuous, and her hips had spread just right. Yuri didn't want to start thinking about her past because she knew that it would ruin her night. She decided to order some drinks, sit back, and watch the strippers dance.

Instead of looking around at the men, Sasha was playing in her phone.

After about thirty minutes of watching Sasha mess with her phone, Yuri interrupted her.

"What are you doing all stuck in that phone?"

Sasha looked at Yuri. "Oh sorry, I'm on Facebook, then I'm switching over to Instagram. I miss this stuff. Do you have one?"

Yuri had Facebook before she was hospitalized but didn't know what the hell Instagram was. She played along either way. "No, I don't have one because I don't like people in my mix."

Sasha laughed, "I know what you mean, that's why some people use fake names, and profile pictures. Girl, I'm loving my android and I miss social media."

Yuri smiled. "So, what's your name on there?"

Sasha hesitated, but answered. "My name is Sasha on there because it's not my real name, Angel."

Yuri thought, *I already knew*, but blurted out anyway, "What do you mean it's not your real name? So, what's your real name?"

"My real name is Sarah. I hate it! So, I changed it to Sasha. Sorry, I didn't think you and I were going to become such good friends. That's why I didn't tell you. Now that I think I'll be sticking around you, I want you to know the truth."

Yuri raised her glass, "Thanks for being honest Sasha, and yes, you will be around."

They toasted and Yuri added, "That's wassup! I knew I liked you for some reason."

They laughed and drank on their drinks

Yuri needed to know more about Instagram, and also to set up a new fake Facebook account. Sasha got back to her phone.

"How does it work?" Yuri asked, masking the embarrassment of her ignorance with a smile.

Sasha was quick to explain, "You can find old friends and family, just about anyone on here. IG is an app where celebrities and regular people post pictures of what they're doing all day; basically virtual fronting and a lot of lying. I prefer Facebook right now, since my life isn't on track, I don't post pictures or say anything. I just read others' post and like them sometimes to let them know that I'm alive."

Yuri realized that this was what she needed. "Can you look up a name for me? It's an old friend that I haven't talked to in a while."

"Sure, what's the name?"

Yuri smiled just thinking about her plan, "Shane Mitchell."

Sasha typed in the name frowning, "Sorry, Yuri, guess he doesn't fuck with the book either."

"Damn, try Chanel Brown."

Sasha tried it, "Three Chanel Browns came up. One from North Carolina, another from St. Louis, Missouri, and one from Los Angeles. Are any of these her?"

She handed Yuri the phone. Yuri looked at the photos and instantly recognized her ex-best friend.

She turned to Sasha, "How do I see more photos of the Chanel from Los Angeles?"

Sasha took the phone and showed Yuri how to click on the picture to get to her profile.

She tutored, "Click on 'profile pictures' and you'll be able to scroll through all her photos."

Yuri looked through Chanel's pictures and noticed that she was looking fly as hell. She also couldn't help but notice how much she dressed like she used to. If she wasn't in a sexy dress, she was rocking True Religion or Robin jeans in most of the pictures. She then scrolled across a picture of Chanel with Shane and their son. Shane's white teeth and deep dimples brought back so many memories. *Damn, he is still so fine*, Yuri thought. Their son, whose name she remembered, Chandler, looked just as fly. Chandler was a cute fair-skinned little boy, dressed in True Religion jeans, a polo shirt with Jordans on. They all looked happy, which made Yuri very resentful. She threw the phone on to the table. It slid off and hit the floor.

Sasha picked it up, "What the hell, Angel! Are you trying to break my phone? What happened?"

Yuri had to think before she answered, she didn't want Sasha to ask too many questions.

"It's nothing," Yuri's impromptu lying skills were on point. "We used to be friends and I saw her in a picture with a female that crossed us both. She said she would never deal with her again, and now they look like they're best friends."

"So, why don't you ask her about it?"

The lies kept coming, "Because when I was in my last relationship, he was so possessive that he made me stop talking to all my friends and family, and they didn't care that I was being abused, and never once tried contacting me."

"Do you want me to make you a Facebook page? It will only take two seconds. Then you can reach out to her?" Sasha asked.

Yuri screamed a little too loud, "Hell no!"

The people at the other table look around to see what the commotion was about.

"If she's cool with her, I would never want to deal with her. I hate them both."

With pure rage and hatred in her heart, Yuri said, "I'm not feeling too good, Sasha. I think that we should call it a night."

As they drove back to Sasha's motel room, Yuri thought about the pictures that she had seen of Chanel and Candice. They were having a ball on several different occasions. She recognized some of the places because she used to travel to Hawaii and the Bahamas on a regular with Shane. Now, he was taking Chanel. She was envious of Chanel and Candice's relationship, but couldn't help but smile because she knew the games were about to begin.

Sasha didn't want to go back to her room. She couldn't hide her disappointment when she asked Yuri to drop her off at the club down the street from the motel. Sasha wanted a drink and it was still early.

Before Sasha got out of the car, Yuri stopped her, "I know that your doctor dude will be popping up tomorrow."

Sasha laughed, "I don't think so. He was upset and the way he choked me the other day, I really don't care to see him anymore."

"I think you like him-"

Before Yuri could finish, Sasha said, "I don't like him. I just need a place to live, and now he's my only way of doing that."

Yuri shook her head. "So, if I get a spot and move you in with me, you'll never mess with him again?"

Sasha almost jumped for joy, "Of course not! Never! I promise never ever eva eva!"

Yuri couldn't help but laugh, "Okay, I'll work on that for us."

Yuri handed Sasha the vial of coke. "Here, take this. I took it from that guy the other night. Don't have too much fun."

Yuri winked at Sasha as she took it and snorted a line before she exited the car. Sasha reached over and hugged Yuri, "Thank you so much big sis. I'll call you tomorrow."

CHAPTER 10

While driving back towards downtown, Yuri decided to get off the freeway and ride pass Magic City. One of the pictures of Chanel and Candice was taken at Magic City. She knew Chanel never liked strip clubs. She was a Ms. Goodie Two Shoes who must have changed her way of living with stealing her life. Yuri was ready to find and kill Chanel, Candice, and Chanel's son.

Yuri watched as all the ballers and gold diggers came and went. After an hour, had passed, she spotted someone she knew. The stripper that was always taunting her with Candice. Her name was Passion. She was being escorted to her car by the huge security guards who took no shit.

She watched as Passion gave him a kiss on the cheek before she climbed in her car and drove out of the parking lot.

Yuri followed closely behind Passion as she jumped on HWY 20.

Yuri thought to herself, *this girl has got to be tipsy as hell swerving all over the place like that.*

Yuri slowed down a bit, then she came up with an idea to get to Candice. Yuri turned on her bright lights, sped up, and pulled up to Passion's driver side window. Yuri caught Passion by surprise, causing her to swerve and lose control of her car. She hit the guard rail, making the car skid and flip over several times. The good part was that they were the only two cars within a six-car distance, leaving no witnesses to see that Yuri had run Passion off the road. It would be hard to believe Passion anyway, because she was drunk, and never should have been driving in the first place.

Yuri kept driving as she noticed the car flipping one last time. People started pulling over to help. She got off the freeway at the next exit and jumped back on, going in the opposite direction so she could get back to the other side to see where the ambulance would take Passion. She didn't care if the bitch was dead or alive, but preferred dead. Yuri felt Passion deserved whatever she got after all the things that they had put her through. Yuri was playing the victim role again, blaming everyone for her mistakes.

Once the ambulance and fire truck arrived, they had to use the jaws of life to pull Passion out of her Benz Coupe. It was a crazy sight. Yuri enjoyed every minute of it.

She knew it was going to be a long night so she decided to take one of her happy pills from her stash. She had a selection of pills that she took with her when she escaped the nut house. She hated the downers, but the uppers made her alive, causing her to do treacherous things.

Once they could free Passion from her car, they strapped her to a gurney, put an oxygen mask on her, and loaded her into the ambulance. Yuri figured that they would end up at Grady since it was only ten minutes away, if that.

She pulled up to the hospital first, watching as the paramedics wheeled her into the ER.

The happy pill, Adderall, which was given to her for ADHD, had kicked in, making Yuri very much alert. She seemed a little off, though she wasn't crazy - but being in the ward made her elevator not go up to the top floor.

Yuri got out of her car and walked into the hospital. She noticed that the paramedic who brought Passion in was talking to a nurse.

Yuri listened as the paramedic gave the nurse Passion's real name. "The patient's name is Gloria Reynolds, thirty years of age, single vehicle accident, the patient seems to be under the influence, they're checking her blood alcohol content now."

The paramedic continued to explain to the nurse that they had found her cell phone and called her mother, who was on her way to the hospital. Neither the nurse nor the paramedic noticed Yuri eavesdropping.

Twenty minutes later, Passion's mother came running into the hospital with a man trailing behind. Yuri sat in the waiting area, giggling as she heard Passion's mom asking to see her. The nurse responded by explaining that Passion was in surgery and was sure she would make it.

Passion's mom tried to ask her more questions but the nurse interrupted.

"Ma'am, I understand that you're worried; however, I need to get back to work. Please try and relax, the doctor is doing everything he can to make sure your daughter is okay."

Passion's mom laid her head on the sexy younger guy's shoulder and cried. His phone rang, and he answered loud enough that Yuri could hear, "Hey Candice."

That got Yuri's full attention.

Jackpot, she thought.

He paused continuing, "Yeah, here at Grady, and all they said is that they think she's going to be okay. Alright, we'll see you soon."

Yuri knew it was time to head back to the car. Now that Candice was on her way, it was time for Yuri to execute her plan by killing her and anyone else who got in her way.

Yuri sat outside in her car bumping to Jeezy's newest song, "Run the Check Up," dancing and singing, especially when Yo Gotti's verse came up. She was crunk off her happy pill. When some type of yellow, convertible coupe that Yuri had never seen pulled up, it was no other than hers truly. Once Candice got out, Yuri would make sure to walk pass and see what type of car that it was. The car and rims caught her attention. She stepped out looking Hollywood, and from the way she was dressed, Yuri could tell that she had to have been at a club. Her body suit was banging! Heels red bottoms as usual. Her shape looked to be different. Yuri knew Candice liked to have cosmetic surgery. More than likely she had had more work done. Yuri thought to herself, *I guess they're right; once you get something done, you just can't stop.*

Candice had the big NWT Boy Rainbow, cross body Chanel bag, that Yuri had seen in Phipps Plaza while she was window shopping. She remembered that it had cost sixty-five hundred dollars. Candice was already a boss chick but Yuri could tell that she had stepped her game up even more. She wondered if Q was still tricking' off, or if Candice still dealt with her old tricks, or upgraded to a few other sponsors. Candice knew how to get to a man's heart and pocket but had never wanted to settle down. Yuri also knew that any man that she dealt with had to be playing with six figures or better.

Candice quickly ran inside the Emergency Room with a female that Yuri couldn't identify following close behind her. As they disappeared into the hospital, Yuri took another pill, just to make sure that she wouldn't fall asleep if Candice stayed all night.

Yuri got out of her car, walking over to the little beauty that sat in front of the building. The car was a 2016 4C Spider Alfa Romeo, Giulia. She tried to remember where she had heard about this type of car. Yuri remembered that Larry had a magazine that came to his condo called the ROBB Report and the car was just featured in the newest issue, costing from seventy to a hundred thousand dollars.

Candice would soon lead her exactly where she needed to go. After that, she would figure out how she wanted her to die.

A few hours later, Candice and the female came out, walking to their car. They looked tired as hell. Yuri knew that this would benefit her because they wouldn't pay too much attention and notice that they were being followed.

Candice jumped on the freeway. The Spider sped off, accelerating up to sixty miles per hour within twenty seconds, but Yuri kept up, not getting too close. Candice got off on the Lennox Road exit. Yuri started thinking she was going to the same condo that she used to live in. Instead, Candice took a right-on Lennox Road to get to her new condo. Yuri recognized the condos that she was pulling into. She was with Candice when she was first considering moving to these newly built condos. They were 4,000 square feet, ranging anywhere from $500,000 to $1.5 million. Candice keyed in a code before driving through the gates. Yuri knew that between her rich men, and her good job as an accountant, she had been living it up. Yuri was extremely jealous. She knew that if Candice was doing it big like that, she could only imagine how Shane was catering to Chanel and that funny-looking kid they had. She hated the thought of it.

It was about five fifteen in the morning, Yuri's happy pill was wearing off. Now that she knew where Candice lived, she could at least try and get some sleep.

CHAPTER 11

At 9:30 a.m., Yuri's phone rang, just a little after she had made herself go to sleep. She decided to answer anyway. "Hello?"

"Angel! can you please pick me up?" It was Sasha.

"Why? What's wrong?" Yuri asked.

Sasha was panicky and sounded as if she had been crying.

"Gary came by not long ago. I had just got in, so I put the vial of coke on the table because I didn't think he would come. He hates it when I do drugs so he made me pour it out in the toilet, beat me, then he raped me! He beat me some more, making me crawl, while he whooped me with a belt. Then, he made me give him head. He told me before that if he ever caught me doing coke again, that he would break my jaw, and he really tried. I'm sorry Angel but I don't know what to do and I don't want him to come back and hurt me."

Sasha started crying again. Even though Yuri was exhausted, she told her that she was on her way.

Yuri hated Doctor Snider with a passion. Yuri thought to herself, *the bastard doesn't want Sasha to do drugs but he was always drugging me up to the point I couldn't even say my own fucking name!*

Yuri had a nice surprise in store for Doctor Snider once she saw him.

Yuri pulled up to the Waffle House. Sasha came out looking battered and restless. She looked around, constantly checking over her shoulder before she jumped in Yuri's car.

"I'm sorry to interrupt your rest but you know I have no one else to call," Sasha whined.

She became furious the very next second and shouted, "I hate him!"

She sobbed uncontrollably after that.

Yuri didn't like to hear her cry.

"So, what are you going to do about it Sasha? Are you going to keep letting him do you wrong? He already fucks you basically for free, and it's only going to get worse."

Sasha knew Yuri was right. "What do I do, Angel?"

Yuri smiled, "You mean, what do we do? We are a family now, Sasha. We are in this together."

Sasha couldn't help but smile. She felt loved, what she yearned for most.

Once they drove off, Yuri called Bliss. Yuri asked her if she found any apartments for her to check out. She told Yuri that she had found three that she might like, and the best part was they were all in Gwinnett County, away from everything. Yuri wanted to stay out of sight as much as she could.

"When can I see them?" Yuri asked.

Bliss could sense her urgency. "I'll be free around two o' clock this afternoon. The most expensive is $950 a month. It's a three bedroom, vaulted ceilings and two and half bath, the kitchen is big with beige granite counter tops. The other two are two bedrooms, two baths, ranging from $750 to $850."

"What street is the three-bed room on?" Yuri asked.

"It's off Hwy 85 and Pleasant Hill Road."

"I haven't seen it, but I already know that's the one I want."

Bliss laughed. "I knew you'd like that one. As I said, the rent is $950 a month. To move in, you need first, and last month rent, plus the $450 deposit. Combined with my $500 finder's and hook- up fee. You'll need $2,850 to move in."

Yuri was more than excited, asking, "How soon can I move in? If I give you the money today when can I move?"

Bliss thought about it for minute. "You can move in maybe Tuesday, considering that today is Sunday, they're closed. Actually, I knew you would like that one, so I already submitted the application, and I'll be picking up your keys tomorrow. So, you can move in probably as soon as tomorrow evening."

Yuri was thrilled.

"You sure know how to get shit done Bliss. Thanks, girl. Oh, you said you would take care of the lights for me too, right?"

"Yeah, for an extra hundred, I got you," Bliss said. Yuri smiled.

"Well, make it happen!"

Bliss laughed.

"I will. Oh, Angel, I have an $800 gift card to Bed, Bath & Beyond. If you want it, I'll give it to you for $350, but you'll have to get it now because I'm short on cash, and I need some Cush."

Yuri wasn't surprised.

"You smoke weed?"

"Hell yeah. Only that good Cali Cush, Girl and it's about to be legal all around the United States." Bliss said. Yuri thought about Shane, who only smoked the best when he did smoke.

"Okay, where do you want to meet, because I'd like to get some, too. Whatever I can get for my hundred."

Bliss couldn't help but laugh. "Let me school you on something really quick, girl, never say whatever you can get, you have to know your grams or you will get fucked out here."

Yuri felt a slightly bit embarrassed that she didn't know anything about weed.

"So, what can I get?"

Bliss decided to help Yuri out. "Well, eighty will get you an eighth, which is three-point-five grams. Hundred and twenty-five will get you seven grams, which is the better buy."

Yuri was trying to keep up. "Okay, I want the seven grams."

"For the record, we call that a Vick," Bliss explained.

Yuri was confused, "What the hell is a Vick?"

Bliss smiled, "Michael Vick, our ex-quarterback, his number was seven, it just sounds good."

They both laughed.

Bliss continued, "Angel, I'm downtown. Can you meet me somewhere around here?"

"Sure, how about on 10th street at the Varsity? Do you know where that is, Bliss?" Yuri answered.

"Of course, I do, I'll meet you there."

Yuri responded, "Alright, give me twenty minutes. I'm leaving Henry County."

"Okay Angel, see you soon."

When Yuri hung up with Bliss, she turned to Sasha. "I found us a place!" She grinned

Sasha screamed, "*Us?!*"

Yuri liked her excitement.

"Yes, I'm taking you with me. But before we move, I need you to call Doctor Snider and let him have one last visit with you."

Sasha frowned with her head down, pleading, "But Angel, I don't want to see him ever again."

Yuri had a devilish grin on her face. "After you see him this last time, I'm sure he'll never want to see you again either."

Now Sasha was confused, "What do you want me to do?"

Yuri was getting a little irritated with the twenty questions. "Didn't I tell you we were in this together?"

Sasha nodded and mumbled, "Yes."

Yuri continued, "So it's what we're going to do to him for thinking he can treat you any kind of way. You must trust me."

Sasha couldn't hide the worry in her voice. "We're not gonna hurt him, are we?"

Yuri smiled, patting Sasha's hand.

"Don't worry Boo, just sit back and enjoy the ride. Now that I'm here I'll take care of my little sister."

Yuri winked at her, noticing Sasha relax just a little.

Yuri met with Bliss and paid her for the gift card. Bliss told her to follow her to the gas station around the corner to meet with her weed connect. Yuri handed Bliss one hundred twenty-five dollars for her weed and watched as she went over to an all-black Dodge Challenger. Bliss climbed into the passenger seat and closed the door.

Once Bliss exited the car, she was smiling as if she had just gotten laid, or had won the lotto.

Once she reached Yuri's car, Yuri smiled.

"Damn girl, why you smiling so hard?"

Bliss laughed, "Girl, wait until you smell this shit. Getting my medicine always makes me happy."

Yuri mused, *I guess she feels the way I feel when I take my happy pill.*

Bliss interrupted her thoughts asking, "Do you want to hang out with me and smoke?"

Yuri had other plans. "Maybe next time. My little sister and I have some business to take care of. Give me a call tomorrow and tell me what's up with the apartment."

Bliss said. "Alright. I'll hit you up tomorrow."

Yuri and Sasha drove around while they smoked a blunt, talking about how they were going to decorate their new apartment.

Yuri treated Sasha to Benihana's that evening. Sasha was very grateful to have Yuri in her life. They started talking about Doctor Snider as their cook prepared the meal in front of them.

"So, Sasha, when that asshole comes to see you, what does he normally have with him?" Yuri asked as she sipped on her Saki.

Sasha thought about it for a minute.

"He usually brings his glasses, condoms, and sometimes he brings his work gloves with him. He always puts his condoms and gloves in a small sandwich bag that he takes with him."

Yuri had a worried look on her face.

"I think that's in case he ever does something to you, like hurt you or even kill you, so there won't be any evidence."

Sasha interrupted. "My, why would you think that, Angel?"

"Because men are crazy and because of how you said that he acted out this morning; you never know what's going through their minds. When men are angry they get extra aggressive and it's an illegitimate excuse, but they don't care." Yuri answered.

After a short pause, Yuri got back to the plan. "So, what else does he have with him?"

"He always has a pack of cigarettes or two, his usual cup of coffee, and he never leaves behind that shitty-ass breath of his." Sasha said.

They both laughed out loud while everyone in the restaurant looked at them.

"It's that bad?" Yuri asked.

Sasha frowned, "Angel, it's so bad that sometimes when I close my eyes, I think I'm at a horse stable working, picking up horse shit."

Yuri almost threw up in her mouth because she knew exactly what Sasha was talking about.

Yuri turned to Sasha, "This is what I want you to do, call him once we leave here and tell him that you liked the way he beat on you this morning. Tell him how much it turned you on, and you want him to do it again. Tell him that after he beats you, you want him to fuck you. Oh, didn't you say he likes the smell of animals?"

Sasha looked disgusted, "Yeah, he loves the smell of the Vet."

Yuri continued, "Well, tell him you went to the Animal Hospital and fucked the vet on the animal table just for him. Tell him that you haven't showered because you want him to enjoy fucking you."

Sasha cut her off. "But he'll hurt me when he doesn't smell the animals."

Yuri shook her head, "No. He won't hurt you because you're going to put this in his coffee." She opened her palm, showing Sasha the pills that she had been saving them personally for Doctor Snider since the day she had left the ward. She wanted to literally give him a taste of his own medicine.

Sasha looked confused.

"What are these, Angel?"

Yuri devilishly smiled.

"Oh, just a little something to relax him so he won't get mad at you."

"Okay, then what do you want me to do?" Sasha asked.

Yuri took a sip of her drink then said, "All you have to do is let me in, and I'll do everything else. So, when I drop you off, I want you to pack all the things that you're going to take with you to our new place. After this, you won't be going back to that terrible place. You must trust me on this."

Sasha smiled. "Okay, Angel. Thank you so much."

Yuri couldn't help but smile at Sasha's excitement. "Oh, so you won't be nervous about anything, I have you a little sugar, so you'll be relaxed."

Sasha looked nervous.

"Angel, he'll know that I'm high and try…"

Yuri cut her off, saying, "Fuck him, and stop being so damn scared! Don't forget to put on that perfume that I gave you." Sasha just shook her head.

"Angel, you're trying to get me killed."

Yuri looked at Sasha.

"You're my little sister. I won't let anything happen to you. Just trust me, please. I'll be right on the other side of the door. All you have to do is let me know when he passes out, okay?"

Sasha was pessimistic about the situation, but agreed anyway. They both finished their drinks and meal. Sasha thanked Yuri. "That has got to be the best meal I have ever had."

Yuri laughed. "I know what you mean. This is my favorite Japanese restaurant. Girl, get used to eating food like this, you're hanging with me now."

Yuri winked at Sasha and they both laughed.

Before Yuri dropped Sasha off, she handed her the powder cocaine, knowing that she couldn't resist taking it.

"Sasha, do you remember everything that we talked about?" Yuri asked.

"Yes, I do. I won't mess up because if I do, I'm dead." Sasha replied.

Yuri stopped her before she got out of the car. "Sasha, I love you."

Sasha lit up.

"I love you too, Angel! See you in the a.m."

Yuri smiled at her. "Okay, see you soon."

CHAPTER 12

Once Yuri was back at Larry's apartment, she cleaned up well. She would see him in the morning before she left for Sasha's. The money for their new apartment would come from Larry. She already planned on hitting up her dad for money to furnish it.

Yuri woke up early the next morning knowing it was going to be a good day. She showered then popped the ecstasy pill that she had gotten from Bliss. Bliss had the hookup for everything, from drugs to furniture to cars. Getting a new car would be her next move.

It wasn't long before she felt the pill kicking in. She had everything planned perfectly because Larry was due home any minute. She heard him unlock the front door. He walked into his condo, shocked to find Yuri wide awake and butt-naked.

Yuri seductively whispered, "Hey Daddy. It's been a long weekend without you. I've missed you and I want to show you just how much."

She licked her lips and motioned for him to join her on the bed.

Larry started undressing, getting more excited watching Yuri spread her legs and expose her clean-shaven pussy. Larry couldn't resist Yuri and she knew it. He knelt in front of her, wanting to taste her wet, sweetness.

Yuri put her hands on the back of his head grinding her hips up against his face. She thought, *I'll make sure that I induct Larry into my pussy-eating Hall of Fame.* Yuri only liked her pussy eaten when they knew what they were doing and Larry was a professional coochie-eater.

Once he made Yuri cum several times, it was Yuri's turn to take care of him.

She flipped Larry over and before she could work her magic, he said, "I have been craving you all weekend."

While putting his dick in her mouth, she whispered, "Well, here I am Daddy, and I'm all yours."

Larry loved it when she talked to him like that. She worked her tongue up and down his hard shaft.

Larry moaned. "Suck it good, baby. Show Daddy how much you want this dick."

He wrapped his hands in her hair and pushed it deeper in her mouth. She wanted to tell him not to touch her hair, but she also knew that she needed to please him to get what she wanted.

She sucked and stroked his dick better than she had ever done before.

She cupped his balls, feeling him tense up, "You like that, baby? You want to cum in my mouth? You want me to swallow it all without letting any come out of my mouth?"

Yuri brought him fully into her mouth, she then made a swallowing motion swallowing all the juices that had built up in her mouth. This action made the muscles in her throat tense up which felt great against his sensitive tip.

Larry squirmed around, trying to stay calm. She then started twirling her tongue in slow sloppy circles around his thick hard, piece of flesh, making sure she had his undivided attention. She moved her head up and down, going crazy on his dick. He tried hard to hold his eruption, but couldn't, causing him to release in her mouth.

As he lay on the couch, he turned to Yuri, "Damn Yuri, I wanted some of that sweet pussy. You were like an animal. What got into you, girl?"

Yuri smiled because she knew the pill had made her super-wild and freaky. She had made Larry cum within ten minutes, giving herself another hour to spare.

She laid back on the bed, still ready to get whatever kind of sex that he could give, saying, "Well, since you wanted to fuck me and you didn't get a chance. Grab my toy from that drawer over there and come fuck me with it until your dick gets back hard, Daddy."

Larry almost tripped over himself trying to get to the drawer. He pulled out the seven-inch dildo and went to work on Yuri. Yuri enjoyed the way Larry worked the dildo. The ecstasy had Yuri extra hot.

She started moaning, "Harder, Daddy, fuck me! Fuck me, Daddy!"

Larry got hard instantly.

He pulled the toy out of Yuri, and climbed on top of her, kissing all over her neck, "I love you, Yuri."

Yuri rolled her eyes but stuck to her script which had turned to real live passionate sex.

"Well, fuck me like you love me."

Larry slowly entered her, stroking her nice and slow. Yuri couldn't put up with the slow fucking - she didn't want to make love; she wanted Larry to beat it up, and curb her sexual appetite. She rolled Larry over so she could get on top. She inserted him inside of herself, riding his dick like the Canadian porn star, Sunny Leone.

Larry grabbed her hips, "Yes baby, ride this dick!"

While riding, Yuri did her famous Kegel muscle squeeze move. She contracted her pussy four counts at a time, then relaxed her muscles, then flexed once more. That was her signature move, and no one could resist from having an orgasm. Larry wasn't anything nice in the bed, and had just as many moves as she did. He pulsed his love muscle, while fully inserting himself all the way up inside of Yuri making her almost jump off, but the pill had her intrigued.

Yuri yelled, "Yes, Daddy! Put this dick up in my stomach."

Larry was on his back, making Yuri buck like she was about to get thrown off a bull, but she stayed mounted, riding him like the professional she was. Larry wouldn't win today but he gave it to her just the way she wanted it.

He made a howling noise and then his orgasm came and could barely breathe, saying, "Yuri, baby, you are fucking magnificent."

Yuri smiled, grabbing the toy off the bed.

She winked at Larry. "Now you just lay there and enjoy the show."

She rubbed the dildo on her sensitive clit while taking her free hand, rubbing her breasts.

She moaned louder and louder while pleasuring herself. "Do you like watching me, Daddy?"

Larry nodded his head, amazed at how she could keep going and yet still be so wet.

She started sliding the dildo in and out, making all seven inches disappear. She worked the dildo until she found her G-spot. She humped and pumped the fake dick while thinking of Uno. She felt her orgasm coming on, she pushed the dildo deeper inside, and held it while she felt all her juices squirt out.

Larry was enjoying the show. Once she took the dildo out of her dripping, wet pussy, she stuck her finger inside, pulled it out, and sucked own her juices. What was left Larry bent down and slurped it up.

He moaned, "Mmmm, this pussy taste so sweet and good."

Larry laid back down, licking his lips in awe of how sexy and nasty his young tender woman could be.

As Larry got dressed for work, Yuri told him that she had found a place. He was happy, but sad at the same time. He would've never wanted his wife to find out about Yuri, so it was good that she would have her own place. The bad part was he knew that he couldn't come and go from her place as he pleased.

Larry turned to Yuri.

"Where is this new place that you have?"

Yuri sat up in the bed. "Gwinnett County."

Larry thought to himself, *at least it's somewhere close to me.*

Yuri walked up behind Larry and wrapping her arms around him, "I need money to move in though, Daddy."

He turned and faced her, without hesitating, "How much do you need, baby?"

Yuri had to resist the urge to smile, "Well, rent is a thousand dollars a month plus a deposit. Then, I'll need the basic things like pots, pans, and other things. So, I need like..."

Larry interrupted her, "Like twenty-five hundred dollars." He reached for his wallet

Yuri looked at him as if he were crazy, "No Daddy, like five thousand."

Larry put his head down, "Yuri, baby, you know I can't pull that much out of the bank without Clara knowing."

Yuri was disgusted,

"Well, I guess I'll take four thousand, and you know that's not shit to you, Larry."

Larry felt defeated.

"I'll get it later and drop it back off. I hope you're here so I can have some more of that good thing between your legs, or better yet what's on your head, smiling. You were great this morning. Damn, baby, you deserve a standing ovation."

While clapping. Yuri bowed, giggling at what Larry had said. She knew she had shown out and this was only the beginning.

Larry gave Yuri a passionate kiss while grabbing a handful of ass.

Once Larry left, Yuri didn't bother to shower. She put on her clothes and headed out. She jumped on HWY 75 South because she knew around this time all the traffic would be going north; therefore, making her trip with perfect timing.

Doctor Snider arrived at Sasha's using his key to walk in. As he entered the room, he found a wide-awake Sasha looking sexy and seductive. The sight of Sasha's naked body turned him on.

Sasha ran to the door and hugged him. She stepped behind him, rubbing on his shoulders, as she steered him towards the bed.

"Are you tired, baby? Or are you ready to fuck me?" She cooed as she reached around, grabbing his crotch.

Doctor Snider jumped.

"Whoa Sasha, you're really freaky this morning. I've never seen you act like this." Skeptical of how she was acting, he asked, "Are you on something?"

Sasha got nervous because she knew that he knew her mood swings.

She played it calm, not letting the cocaine take control. "No baby, absolutely not, I'm just happy to see you and I promise that what happened yesterday will never happen again."

Doctor Snider looked at her for a minute before responding, "That's a good girl. Now come around here and give me a kiss."

Sasha walked up to him and kissed him. He shoved his tongue down her throat without warning almost making her puke. She wasn't expecting one of his wet, sticky kisses, not to mention how bad his breath smelled.

Doctor Snider put his cup of coffee on the table, "I'm going to the restroom. When I come back out, I'm going to devour your sweet deep pussy."

Sasha faked a smile, "I can't wait, baby."

Once he was out of sight, Sasha grabbed the secret potion that Yuri had given her to put in his coffee. Sasha was so nervous that she almost spilled his coffee. She was finally able to get it all in. She stirred it with her finger and laid back down quickly before he finished.

She then thought about everything Yuri had told her to do, making sure she didn't forget anything.

"Damn," she whispered.

She ran over to her bag and sprayed the perfume all over herself. Before she had a chance to put the perfume back in her bag, Doctor Snider startled her by coming out of the restroom. He walked over and took a sip of his coffee.

"Come here, Sasha, massage your man, he's tired."

Doctor Snider had already undressed in the restroom. Sasha realized that even though he wasn't a bad looking older man, his body showed that he was sixty. His skin was wrinkled and hung all over, turning Sasha off. She thought, *what the hell was I thinking?*

As he took another sip of his coffee, Sasha massaged his dick. "Mmmm... hmmm," she moaned. "Baby, I've missed you." She wondered how long it would take for whatever she put in his cup to kick in.

Doctor Snider instantly became aroused once Sasha started talking in her little girl voice. She knew that her child-like voice always turned him on. *Does this motherfucker like kids?* She wondered.

The voice made him eager to get between her legs. As he grabbed her trying to smell the fragrance that would be on her, he stopped. "You smell like that perfume again. Why?"

His whole body tensed up, while his face turned red.

Sasha was now scared. "Because I thought…"

Doctor Snider quickly interrupted, "You thought what, black bitch?! Didn't I tell you that I didn't want you smelling like someone who was special to me?!"

Sasha whined, "I thought I was special to you, Gary."

Doctor Snider backhanded her as hard as he could. "You're a cheap black slut, who lives in a motel, with a fucking drug problem. I fuck you, and put my cock in your mouth, when I want, with no strings attached. So how special do you think you are, you fucking cunt?!"

Sasha knew she was in trouble. Doctor Snider grabbed her by her hair, throwing her to the floor. He put on the rubber gloves and condom. The madder he became, the harder his penis got. He held Sasha down by her neck, lifted up her negligee, going inside her. Every time he smelled the fragrance, he choked her harder.

She heard him screaming that name again, "Yuri! Yuri! Yuri!"

Tears streamed down her face because she saw her life pass by, the good, bad and the ugly. She felt that she was going to die.

The next Yuri that came out of his mouth was his last - he fell off her. She coughed, holding her neck. She finally got up, kicked him onto the floor, the pill had kicked in right on time. "You pussy-ass cracker! Fucking fuckboy nigga! I hate you! Aarrggh!"

Screaming to herself.

She jumped up and wondered where Angel was. She was totally panicking, not knowing if Doctor Snider was dead or alive. The knock on the door startled her half to death. She looked out the window to see Yuri. Sasha opened the door.

"You're late! What the fuck, Angel. He was about to kill me for wearing that fucking perfume!" Sasha turned her anger at Angel.

Sasha ran over and kicked his lifeless body again. The 'umph' sound he made let her know he was alive. Even though his body jerked, he remained unconscious. Yuri checked his pockets. She found a Viagra pill and shoved it in his mouth. She pulled the plastic ties out of her bag, tying both sides of his hands and one side of his feet to the head and foot rails of the bed, then gagged him with a bandanna. She had to make sure he was unable to speak because she didn't want him to say her real name.

Sasha gathered all her belongings in the room just in case he wanted to go to the police. She already planned on going herself to tell them that he raped her. The room wasn't in her name, so there was no way it could be turned on her.

After what seemed to be an hour, he started coming to. He saw Yuri's naked body standing in front of him. He thought he was delusional but what he was seeing was Yuri live in the flesh.

Yuri got Sasha to snort more powder. Sasha was spooked, standing in the corner, not knowing what to do.

"Mmmmm," Yuri moaned to herself while playing in her pussy.

"Get naked. If he wants a show, let's give him one," she told Sasha, while sucking her juices from her fingers.

Doctor Snider's eyes were totally opened now. Yuri pulled Sasha to her and started sucking on her titties, causing Sasha to jerk and shake her head. Sasha felt weird. "What are you doing, Angel?"

Yuri smiled, "Giving him a show. Don't be scared." Yuri had a woman go down on her before but hadn't ever been the aggressor with a woman. She would have to be the aggressor with Sasha, because the girl had never been with a woman. It was strange, but once Yuri started caressing and sucking on her breast, it all felt so natural.

Doctor Snider watched with excitement. Yuri gently laid Sasha down next to his loose foot on the bed and ate Sasha's pussy like no man had ever done before. For it to have been Yuri's first time, she ate Sasha's pussy like a pro.

"Ohhhh," Sasha moaned with pleasure as she arched her back.

The molly had Yuri going, and she enjoyed her new venture of eating Sasha, all while turning the pervert Doctor Snider on.

Doctor Snider's dick stood straight up as he watched Yuri turn Sasha out.

"Aaahh, aaahhh... Oh shit, Angel," Sasha moaned, while grabbing the back of Yuri's head.

Yuri was making her feel like no man had ever done before. When she came in Yuri's mouth, Yuri sucked on her pearl tongue, making Sasha go ballistic. The slurping sounds echoed throughout the room as Yuri swallowed Sasha 's cum.

"Oh - I love you!" Sasha cried out.

Doctor Snider tried to break loose; he wanted in on the fun, but unfortunately, he was tied up.

Yuri asked Sasha if she wanted a taste, pointing toward her own lower lips. Sasha was more than ready. Spreading Yuri's legs, apart, she dove straight in. She went down on Yuri, moving her tongue in and out of Yuri's wetness. She wasn't a pro, but by the time Yuri finished with her, she would be one of her sex slaves, like everyone else. While Sasha was licking Yuri's clit, she moved her head from side to side, really getting into it. She pushed three fingers into her pussy, getting them good and wet, shoving them underneath the bandanna that was in Doctor Snider's mouth, letting him taste her sweetness. This drove him wild. Making him try and brake the plastic restraint lose. At this point, the Viagra Yuri had shoved down his throat kicked in; he was stuck on stupid, with a rock-hard dick, and no ability to relieve it.

After Yuri got tired of Sasha 's fouled attempt to make her cum, she pushed Sasha's head back, gripping her hair, and began kissing her, while grinding sexually, bumping pussy to pussy.

Sasha squirmed and moaned as did Doctor Snider. When she was sure neither one of them could stand it a minute longer, Yuri finger-fucked her until she climaxed,

Sasha went wild. "Awe awe aw, ooh, ooh-Jesus!" Sasha screamed, squirting out her juices everywhere.

Once Yuri finished her off, she told Sasha to go clean up while she talked to him about how he had treated her. Sasha felt in lust with Yuri now, and did exactly as she was told, without questioning. Once the bathroom door closed, Yuri took the gag out of Doctor Snider's anxious mouth.

"Well, did you enjoy the show, Doctor?" She asked, seductively.

"Yuri, I love you" was the first thing he blurted out. Yuri hopped on his face, sitting her hot, wet pussy in his mouth, knowing that he would enjoy it.

"You don't love me, your sick motherfucker! You loved raping me - fucking and eating my pussy while I was incoherent, didn't you?"

This line of questioning, the accusations and insinuations was all turning Doctor Snider on even more, he was one sick puppy.

He licked and sucked on her pussy while she talked trash to him.

He thought to himself, *while she thinks she is torturing me, this is hands-down the kinkiest and most exciting thing that has ever happened to me!* He laughed, and sucked on her pussy even harder.

Once Sasha came out of the bathroom, Yuri told her to get dressed. Sasha ran past them and started putting on her clothes. When she was completely clothed, Yuri directed her to where her own outfit was.

"Now get that dress over there and slide it over my head," Yuri told Sasha, while Doctor Snider was still licking her cunt.

Sasha immediately did everything, exactly as Yuri instructed her.

She finally became jealous saying, "Angel, he's enjoying sucking your pussy!"

"He won't for long," Yuri replied, as she spun around on his tongue, now facing his blood-engorged dick. She lifted up and let him eat out what he really liked. He licked and sucked all up her ass for all he was worth. "Eat these cookies! I wish I had to shit, because it would be all in your mouth, you nasty, funky-breath bitch!

Sasha looked at Yuri in a confused manner, asking, "How do you know he likes to lick ass? I never told you that part."

Yuri paid her no mind.

"Pass me the bag!" Yuri demanded, then removed the utensils, and put on the latex surgical gloves.

Sasha had her face scrunched, wondering what the hell Yuri was doing. Doctor Snider wasn't even aware of what was about to happen to him, since he was completely caught up in his obsession with sucking Yuri's butt. Yuri unwrapped the scalpel from the cloth that it had been wrapped in. She rubbed on Dr. Snider's dick, making sure it was at its hardest peak, moaning, and calling out the first half of Yuri's name.

"Oh, Yu..." was all he could get out before Yuri sliced his dick off. "Ahhh! — *What the fuck?!*"

Doctor Snider screamed. Yuri jumped up covering his mouth back up, regagging him to shut him up. He tried to grab his prick, realizing too late that he was still tied up.

Sasha screamed, as well.

"Angel, are you crazy?!"

"No! Now grab my bag and go start the car up!" Sasha looked around the room once again, making sure she hadn't left anything behind. She ran out the motel door, almost tripping over the boxer dog that was always out next door. She ran down the stairs, taking them two at a time, shaking, hoping she wouldn't pee on herself.

Yuri cut the plastic wires that were wrapped around Doctor Snider's leg.

"This is for fucking me, and all the other people at the crazy house, and for abusing Sasha! You're damn lucky I didn't jam your pink skinny dick down your motherfucking throat, or shove it up your flabby, flat ass!" By this point, Yuri was screaming in his face, as tears streamed from his eyes from the excruciating pain that he was feeling. "Oh, and I'm pretty sure they will be able to put it back on before you bleed to death, because I didn't hit a major artery or vein. You may want to grab that ice bucket and put it on ice, but I'd hurry up if I were you. Drive yourself to the hospital." She teased him sarcastically. "Don't wait too long, or you'll pass out." Yuri couldn't help the evil smirk on her face as she continued, "I'm sure you don't want your wife to come here and see you in this raunchy-ass motel with your dick cut off in your hand. Now wouldn't that certainly be hard to explain. I'm sure you'll create some lie that she'll swallow about all this, but finding you here would make it pretty tough."

She threw her head back and let loose with a semi-hysterical devil-laugh as she cut the last of his bonds, freeing his hands.

He grabbed for his penis in a curious way, his fingers finding nothing but a bloody stump. Yuri waved it at him.

"Bitch, you cut my dick completely off!" He yelled.

She laughed at his horror, as she walked out of the motel tossing it in his general direction, over her retreating shoulder, as it hit the wall. Doctor Snider rushed to put his shirt and pants on, hoping he could make it to the hospital in time for them to successfully reattach his penis. Once he picked his limp member up off the floor, he barely made it to the open door before the severity of his situation hit him full-force, and he dropped to his knees. It took a moment for him to clear his head enough to get to his feet, and unsteadily made it through the door. As he walked out, he stumbled over the boxer, dropping his slim pencil pecker. The dog took a sniff and picked it up. Doctor Snider tried grabbing it out of his mouth, but the dog clamped down harder on his prize and growled threateningly. The two struggled over the bloody hunk of flesh, each tugging for all he was worth. The boxer must have thought that it was a toy because he wouldn't let go, clamping down tighter, as Doctor Snider sweated almost passing out. He fought the mean animal with everything he had over his manhood. Eventually, after several minutes of scuffling, the dog grew weary, the Doctor gave a mighty tug, snatching it from the dog. He pulled so hard he threw himself off balance and flipped backwards down the entire flight of stairs, knocking himself unconscious.

Yuri took Sasha down to the Hilton, where she already had a room reserved through Brandon, the supervisor that she screwed for hotel favors. Sasha admired the room, but told Yuri she was scared about what had happened with Doctor Snider, and didn't want Yuri to leave her there alone. For the rest of the day, Yuri promised her that everything would be okay and that Doctor Snider would never go to the authorities and talk for so many different reasons.

Throughout the day, they made love to each other. When the six o'clock news came on, the featured story was about how Doctor Gary Snider's penis was cut off, and how he fought with the dog to get it back. They laughed hysterically. Knowing how playful the dog was next door. Yuri fell off the bed onto the ground laughing so hard that she started to cry. Sasha joined in making her relax. The news also said they had no suspects in the case, and were looking for leads. Yuri turned to the next channel. They made the story seem even funnier, and they laughed some more. Their story had a witness leaving the Waffle House, who was funny as shit the way he told the story made Yuri run in the bathroom and tinkle. He explained how he had never seen a grown man fight over his manhood "literally," even though he didn't know what it was at the time until Doctor Snider fell down the stairs and passed out. The comedic witness said once he ran over to help out, and give him CPR he stepped back when he saw what appeared to be a human penis a few feet from the victim. He said once he saw that, and knew it was what he and the dog were fighting over, he wasn't giving him shit, and called the paramedic. Yuri said this shit is funnier than watching Kevin Hart.

Sasha had a sobering thought.

"But Angel," she ventured, "What if he tells them it was us?"

"Trust me, he won't," Yuri assured her.

"I do trust you, Angel I'm just scared," Sasha sighed, as she leaned her head-on Yuri's shoulder. She felt safe and content in her arms.

Always the opportunist, Yuri knew this was the perfect time to take full advantage of the girl.

"Sasha," she started, softly, while stroking her hair. "Do you remember I told you about some problems I had with that Chanel girl?" Sasha nodded, and Yuri continued, "If you and I are going to be together, I'm going to need you to assist me in finding her. She really fucked my life up."

"How did she do that?" Sasha asked.

"I don't really want to talk about that right now?" Yuri responded, "Come here and let me take care of you. That's all I want to do."

Sasha shifted her position, and Yuri began rubbing her clit, getting her pussy wet again, thrusting three fingers inside and out of her, gently and teasingly at first, then gradually faster until Sasha was completely aroused.

"Yes, Angel, yes!" Sasha moaned.

Yuri knew that her plan was about to go well, anyone that she felt, destroyed her life, she was coming for them all. She thought one down and a few to go. She licked on Sasha's clit as her fingers continued their mission. In no time at all, she mastered the art of eating Sasha's pussy that evening, and not only did Sasha enjoy it, but Yuri did, too.

CHAPTER 13

Yuri and Sasha moved into the new apartment together. Yuri couldn't help thinking to herself how everything was going as planned. Her dad had sent enough money to pay for three months' rent, and Larry's contribution paid for the furniture. All Yuri had to come up with was a little for the odds and ends, and she had Bliss that could give her gift cards for that. Sasha and Yuri had been selling a lot of pussy since they had moved. They both had a nice chunk of change stashed up.

Sasha had hooked back up with the white guy she had met at Billiards. His name was Kevin Choice. He was thirty-five years old. He had an impressive athlete's build, soft wavy brown hair, and perfectly straight, white teeth. As pleasing as he was to the eyes, Kevin's best attribute was that he worked for a very wealthy business tycoon, importing computer microchips, pulling in a comfortable seven-figure salary. Plus, he had franchised a couple of Steak and Shakes restaurants, in Sandy Spring Georgia. Kevin had a girlfriend who was mixed Japanese and black – and best of all, she lived in Japan. That made it easy and convenient for Sasha to be with him, as much as he liked her to be. She didn't deal with any other tricks, and felt stress-free whenever he was in town. Sasha didn't mind how much he talked about his girlfriend, Niko. Although he loved her, he liked Sasha's deep-tight wet pussy, and she knew that she was satisfying his sexual appetite while his lady was unavailable also, leaving no room to catch feelings. Yuri had made sure Sasha whipped it on him every time. Kevin bought Sasha a 2012 Honda Accord, during her second month dating him.

Needless to say, Yuri had made Sasha fall so deeply in love with her, and their new lifestyle, that Sasha was her puppet. They used Sasha's car whenever they went out searching for people that Yuri had it out for, so that no one would guess it was Yuri.

They had been following Candice for months. Finally, she had led them to Chanel. They had just about given up stalking her for the day, thinking Candice was just going shopping at the Phipps Plaza, as she did often.

Sasha noticed Chanel from a Facebook picture. She had just stepped out of a Bentley Convertible Coupe. Sasha was in awe of the fashionably dressed woman in the five-inch stiletto pumps, J-Brand jeans, and tank top. What caught Yuri's eye was the sparkling 6-carat rock on her left ring finger, and the eleven thousand dollar Hermes Birkin bag that dangled casually from her right forearm. Chanel's shiny black hair was damned near to her ass now, all natural, all hers.

Yuri thought, *this pretty bitch has stolen my life, looking like a million dollars and a Dope Man's Bitch,* which is what she was. Yuri's skin boiled at the thought. She then watched Candice hop out of her second car, a midnight black S-550 Benz. She hated them both with a passion. Candice's body was on kill. She could make men that were with their women look at her; she even made the women look. She demanded attention, making Yuri envious of her. Yuri wasn't doing bad herself, but she knew that Chanel and Candice were winning.

It didn't matter, Yuri thought, *they're both going to pay, so they had better enjoy this time out.*

Two long hours of stewing later, they emerged from the mall, Chanel carrying a Versace bag and Candice with several bags from all different designer stores. Yuri knew that Candice had been giving Chanel shopping tips, because she had been a plain-Jane, Victoria's Secret sweat suit kind of girl. But cash rules, and her real-estate mogul fiancé - whom she probably didn't know was a drug dealer - had a whole lot of it; he had Arab money. After they talked for a second outside their cars, they hugged and parted ways.

Yuri followed Chanel up 85 North to the 400N freeway. She got off on Exit 11, making a left turn onto Windward Parkway. After another mile, she pulled into a plaza where the Listen and Learn Day Care Center sat. She watched as Chanel stepped gracefully from her car, went inside, and minutes later appeared with her son. She carried him out, kissing his chubby little cheeks, while he showed her something that he must have made, even though he was only eighteen months old. Yuri judged that it must have been a pretty good pre-school. Chanel locked him securely into his car seat and sped off. After fifteen minutes, she was in the John's Creek neighborhood, never once noticing that she was being followed.

Yuri turned to Sasha, saying, "I hope you're paying attention to all of this."

"All of what?" Sasha asked.

She had been paying attention to plenty, studying Chanel like a small child examines a rare and beautiful new creature.

"How this dumb bitch is letting us follow so close behind her, without once looking back," replied Yuri. "I would have thought that her dope dealing boyfriend would have taught her better after all of the shit he's been through."

"Yeah, I was thinking the same thing, Angel, but she sure is whipping the hell out of that super bad ass Bentley! She's sauced up."

Yuri raised an eyebrow at Sasha's obvious hero worship. She was already feeling jealous.

Chanel pulled up to the elaborate entrance of the gated community. *Damn,* Yuri thought, *how are we going to get in?* Just then, a car pulled up, directly behind Chanel's, and seeing her opportunity, Yuri pulled up close to his fender going in on his bumper. She never took her eyes off Chanel's back tail lights, following her onto John's Crossing. She went up the hill and turned into a circular driveway, coming to a stop in front of a four-car garage. Yuri stayed three houses down, just watching to see if this was her home. There was a black Phantom siting partway around the curve of the driveway. After a brief pause, Chanel continued to the front of the house, and then stopped again. Yuri wondered what she was doing, when, to her surprise, Shane opened the stained glass double entry doors, and stepped out. She could see the crystal chandelier sparkling through the magnificent design of the emerald green leaves, pink and purple flowers, and brightly colored monarch butterflies in the expensive custom glass panels. The colors reflected off the slate entry foyer, dancing like so many precious jewels. He opened the passenger door of the car, leaned across the seat, kissing Chanel. He then reached into the back seat, took the baby out of the car seat, and headed back into the house. As the door closed, Yuri noticed the rest of the home for the first time. It was a three-story brick structure home, with stately columns, wraparound gleaming white-railed porches, and ornate crown molding. The five wide steps leading up to the breathtaking doors were classy and inviting.

Pulling her from her thoughts, Sasha whispered, "Damn, her husband is fine as hell. I wouldn't mind fucking him!"

Yuri snapped, "That's not her fucking husband, and bitch, you won't fuck anyone unless I tell you to!" Sasha shut her mouth, knowing Yuri was having one of her spells, and now that she had seen what was in front of her, that her day wouldn't go well. Sasha wondered what could Chanel have done to Angel to make her hate her so much.

Shane had on sagging jeans, but not hanging too low. His belt was still on, but was unbuckled, like he had been relaxing. The wife-beater tank showed every muscle in his toned arms, and clung to his rock-hard abs, looking as if he had never missed a day at the gym. Yuri remembered the last time that she had contact with Shane was when he had gotten shot, and learned everything that she was doing with Uno – setting Shane up, and sleeping with Spida in the hospital as he laid there helplessly and unconscious while Spida put his dick in her mouth to blackmail her. Before Shane shut the door on his more than two-million-dollar house, he had blown Chanel a kiss, which she caught, and then sped off again.

Yuri followed her to the next stop. The sign read 'Wonderful Weddings'. She must have had to meet with someone about their wedding, which wouldn't be taking place, if Yuri had anything to do with it. Before she got out of the car, she put her roof up, got out of the Bentley strutting like a diva. After waiting for thirty-five minutes, Yuri thought, *I have all the information I need.*

She put the car in gear and drove away, leaving a cloud of dust in her wake.

Fifteen minutes later, she was back at the daycare center. She boldly walked in. A young black woman came forward, to assist her. "Welcome to Listen and Learn, my name is Tangy. How may I help you?"

"Hello, Tangy. My name is Carla Coleman, and I was trying to find out some information about your day care. I'm new to the neighborhood, and wanted to see if you have any openings, currently, for my two-year-old daughter, Sanai?" Yuri asked convincingly.

"Yes, actually we have two spaces available in that age bracket, right now. The Carson twins just moved, and there is no waiting list for two-year olds at this moment. What are your hours? We operate from six o'clock in the morning. All kids have to be here before 8:30a.m. with the last child needing to be picked up by six o'clock p.m., on the dot. For every ten minutes that you're late, there is an additional charge of twenty dollars, which needs to be paid in cash, at that time of pick up," Tangy recited as she looked Yuri square in the eye as she delivered the information.

Yuri thought about how expensive it was to raise a child in this day and age. .

"When I kill him, it will be less money Shane must spend," Yuri muttered under her breath, as Tangy continued to yap about all the virtues of the daycare, information that Yuri didn't care to hear about.

Thanking her, she took the application and left.

Once she was back in the car, Sasha asked, "So what did we come back here for?"

Yuri smiled and responded, "All part of the plan, girl. We are going to kidnap their baby and see if we can get ourselves an easy meal ticket."

Sasha looked at Yuri, saying nothing for a while, but knowing now that she was certifiably a nut case. In the past few months, Yuri had Sasha doing things she never would have considered before. They had robbed several white men, and a couple of drug dealers. Sasha was sitting on twenty-five thousand dollars from her licks that they had pulled off, but the more coke she sniffed, the more she didn't think twice about drugging and setting people up. What she did do was try and save for a rainy day. Yuri had turned Sasha into a psychopath, just like she was.

As she thought it through, Sasha's eyes lit up, as she excitedly asked, "Do you think they'll pay a million dollars to get the boy back?"

"I am positive. Shane loves his family and its straight loyalty with him," Yuri answered, eyes narrowing, as she allowed her anger to simmer. "He would die for what he loves."

"Well, I'm down!" Sasha nodded, daydreaming of a duffle bag filled with stacks of hundred dollar bills.

CHAPTER 14

Two months later, Yuri's stash had grown to over seventy thousand dollars, and Sasha's wasn't far behind. Yuri was back to popping ecstasy pills and molly's like they were candy; the men she dealt with loved her on a pill. She would do the unthinkable; she was any man's secret fantasy; men and women yearned for her love. Yuri had taken her hustling game up the road, and the last couple of months had been extra good because the white men in Chattanooga, Tennessee went crazy over the way Yuri and Sasha would say they were sisters, and then perform oral sex on each other. They were getting paid to do what they would have been doing at home anyway, cashing out, plus anything else they had to offer.

One night, the trick they had met with wanted a threesome, and aside from joining in, he told them that he wanted his ass licked. He also wanted to be fucked in the ass before fucking them both in their asses. Yuri used to like screwing Chance in his ass, but doing it to someone she didn't know seemed gay. The way he had asked for it made her think he was a sick motherfucker. For this, she put an extra sleeping pill in his drink, took the four thousand dollars that he had paid the two of them for the evening and put it safely away in her bag. He made Yuri think about Chance, and how she was the cause of him killing himself, when she had sent the tape to Shannon of her ramming the eight-inch dildo up his ass after she had drugged him.

The guy brought her back from her thoughts, telling her, "Its show time. I'm ready to take some dick." Seductively, she removed her expensive designer clothing, followed by an elaborate show as she helped Sasha out of hers. The man watched, stroking his hardness, eager for the real action to begin. Yuri and Sasha took their time, pleasuring one another, as Yuri wondered when the pills were going to kick in and knock him on his ass.

Once the girls were done, it was his turn. He eagerly pulled out the nine-and-a-half-inch dildo that seemed to be his best friend, by the way he had it securely packed. Yuri made a big show of lubing it up with his special brand of KY warming jelly, and was about to insert it in his butt when he fell flat on his big fat fleshy face. They looked at each other, then at him, and laughed hysterically.

"Thank goodness that shit took over fast, but since he wanted this big ass dick so bad, and it's already lubed up, I'll give it to him!" Yuri said. She slowly pushed it inside his butt, inch by inch, turning it as she pushed it all the way until it almost disappeared. They giggled.

"Damn, that was easy, he sure likes a big fat, black one..." Sasha said.

"Just like we do," they sang in unison.

They continued to laugh as Yuri emptied his wallet. There was an additional six hundred dollars in cash, plus his credit cards and identification, which she would give to Bliss, who loved playing with peoples' identities. She also helped herself to the Rolex on his arm, knowing it was worth between five and ten thousand dollars based on the two others she had retrieved in the last few weeks. She wasn't done until she had his platinum wedding band, wondering if his wife fucked him in the ass with big dildos like this. If so, he was getting more dick than she was! She smiled at the thought, as they dressed and left him sleeping. Yuri was getting worse with each robbery, or better, depending on your outlook.

The best payday finally came when she met Bilal. He was from Memphis Tennessee, and somewhat reminded Yuri of Spida, making her dislike him from the beginning. They had met him during their last two weeks on their Memphis tour, on Bill Street. He was with a couple of his boys, eating at a small diner, after the club. As Yuri walked by, switching her fat ass, Bilal and his boys could only stare, mesmerized. Sasha had their attention as well. When they sat down, Sasha said, "Damn, Angel, big boy sizin' you up."

Yuri smirked, "He must want to get robbed."

They laughed. The waitress walked over to take their order. Once they ordered, she told them that the young man over at the other table was paying for their meal, Yuri looked at him, nodded and smiled, flashing him her well-maintained teeth, from between slightly parted, Passion Punch lipstick. He had the look of love in his eyes, which matched hers when she noticed the diamond link chain around his muscular neck. She was sure it must be worth well over fifty thousand dollars. It was when she spotted the Audemars Piguet watch that he wore that her interest was really sparked.

She knew that Shane had just bought an AP right before they had broken up. It had set him back one hundred thousand dollars, even though it was play money.

"That fat nigga got it popping," she told Sasha. "Watch this!"

Yuri slid gracefully out of the booth, sashayed over to the cats, and purred, "Thank you, big boy."

He said, "The pleasure is all mine. What's yer name, baby girl?"

"Paris," she responded, lying effortlessly, "And yours?"

"Bilal, baby girl."

"Nice to meet you, Bilal."

"The pleasure is definitely all mine," he said again. "Who's yer friend over there?"

"That's my little sister Milan."

"Well me and the little goon want to take you and your little sister out one day, if that's possible."

"Well, we'll only be in town for one more week," Yuri teased.

"Where you from?"

"L.A." she replied

"Cali Girls, huh?"

"Yep."

"Well, I wanna get to know you before you go!" He noticed a change in the way Yuri was looking at him, and asked, "What's wrong, baby? Why you muggin' a nigga like dat?" Yuri snapped out of her mean stare.

"I'm sorry, you just look like this no-good nigga that I used to know. I hope you won't treat me like he did."

He laughed in a deep, warm, inviting way. "Baby, I can show you, better than I can tell you."

Yuri looked over to her table and saw the drinks arriving. "There's my juice, so I'm gonna go."

"Okay, baby girl, but before you leave, I'll get your number, if that's okay?"

"Cool, baby, it's all good." Yuri walked back to her table, switching as hard as she could.

Bilal's mouth was on the ground.

"That's gone be my nex' baby momma," he laughed, telling his boys, as they ate on their steak and eggs.

"So, what's up with him, Angel?" Sasha asked.

Yuri smiled in his direction, then turned back to Sasha, saying, "He is most definitely gonna get fucked, then hit!"

They laughed, slapping hands as the guys looked on, knowing surely that the ladies were talking about them, but they didn't know what they had in store. Yuri filled Sasha in on the details as they ate, letting her know that one of the little cats with him wanted to get at her, and that their names had now changed to exotic cities and countries, Paris, and her sister, Milan.

"I like it," Sasha said, with a dreamy look in her eyes.

Once Bilal and his goons, as he called them, were done eating, they came over to Yuri's table, giving her his business card.

"Oh, and dis my lil goon, Po Boya, but don't let the name fool you," he said grinning.

Sasha was sizing him up. She liked what she saw. He was just as icy as Bilal, and much sexier, with golden-brown skin, six-foot frame, hypnotizing dark chocolate brown eyes, perfect line on his head, and tight athletic build. His size 36 Levi 501's and Prada tee shirt fit like a second skin on his toned arms and six-pack abs, the Prada sneakers set it off. Sasha thought she was in love already.

Yuri was also checking him out as she thought, *Damn, I get Fat Ass who looks and is shaped like Spida's bitch-ass, and she gets him.*

Po Boy gave his number to Sasha, telling her to make sure she called. They watched the men as they walked outside to their cars. Bilal and one cat jumped into a 2017 Range Rover, While Po Boy got into the new Escalade, sitting on big rims. They were in for a rude surprise.

After letting them chill for a few days, and not trying to look thirsty, Yuri finally called Bilal.

It was as if he had been holding the phone in anticipation since they parted; he answered on the first ring.

"Hello."

"Hi, Bilal. This is Paris. The chick you met the other night."

"Hey, Paris, baby, I know exactly who you are! Damn! What took you so long to get at a nigga?"

"I had a few loose ends unfinished, but now that I'm done taking care of my business, I'm ready to see what's crackin' with you." She responded.

She could hear the smile in his voice as he said, "You sound East Coast, but when you said crackin' I heard that Cali come out of ya. Were ya born in L.A.?"

"No, I was born in Jersey, but moved to L.A. in tenth-grade, so I've been out there about seven years. That's probably why you still hear my East Coast accent. I'm East Coast to the heart with Cali swag."

"What do you like to do, Ms. Paris?"

"Since you asked, shopping, shopping and more shopping."

They laughed together.

"Where yo man at, ma. I know you have to have one as sexy as yo ass is?"

"He couldn't afford me, so I dumped him in the dump that I found him in," she joked.

"Oh yeah?" He asked.

"I'm just kidding. I don't have one. Where's your broad?"

"Where she's supposed to be."

"Does she know that you be trying to take other women out?"

"I'm sure she does, but I pay the cost to be the boss, so she knows her place."

Yuri responded sounding serious, "I don't like hollering at other broads' men, that shit is bad karma, I wouldn't want a chick on mine so maybe I need to pump my breaks on letting you take me out." Trying to let him know that she practiced integrity.

Bilal came right back at her. "So, don't holler at me, just talk to me. Let me take you out just once."

"Where are we going to go?"

"Wherever yer sexy ass want to go! I just wanna get to know ya, plus, I be in L.A. a lot, so we just may become really good friends."

"Sounds great!" Yuri said with mock enthusiasm.

"So where are you staying?"

"Over here by Memphis International, at the Marriott. We may leave Thursday, so I wanted to be close enough to the airport to make returning the rental car and hitting the road easier."

"Are you planning to leave Thursday because you have to get back to work?"

"No, I have my own business. I have a couple of boutiques back home."

"So, what if I paid the bill for your room for a few extra days, and for the rented wheels, would ya stay?"

Yuri knew she hadn't planned on leaving for at least another week and a half. He was playing right into her hands.

"Bilal, I'm running out of clothes and I don't like wearing the same thing over while I'm out of town. Just meet me for dinner tomorrow, and we'll talk about it more. I'm handling some things tonight, but I'm all yours tomorrow."

"That works. I'll tie up some loose strings tonight and clear my appointments for the next few days, all for you. And plan to bring yer sister, so her and Po can chop it up."

"Okay, just call and tell me where you want us to meet and I'll be there."

"Will do, baby girl. Holla."

Yuri disconnected the call and turned to Sasha, "We'll be in a suite somewhere else after tomorrow."

"Why do you say that Angel?" she asked, head tilted like a puppy or a young child.

"Because he wants to put us in one, and that will make my plan go even better. We 're going to go out with them tomorrow night. Don't get freaky and give that nigga any pussy. We must play hard to get for a few days, then we're going to break their ass off, and rob one or both of them. I can get my people in DC to cash me out at least eighty grand on the watch and necklace alone.

Sasha's phone rang. "Angel, this is the trick I' m supposed to get with tonight, should I answer?"

"No, fuck him! He's only working' with a thousand dollars. We 're about to spend that on dinner tomorrow night. I'm going to get some sleep."

As the door came crashing down, Yuri jumped up terrified. With all the noise from the door, Sasha didn't even stir. She remained fast asleep, which amazed Yuri.

The guy ran straight at her, with a scarf wrapped securely around his face, and a Beretta 9mm pointed right at Yuri's forehead, yelling, "Put your hands up, bitch!" Yuri did as she was commanded. She was stuck and had nowhere to run. "Bitch where's the money and jewelry you stole from my brother?"

Yuri stuttered, not able to get her words out.

"I, I didn't…"

He hit Yuri across the side of her head with the butt of the gun, making blood splatter on the pillow and the walls, screaming while his thick spit flew on her face,

"Bitch, do you think I'm playing with you? What makes you think you can run around here stealing from mothafuckas and nothing happens to you? Now where is his shit? you have five seconds to give it back, or your brain will be all over this hotel room! Five – four – three -" she cut him off.

"Who is your brother," she asked, "because I don't know who you are?"

She had robbed so many men in the last few months that she really didn't know whose brother he was.

"You don't know? Well, I bet you will when I put a bullet in your bitch ass skull!" He took a potato out of the brown bag that he was carrying. "Better yet, I'll let you watch your lover die first!" he said calmly. "My brother told me how you bitches say ya'll sisters, fuck a niggas mind up, then rob him! Well guess what? Neither one of you hoes will be doing that shit again!" He positioned the potato at the end of the gun. "What number was I at? Three – two -" He pressed the gun to Sasha's temple. Yuri closed her eyes, and he continued. "Look, bitch! Say goodbye, unless you don't know her name either."

Yuri screamed. "Noooo!"

Sasha shook her, "Angel, wake up! Wake up, you're having a nightmare, wake up."

Yuri jumped up, "No!"

She looked at Sasha, who was watching her and looking worried.

"Are you okay? You were dreaming."

Yuri looked around, wiping the sweat from her eyebrow. "Yes, I'm okay, and I'm glad you are, too."

"Why do you say that? Was your dream about me?"

"Stop always asking why Sasha."

"Just come here and let me hold you. Sasha crawled under Yuri's waiting arms. They fell back asleep without a worry in the world.

Bilal called while they were in the shower. When she called him back, he told Yuri to meet him at the casino in Tunica at seven o'clock that evening. It was about forty-five minutes outside of Memphis on the border of three states. He gave her directions, but she programmed it into the navigation system on the rental car instead, and told him they'd be there.

Yuri and Sasha carefully decided what they were going to wear for maximum tease-appeal. Sasha wore a pair of leggings to show off every curve on her small, sexy frame, with a tiny, tight blouse, her Jimmy Choo heels set the whole outfit off. She also had the matching Jimmy Choo clutch. Sasha's gear was straight on point now that she had been with Yuri. Between the white boy, she was dating, Kevin- who loved clothes himself - and Yuri hitting their licks, she had totally stepped into dime piece status. Yuri always had it going on; she just had to get it back, and this time was nowhere as easy as the last. Yuri's ass was fat, so she always made sure she wore a pair of tight fitting jeans. She wore the J-Brand jeans with a black low cut shirt that showed off her firm real 36B breasts, with the back out, and a sexy pair of Christian Louboutin heels. Once she had hit the fifty-thousand-dollar mark, the first thing she bought herself was the $11,550 Hermes bag.

When she did, Sasha said, "Damn, you're paying twelve stacks for a bag? You're the shit! I could never do that!"

Sasha had been doing better since then. Yuri wanted her to take her money and go back to school and finish getting her degree, even buy herself a house. Really do something with her money that she would appreciate.

They finished dressing, put their sexy fragrance on, and headed out. When they arrived, Yuri called and told Bilal they were outside. He told her they were on the inside so she should park the car and come in to their table. When they found their way in, Yuri and Sasha walked around a while before they found the table where Bilal and Po Boy were gambling. There were two White men and an Asian man at the table, also.

Bilal noticed Yuri walking up, saying, "Damn girl, you lookin' real suave and sexy."

He then threw the dice, throwing an eleven. He continued to pass on the dice. "And your ass is good luck!"

The dealer pushed fifteen hundred dollars' worth of chips to him on the hit, and then another three grand that he won on the field.

"Get over here, baby girl!" He called out.

Yuri cozied up beside Bilal. Sasha mirrored her action, taking her place beside Po Boy.

"What up, Milan?" he asked, while sipping on a glass with some type of cognac.

"You," she responded seductively.

"I'm glad you came, boo. We haven't got to talk because I been so busy, but after we leave this table, we'll chop it up, so we can get to know each other better."

They gambled for the next five hours, forgetting all about dinner. When they walked away from the table, Po Boy had won thirty thousand dollars, but given back ten. Bilal had started off with twenty thousand, and pretty much had broken even. Sasha had even got a piece of the pie, walking away with three thousand dollars after starting off with two hundred of Po Boy's chips. They had been at the table for seven hours. Bilal hated breaking even; his motto was 'Make me or break me!' Yuri was glad he hadn't lost more as it left more for her.

Bilal finally took a good look at Yuri, from head to toe. He was a boss, but it would be the first time that he seen a chick carry a real Birkin bag in his presence, without being a celebrity. He knew that it was a sign of wealth. He thought she either had a good ass job, or a drug dealer was sponsoring her.

He bought his girl Louis Vuitton, and Celine bags, but Yuri was bossed up with the Birkin bag, her real hair hung down her back, moving with body, just like her fat ass. She had to be doing it big.

He thought, *Damn, if her pussy is as good as the rest of her looks, I just may leave ol' girl and wife this bitch!*

Po Boy was digging Sasha, as well. He was totally digging her innocent ways, and her shyness, but he could tell she snorted dope by her runny nose, that at times she hadn't seemed to notice it running, until he handed her a napkin making her feel guilty. Her frame was small, but she had decent curves. Her flat stomach turned him on, as did the camel toe between her legs.

He thought, *I bet her little ass has a big, deep, tight, wet pussy! Man, it's on!*

They left the casino and went out for breakfast. Yuri had already told Sasha to follow her lead, since she knew nothing about L.A. In case they asked. Yuri had schooled her on Crenshaw, South Central, Englewood, and the surrounding cities. She knew that the Bloods were in Englewood and the Crips in Compton. She also told her about Roscoe's Chicken and Waffles, and Crustaceans. She told her to tell them she was from someplace down in the country called Cuthbert Georgia, and had just moved to Cali with Yuri. That they had the same dad, and that's all they needed to know, if they asked. Sasha was all gamed up and on her shit. The good part was that Po Boy didn't say much - Bilal asked most of the questions, leaving Yuri to answer, although they both said that they wanted the ladies to stay in town longer.

Yuri reminded Bilal that she had told him that they were running out of clothes, and that their cash was getting low. Bilal responded with, "I got you, boo. We can go grab some things tomorrow. I'll put you up in a hotel of your choice, and we'll go take care of the bill on the car."

Yuri smiled, asking, "And what are you expecting in return for all of that?"

"Baby, not a thing. Just for us to get acquainted. I'm not a trick, if I spend it on you, means it's much more where that came from. I'm not just trying to buy some pussy, I'm a real one out here. Po said he'll take Milan shopping, too."

"That's cool, she'll love that," Yuri replied.

After they ate, they talked some more. Yuri told Bilal they would check out of their room in the morning, asking if there was a Residence Inn around because that was more private. Bilal gave Yuri a thousand dollars to take care of the car, and said he'd go get the room. He smiled at her, adding, "We'll go shopping once you call."

Yuri agreed, giving him a gentle kiss on his cheek. She let Sasha finish talking to Po Boy. They took it in at two in the morning.

Once they were at their room, Yuri and Sasha high-fived one other. "Sasha, they are really feeling us and baby, we are going to take these niggas by surprise!"

Sasha was liking Po Boy, but what Yuri said, went, and that was it, even though Sasha thought he was a keeper.

The next morning, when they checked out, they were given an envelope with a room key and directions to a Residence Inn across town. Yuri programmed the address into the GPS, and they were there in just under a half hour. It was a nice two-level suite, with spacious rooms upstairs and downstairs, large and secluded enough for Yuri to carry out her plan.

They settled in, showered, and got dressed for the day, then called their guys. Po Boy told Sasha that they were handling business, but to be ready around two o'clock, and he would swoop them up and they'd meet up with Bilal. She said they'd be ready. Bilal didn't answer, but Sasha told Yuri what Po Boy had said.

At 2:30p.m., Po Boy picked them up. After driving over twenty minutes, they stopped at a house, in a well-maintained development in a middle-class area. The homes were all different, unlike a lot of communities, but the styles were very nice, and the landscaping was lush and meticulously mowed. Every driveway held newer model cars. Bilal's Range Rover sat outside of the home, with another Escalade, and a black 2017 BMW 750i. Po Boy said he'd be right back, hopped out from behind the wheel, and disappeared into the upscale house.

After five minutes, though it seemed like thirty, all the men came out through the front door. One of the men carried a huge cardboard box, like you'd receive from UPS or FedEx delivery. They all looked around cautiously, like they expected something to happen. Po Boy had his hand inside his jacket. Yuri could tell he had a pistol, and was prepared to use it, if necessary. Bilal shook the other guy's hand and jumped into his truck. He rolled down the window motioning for Yuri to join him. She stepped from the backseat of the Escalade looking as fly as she had the day before. He was digging her style, and her body.

When they arrived at the mall, Yuri and Sasha each went their own way, man in tow.

Yuri's first stop was at Neiman Marcus. She selected two pair of five-hundred-dollar Robins Jeans, so she could see where Bilal's head was at, and then added two silk tank tops, at one hundred seventy dollars apiece. Bilal paid the cashier with stacks of all hundred dollar bills without a problem.

Next, she went to the shoe department, and being a Louboutin fan, she first chose a pair of Red Bottoms, followed by Giuseppe Zanotti, for which he chalked off an additional twenty-four hundred bucks. She smiled seductively, thinking *he hasn't said a word, let me press my luck one more time and see how this will play out*, as she led him to Intermix. She knew just how to charm him, working her magic, as she took his hand and guided him to a chair just outside the fitting room. She winked over her shoulder, as she located the sexiest dress in the store, in her size 8. She breezed by him, the scent of her expensive Creed Millesime perfume, lingering in her wake as she entered the dressing room to model it. The beautiful emerald green silk dress, was nearly weightless in her hands. It reminded Yuri of the gown that J-Lo had worn to the Grammys in 2000 when she was dating P. Diddy. The front was so low cut that there wasn't anything but smooth, caramel skin, from her pulsating throat to her flat belly. Yuri wore neither panties nor bra. When she stepped from behind the curtain, Bilal couldn't even speak. His mouth just hung open.

Yuri sauntered over to where he sat. She had on the Giuseppes that he had just purchased, which were perfect with the emerald dress.

She turned around, hand on one hip, and purred over her shoulder, "How does it look, bae?" as she batted her eyelashes, smiling wickedly.

Eyes full of lust, Bilal found his voice, and croaked, "Damn, baby, you look sensational!"

He sounded like a love-struck man, completely under her spell.

"I feel sensational as well," she whispered, raising an eyebrow, seducing him with every syllable.

Bilal's dick instantly grew, with his heart banging in his chest. He had to adjust himself, as he was bursting out of his pants. He had to take a moment to gain his composure. Yuri knew her shit.

She waited until he looked okay, and asked, "We gonna get it, Daddy?"

"Hell, yeah, baby," he responded without hesitation.

The dress was made by Tom Ford, the tag reading forty-two hundred dollars, but at this point, Yuri had turned Bilal on so much that he would have dropped fifty thousand dollars on her, without blinking twice.

Yuri continued sweetly, "So, Daddy, how long do you want me to stay? Because that's only three outfits."

She looked at him expectantly, but with innocence in her eyes.

"I want you to hang out with me for at least a week, if not the rest of your life," he responded, meaning every word.

Yuri hugged him tenderly, not leaving much to the imagination in the emerald dress, saying, "Well, then I'll need to grab a couple more changes of clothes, if that's alright with you?"

Yuri concluded her shopping spree with two pair of True Religion jeans, an assortment of D&G and Rag & Bone tee shirts, and a couple of Juicy couture sweat suits, for an additional six grand.

Once she met back up with Sasha, she was very proud of her protégé. Sasha had chosen a few similar items, with some differences. The girl had a shoe fetish for Jimmy Choo, though she never could afford them. Now she had three pairs of shoes, two shopping bags from True Religion, and a variety from every other expensive store that she claimed she'd never buy shoes or clothes from with her own money. However, this time it was all Po Boy's money, and she went deep down in his pocket. It seemed that these cats had bottomless pockets to spend on chicks that they barely knew, which meant they had to be loaded. Yuri wondered what their motives were.

When they had met back up, Sasha and Po Boy were hand in hand. Yuri couldn't help but notice what a cute couple they made.

Yuri didn't like looking Bilal in the face because it gave her flash backs of Spida, and how he used to make her fuck and suck on his small member. Even though Bilal looked much better than Spida, there was a slight resemblance. He was all good for what was going to go down.

In the short time, Sasha had started liking Po boy and decided she would try talking Yuri out of robbing Bilal, one last time. As much as she had fallen for Yuri, she felt like this could be real love with Po Boy. He was twenty-three, and felt so right for her. He thought she was twenty-one, though she was nineteen. Still - that wasn't too young.

After tearing down the mall, they ate at a five-star French and Creole restaurant, Iris. The cocktails were some of the best Yuri had ever tasted. They ate and drank, having a great time with these cool cats who would soon regret meeting them and hating their guts.

After dinner, they went back to the hotel. Once they finally arrived at the room, Po Boy said, "I couldn't wait to chill, and fire this bomb shit up!"

Yuri wanted to make sure they knew she was from Cali, so she looked at him and commented, "If you're not smoking Cush, please don't light it in here. We don't like smelling bullshit weed."

Thankfully, she had paid attention to Shane's one-liners.

The two guys laughed.

"That's how you feel, baby?" Bilal asked.

"Hell, yeah!" Yuri answered.

Po Boy fired up his blunt, making Yuri think about Shane; he was most definitely smoking Cush. It smelled wonderful, she sat back and took in the exotic aroma.

Po Boy passed it to her so she could hit it, but she shook her head, just enjoying the smell.

Bilal pulled a fifth of Remy Martin 1738 out the bag, and took a swig to the face. Yuri couldn't help but think how this nigga was now even acting like Spida! She had seen Spida hit the Remy Martin VSOP bottle on several occasions. She was starting to make herself hate him.

By the time, Bilal and Po Boy finished the bottle, they were both ready to see what was up with the girls. To their surprise and delight, they were both anxious to give them what they wanted.

Yuri and Bilal went upstairs, and she headed straight into the bathroom for a shower. When she came out, Bilal was sprawled across the bed, his watch and chain dropped on the nightstand carelessly. She knew then that the day she decided to take it, it wouldn't be hard to do; he didn't even know her. When Bilal caught sight of Yuri in the Cherry Blossom Temptation satin and lace, boy shorts and strapless push-up bra ensemble, his manhood instantly grew. Yuri saw what she was working with, and was somewhat pleased.

As much as he reminded her of Spida, his package was thankfully much larger. She had not had any dick in over a week, so she was planning to break him off. He had certainly paid enough! What really turned her on was when she heard Po Boy banging Sasha out. Sasha moaned loudly from downstairs.

Yuri could hear Po Boy slapping her ass, saying, "Take this dick, girl!"

Bilal didn't waste any time. He immediately slapped on a rubber, grabbed Yuri, tossed her onto the bed, and in one smooth motion, pulled aside the skimpy crotch covering and plunged his cock into her already wet pussy.

Fucking like a porn star, he panted, "Fuck some foreplay, I want twelve-play, baby!"

Bilal tried to beat the brakes off of Yuri's love- nest. For such a big guy, he had quite a playbook of complicated positions. What he didn't know, was that Yuri had popped an X-pill while she was in the bathroom, and was ready for whatever he was coming with.

As Bilal thrust repeatedly into Yuri, she formulated a plan. She asked him to lie still, even though he was on top, and she really started working him. She moved her hips in a circular, corkscrew pattern, and then added her Kegel squeezes, gripping his penis and thrusting him in and out, like she was giving him the best hand job of his life, but with the added benefit of her soft, wet pussy being part of the equation. This move never failed her, as evidenced by his loud, pleasurable moaning. She was a woman on a mission, and even her missionary position turned a nigga on.

After forty-five minutes of super sex, Yuri begged Bilal to finish, in her sweet, sexy voice, which really turned him on – he loved it.

"What you want me to do, Paris?" he asked

"Please cum all over me, baby! I want you to take that condom off and splash your cum *all over* my tits." This excited Bilal. He was really feeling Yuri. He thought there's nothing like a classy, nasty freak. He pumped and pumped, going hard and fast, pulled out, at the same time peeling off the condom, and nutted on her breast and her belly.

It seemed like she and Sasha were both finishing at the same time, if her screams of ecstasy were any indication - "Ohhhh, damn Po, oh shit, ahhhhh!"

She knew the sounds from the many times she herself had made Sasha cum. To Yuri, it even sounded as if he had done a better job.

Yuri and Bilal cuddled in bed, worn out, but happy. Yuri turned toward him and said, "I know that you have set it out for me. Thanks. You got your paper right, and you're working with some good dick. Now tell me more about the man that I'm lying here with, trying to make himself my future baby daddy."

Bilal laughed.

"Oh yeah, baby." He took a deep breath of her musky scent, and continued, "Well, my name is Bilal Sands. I'm thirty-one years old, and was born and raised right here, in Memphis. I grew up poor as hell. I wore one pair of shoes a year, growing up. When I'd see other kids in school getting fresh kicks throughout the year, I swore to myself that when I grew up, I was gonna have every pair of shoes in the world!"

"So, what do you do for a living?"

"I'm pretty sure you know. That's all I'm gonna say, babygirl. I'm about my chedda. Ask me no questions about that, and I'll tell you no lies."

"Okay, boo, so what's up with your girl?"

"We've been together for six years. We have a five-year old son, and a three-year old lil princess. I keep them out of the way, because niggas be on bullshit."

"What you mean?" she asked innocently.

"I have been in these streets grinding for a while, and if theses niggas don't tell on you, they tryin' to rob you. So, I have to watch out, and be careful."

Yuri's thoughts went to the fact that he was lucky she wasn't working with someone, because he could be getting robbed right now - not only was his jewelry over on the table, but so was his gun, with the silencer on it.

She told him she was thirsty, and so went downstairs to get something to drink. When she reached the bottom landing, she peeked in on Sasha. Po Boy was sprawled out, dick hanging across his leg, with his gun right next to his trigger hand. She knew that he couldn't be around when she planned on jacking Bilal. She grabbed two strawberry kiwi juices out the fridge, and went back upstairs. Bilal was fast asleep, never trying to sit his gun next to him.

A week had passed fast. Yuri was ready to get what she had been waiting for. Sasha had fallen hard for Po Boy. She didn't even care about Yuri going down on her anymore, and had no interest in the other tricks that she had been getting money from.

Po Boy's hot young ass was turning her on and out. He made her feel alive and beautiful. He talked to her like no man had ever done. Even though he was only twenty-three, he had a whole lot of sense. He told her she was gonna be his girl, and that he wanted her to come back to Memphis at least once a month, and that he would also make trips to California. Sasha wanted to settle down and be wifed, but Yuri was on some other shit. Every time she got on Facebook and saw Chanel happy in her life, things would get even worse. Yuri was obsessed and vengeful.

The day before they were to leave had finally come. Yuri sat with Bilal, and dialed Southwest Airlines. She made reservations to fly to L.A., in the names Paris and Milan Jackson, leaving Tennessee Saturday, at 11:45 AM. The first-class tickets, which Bilal gave her the money for, were five hundred dollars apiece. Yuri had stashed twenty thousand dollars in cash, from all the tricks they had turned, plus three Rolex watches, and a diamond wedding ring; if everything went according to her plan, she would have an extra sixty to eighty grand from Bilal. She started packing while Bilal talked to Po Boy. Everything was going super, because Po Boy had to make a run to Chattanooga, so he wouldn't get in her way.

Yuri told Bilal, since it was their last evening together, that he should stay and make love to her all night. He told her that's why he sent his dogs off, so the last night would be special. Bilal said he would get Milan her own room, so they could do some real freaky shit, up and downstairs. He told her that he had to get his shipment from the Columbians, and give it to Po Boy, but that he would be back by midnight. Yuri hugged him ultra-close and seductively stuck her tongue in his ear before he left, whispering that when he brought his ass back, she was going to fuck him so good, that he could never forget her.

Smiling from ear-to-ear at the thought, Bilal's cock jumped to attention, but he knew he had to go get his paper.

He kissed her passionately, and said, "I'll be back as soon as I can. Keep it wet!"

Once he was gone, Yuri started setting everything up. She put the Veuve Clicquot Ponsardin champagne on ice in the wine bucket, arranged dozens of scented candles throughout the suite, then called Sasha's room and told her to come back over. Sasha told her that as soon as she got off the other line with Po Boy, she'd be there. She clicked back over.

Po Boy said, "You're leavin' tomorrow, boo, and I won't see you before you go, because you know I have to make this move, and I won't make it back until after your plane takes off, but I want you to know that I'm really feelin' ya, and I want to see you again. I don't care if I have to come to Cali, I will, 'cause I'm gone make you my girl."

"I would love for you to be my man. I think we make a perfect couple, Sasha giggled shyly. I can't think of anyone else I'd rather be with!" She responded.

"Well, Milan, my man 'B' just pulled up, so I'm gone holler at ya. Call me when you get to Cali, ma."

"Okay, baby, I will. Meeting you was the best thing that's ever happened to me, and spending the week with you has spoiled me for any other man, Po Boy. Oh, before you go, I just have one question, what is your real name?"

"Po," he responded. "We'll talk about all that the next time I see you, okay? Bye. Holla."

Sasha shook her head and thought, *He is a for real goon. I couldn't even get his real name!* She grabbed the couple of things she had brought into the new room, and left out, knowing she wouldn't return. Once she got back to the original suite, Yuri told her that she was to be in the closet when Bilal got there. She knew he wouldn't check, because he was careless, by everything she had observed all week. Po Boy was his lookout, and without Po Boy around, she knew that she would catch him slipping. They talked and put their plan in motion.

Yuri finished packing up her bags, taking all their things down to the car. They went back to the room, wiping as many fingerprints off of things as they could. It helped that they had not used anything in the kitchen, except the fridge, and each of them could easily retrace her steps. It wouldn't really matter, once Bilal woke up from his nice, long sleep. By then, the girls would be long gone, and Yuri knew, from experience, that drug dealers didn't call police. It was going to be all good.

Yuri decided on not popping a pill, because she might get paranoid. The pills sometimes made her feel guilty about most of the things she did, and she was going to get Bilal tonight - she wasn't taking any chances.

He called at 12:35 AM, and apologized for being late, explaining that he'd had a small setback, and he was on his way. Yuri woke Sasha up, telling her that he'd be arriving soon, so she needed to take her position.

Yuri got the champagne ready. She dissolved two of the pills she had brought from the hospital in his glass. They were her last two. She hoped this would be the last time she stole from a trick.

When Bilal showed up, he used his card key to get in. Sasha curled up in a ball on the floor of the closet, as quietly as she could, although the music Yuri had playing was just loud enough to mask any sound of movement.

Bilal kissed Yuri, taking a moment to admire the sexy lingerie on her amazingly tight body – the same lingerie that he had paid two hundred and fifty dollars for. He told her that he needed a shower, and wanted her to join him. That was no problem for Yuri, she was naked in under three seconds. Bilal liked that she wasn't shy.

He took off his diamond link chain, ring and watch, and set them on the table, as usual. Yuri suggested they do a toast to start their night of bliss, but he wanted to wait until after their shower. As the water ran over their bodies, they took turns soaping each other down, and talked about Po Boy going to Chattanooga. He casually mentioned that when Po got back, he'd be three hundred thousand dollars richer, and that he wanted to take her to Paris.

"Picture that," he mused, "Paris in Paris!"

Yuri was conflicted - should she not do the move? He wanted to do big things for her, and the twenty grand that she had come up on, plus the sixty to eighty thousand that she was anticipating from that night, wasn't anything compared to what Bilal was talking about.

After they made love in the shower, and then on the bathroom counter, they headed to the bedroom. After a few minutes of cuddling, Yuri hopped up, coming back with the two glasses, suggesting, "Let's make a toast."

He looked curiously at the one she offered him asking, "Why is mine bubbling more than yours?"

Even though she noticed too Yuri gave him a confused shrug and responded by saying, "What do you mean?" Then she noticed the medicine had fizzed his drink up like an Alka-Seltzer.

"You drink this one, and give me that one." Bilal said, handing her his glass.

"What does it matter?" Yuri countered.

"It matters a lot, and why all the questions? Just drink it!"

When Yuri didn't want to drink it, Bilal became enraged.

"What's up, babygirl, you makin' a nigga think you put something in my cup! Now you either gone drink it, and prove to me that it's clean, or I'm gonna force it down your muthafuckin' throat!"

Yuri became nervous. Sasha was silently praying, *Oh shit, don't drink it Angel!*

Unfortunately, Yuri had no other choice but to drink her own poison. She took the glass indignantly, gulped it down, and handed him back the empty champagne flute.

"Good girl, but I don't want a drink. Just give me some of this pussy." Bilal said with a grin. After ten minutes, Yuri began feeling the effect of the pills. Luckily, she had built up somewhat of a tolerance to them, so it didn't automatically knock her out. While Bilal fucked Yuri, Sasha remained hidden in the closet, knowing that everything wasn't going as planned. Yuri slowly started to nod out.

Bilal growled, "Bitch, you must've put somethin' in that cup, because you lookin' crazy like you tired and possessed!"

As she went out, he ranted at her limp body, he continued pounding his dick into her again and again.

"Bitch, I'm gone fuck you, then kill yo scandalous ass! I don't know who you thought you were fuckin' with," he threatened as he slammed into her, harder and harder, trying to get off.

Sasha put on the rubber gloves and slowly opened the closet door. She crept along the floor, to the table, reached up, grabbing Bilal's gun. He turned at the sound, and saw Sasha standing with his gun pointing at him.

"Milan, what the fuck you doin' in here?!" He yelled, getting off Yuri's limp body. As he turned to reach for Sasha, she shot him twice in the chest. She didn't realize she'd pulled the trigger, the silencer made the gun have a light thumping sound. Nothing like the regular sound of a nine millimeter.

Bilal looked down, grabbing his heart. He looked at the small hole in his chest, while his blood flowed down his chest to his stomach, sinking slowly to his knees. Then he fell to the carpeted floor with a thud.

It took Sasha a second to register what had just happened, as Bilals lifeless body lay on the floor. Although she was in shock, instinct kicked in; she ran to the bed to her friend.

"Angel, get up!" she screamed, as she shook Yuri by the shoulders. "Get the fuck up now!" Becoming hysterical, she slapped Yuri across the face.

Yuri came through groggily, asking, "What's wrong, Sasha?"

"We have to get out of here right now! Please get up!"

Sasha helped Yuri slip into the dress that was left out for her. She then took the pillow cases off the pillows, walked around the side of the bed, past Bilal's body to get to the nightstand, where his watch, chain, and ring were sitting. She turned away from him, so she wouldn't have to look at his open, accusing eyes, then went into his pants pocket, grabbing the stack of money out of it. She shoved all of it into the first pillow case, and took the two champagne glasses and the bottle, jamming them into the second one.

She ran to the door, peeked out cautiously to see if anyone was on the walkway, then jogged to the car, tossing everything into the backseat. She started back up the stairs to retrieve Yuri, but had to sit down halfway up, to breathe. She inhaled and exhaled, deeply, trying to regain her composure, then ran up the rest of the stairs, to help Yuri out and down to the car.

Sasha had been driving for an hour and a half, when Yuri began to stir. Sasha saw that Exit 24 had gas and food, and turned on her signal. She needed to fill up and use the bathroom, and figured that Yuri would probably need to, as well. As soon as she pulled into the station, she cut the engine, ran around to the side of the building, and threw up. She had needed to do that for a while. She kept her head down, between her knees for a couple of minutes, and cried.

She wiped her mouth with the back of her hand, fixed her ponytail, took a few cleansing breaths, and entered the store. She paid for the gas and a bottle of milk for Yuri, and a Mountain Dew for herself. She got the key for the bathroom, and headed out the door. Yuri was still asleep, but she roused her enough to get her to drink the milk. She wiped off and returned the key, and got back on the 75 South, heading to Atlanta. Two more hours down the road, Yuri regained consciousness.

"Where are we?"

"We're on our way back to Atlanta."

"The last thing I remember, Bilal was telling me to drink his glass of champagne. I think he knew I was going to drug him or something."

"Yes, and when you started nodding out, he said he was going to kill you! That's when I snuck out of the closet. He heard me, and charged at me, and I shot him with his gun."

"You *what?!*"

"I shot him, Angel!"

"Damn, Sasha, we were just supposed to take his shit!"

Sasha cried, as she sped along the highway.

"This is all your fault, Angel! Fuck! I didn't even want to do this shit! I was protecting you, bitch! And now I'm a fucking murderer!"

"Slow down, and calm down. We have to figure out what to do. So, did you get the jewelry?" Yuri calmly told Sasha.

"Yes. I also took the bottle and glasses you drank from, and a wad of cash from his pants pocket. It's all in the backseat."

Yuri counted out the fourteen thousand dollars that was in the pillow case, then she stroked Sasha's hair, saying, "I'm sorry, baby. You did a great job!"

"Angel, I killed someone that didn't deserve to die!" She cried.

"It's okay. Stop at the next exit so I can use the bathroom, and I'll drive so you can relax."

Before they came to the next exit, Sasha saw a sign that read: CHATTANOOGA 76 MILES. She thought about Po Boy, and how he would react when he found out his boss was laying in the hotel, dead. He would surely go after the person who did his boy in.

CHAPTER 15

It had been two days since the murder, and Sasha was on pins and needles. Yuri didn't care. She was setting up the deal with her Russian connect back in D.C who owned the pawn shop. He had already told her that all he would pay for the chain, watch, and ring was forty-five thousand dollars. He was becoming concerned. He knew that Yuri was stealing the jewelry, instead of getting the pieces in a more legit way, but he was still interested, at a reduced price, after he felt that's what pawn shops do. She told him that she would fly in on Thursday to make the transaction.

Once she hung up the phone, she let Sasha know that her intention was to go pick up the cash, and once she came back, they would split the whole thing down the middle. Yuri felt that would be fair, because of the loyalty Sasha had shown when she was in trouble. They had made twenty thousand dollars, then fourteen from Bilal's pocket, plus the jewelry, which put them at just under eighty thousand dollars, way less than Yuri had expected to pull. This enraged her.

Fuck stealing! She seethed, and turned her attention and anger back to her vengeance on Chanel.

While Yuri was in D.C., Sasha got a call from Po Boy. He was in a rage.

"What the fuck happened to my Boy Milan? The maid found him dead the other day, in the hotel room, while I was in Chattanooga!"

"Po, I was going to call you but I was so scared," she explained. "I was in the other room, Po, Paris came running to my room, she was screaming that she thought that someone had followed Bilal into the suite, robbed and shot him! She said it looked like a hit to her. Luckily, she was in the bathroom, so they didn't know she was there. As soon as they ran out, she came to my room, terrified, shaking, and pretty hysterical. We just wanted to get out of there, so we just packed our things and left quickly, in case they realized he was there with someone, and came back to hurt us. I was so terrified, that I didn't even think to call you. I'm so sorry, baby. I really am!"

She was crying as she talked, and had to stop, because she couldn't control her very sincere sobs. He didn't have a clue that she was apologizing for killing his big homie, but she was.

"It's gonna be okay, Milan. I think I know the niggas who did it, and I'm gone kill they kids' mommas, and everyone they know! Look, ma, I'm on a mission, but you'll hear from me soon," he hung up the phone.

When Yuri got back from D.C., she had sold Bilal's jewels, getting an extra five thousand bucks. He had decided to give her fifty thousand, instead, once he saw the goods and the clarity of the diamonds.

Yuri was tired, the trip having drained her. She had visited Chance's grave. She told him how sorry she was, for what she had done - making him so upset to the point that he thought there was nothing he could do other than hang himself. She told him not to worry, because he wouldn't be alone. Soon, his sister and nephew would be lying right beside him.

Yuri was an extremely sick person, and getting worse by the day.

After Yuri took out the rent, grocery, and car payment money for three months, she handed thirty-five thousand dollars to Sasha, whose eyes lit up.

"Thank you, Angel!" She said, then gave Yuri a big, wet kiss.

"Sasha, that's nothing, so don't run around spending, like you have a million dollars."

"Angel, I like cheap shit, it's you that drops ten stacks on bags!" Sasha countered playfully.

Yuri knew she was telling the truth, and laughed, "You're right, you do sit on cash. Well, we're gonna go out and celebrate tomorrow, so let's get some rest."

"I'm gonna go hang out with Kevin tonight, so I can spend his money on something new to wear tomorrow night."

"Sasha, with all that shit that Po Boy bought you, you're telling me that you don't have shit to wear? You just like that white boy."

Sasha shrugged her shoulders and looked down at the floor. "He's cool, and he helps out, and you know it. After all, I wouldn't have the Honda if it wasn't for him."

"So that's why you're looking' and smelling' so good."

"Yup, and the stakes have gone up, bitch, you done turned me out!"

Yuri giggled. "See ya later, bitch. Have fun. Suck it easy."

"You're silly, Angel. It's 'take it easy'. See ya later, Angel." She kissed her tenderly, on the cheek, as she headed for the door.

Yuri woke up to the stereo bumping 36 Mafia. Sasha was cooking and singing loudly, *"You know, it's hard out here for a Pimp."*

"Can you sing any louder, hoe?!" Yuri screamed.

"Yes, I can," Sasha came into the room, singing louder, and began jumping on the bed.

"Stop it, Sasha!"

Sasha jumped right on top of her. "Get up! It's going to be a good Friday; I've even cooked for you."

"Sasha, Kevin must have put it on you!"

"Girl, it's the other way around - I put it on him, and he laced my pockets!"

"You probably got five hundred dollars from his ass."

"No, honey, he did some kind of move on the computer software gig, and I got four thousand"

"Okay! Let me hold something!"

They both laughed.

"You go to the mall with me, and I'll buy you something, but you have a seven-hundred-dollar limit!"

Yuri chuckled. "And what can I buy with that, some perfume?"

They giggled some more. "You're an expensive chick, Angel!"

"You haven't seen nothin' yet!" They ate, dressed, and headed out.

Yuri pulled up to Phipps Plaza saying, "I'm not buying anything but what you get me."

Sasha looked at her with a pleased grin, knowing that is was impossible. They always walked through Saks Fifth Avenue first, because that's where they parked. As they entered the store, they were greeted by a huge sign announcing 'NEW SHOE ARRIVALS'. Yuri checked out all the Louboutin heels, but kept walking. Sasha's first stop was Jimmy Choo, where she bought her a six-hundred-dollar pair.

"These are all I really want, so let's get what I'm buying you, and on the way out. I can go upstairs in Saks, and grab a cute shirt off the sale rack."

"Just give me the seven hundred dollars, because I'm going to add nine more to it, and get those shoes I was looking at," Yuri said.

"Damn, Angel, sixteen hundred for some shoes? I thought you weren't spending any money?"

"What bitch you know can come and see some shoes she loves, and walk away?"

"I knew a lot of them, before I met you!"

They laughed and headed to the cashier, arm in arm, before deciding to go upstairs, where Sasha bought a couple of tops.

They came down the escalator to the Shoe Department, where Yuri walked straight over to the Marchavekel Knotted Lame D'Orsay platform - Red Bottoms. When the saleswoman hurried over, she asked for a size seven.

"No problem. You look really familiar. Do I know you from somewhere?"

Yuri said she didn't think so, but the lady persisted. "I never forget a face, and I'm certain I've seen you before."

"Maybe you sold me some shoes, here."

"I just started working at this store. I used to work at Neiman Marcus across the street." As she said it, Yuri remembered that she was one of Shane's personal shopper friends. "I'll go get your shoes. What did you say your name was?"

"Angel."

"I'm Symone. Nice to meet you. I'll be right back with your shoes."

When she walked away, it all came back to Yuri, she could never forget Symone. She was one of the prettiest Ethiopians that she'd ever seen, and her body was super bad.

She came back with two other pairs of shoes, as well. Yuri tried them all on, and they were perfect.

"I'll take them all!" She declared. The others were hot Manolo Blahnik. It was as if the chick knew Yuri's style. She took Yuri's cash, handed her the bag and her receipt, and asked if she'd like to leave her phone number, in case they got in shoes that Symone thought Yuri might like.

"No, that's alright. I'll just keep your card and call occasionally." Yuri answered.

"Wow, you even sound like that female, are you from the East Coast?" she asked, puzzled.

"I'm from Pittsburgh," Yuri lied.

"Oh, okay. Well, it was a pleasure meeting you, Angel, and I hope to see you again soon."

"The pleasure is all mine, Symone. I'll be in touch."

Yuri could not run away fast enough. She was very uncomfortable under Symone's scrutiny.

When they got to the car, Sasha inquired, "Damn, are you sure you didn't sleep with her, or her man, because she definitely knows you."

"She's probably seen me in one of the clubs. Like they say, 'we all have a twin out there, somewhere'. Ya know?"

CHAPTER 16

On an unseasonably warm May evening, Yuri pulled out the strapless, royal blue Max Mara mini dress.

It really showcased the new Louboutins, which, in turn, complimented the dress. The whole outfit worked well together. She went to see what Sasha was wearing. The Jimmy Choos were on the bed, next to the sexy red back-out blouse she'd purchased, and a pair of J-Brand leggings, which she knew hugged her like a second skin. Sasha loved her leggings. They showed off every curve on her sexy, petite frame. Sasha had stepped up her game to the fifth power, and made Yuri proud.

Once they were dressed, and smelling good enough to eat, they each popped an ecstasy pill, and headed out. They pulled up to the Compound at 12:40 a.m. Yuri knew that it should have been jumping by then. As the valet parked the car, they strutted straight to the front of the line door. Yuri paid five hundred dollars to get their own VIP section, and was escorted straight to the back.

Yuri moved through the crowd confidently, totally feeling herself. She knew that everyone she'd hung out with in Atlanta partied there, but after popping the X-pill, she could care less who she saw. Sasha was right behind her, dancing, shaking her ass, and swinging her hair. Just before they were about to enter the VIP section, Yuri stopped dead in her tracks, as if she'd seen a ghost. She was stuck to the floor.

The hostess who was directing them said, "Come on, I have to get back up to the front."

Yuri took the bottle from her haltingly. "Sorry. I'll see myself up."

"Well, let me put your bands on, so you won't have a problem getting through the ropes," the hostess pointed, as she continued, "That's your section right there, thank you."

Sasha was confused. "What are we waiting for, Angel? It's popping off up there!"

Yuri just stared, paying her no mind. Sasha kept dancing, right around where Yuri stood. After ten minutes, Yuri finally grabbed Sasha by the hand. "You see that bitch right there?"

Sasha followed Yuri's gaze. "Yeah, isn't that the chick that was at Phipps that day?"

"Yeah, that's the hoe."

"Her dude is sexy as fuck!"

Yuri took one last look at the dude then turned to look Sasha right in the eyes. "Go up there and dance on that nigga. Get him to talk to you any way you can. I want to know who he is, where he lives, his number, whatever you can get!"

"Girl, you're trying to get my ass kicked!"

"That bitch not going to do shit, bitch, quit acting like a punk and go, now!" Yuri handed Sasha the Moet bottle. "Hit this and go!"

Sasha grabbed the bottle and went through the security ropes, waving her band like she owned the place. As she walked past the guy, she bumped him good, pushing him right into Candice. He looked at her like she had lost her mind, but also checked her out. She gave him her best come-fuck-me-smile as she headed over to the rail that overlooked the dance floor. She swung her hips seductively and danced to 'Juju on that Beat'. Sasha could dance her ass off, and guys were stepping up, and getting on her. She paid none of them any mind; her eyes were on Candice's man. He watched her move her body, like fluid sex, consuming him with her gaze. She turned him on. Even Candice felt that her guy wasn't focused on her.

He leaned toward Candice saying, "I'ma be righ' back, shawtee." Candice nodded and started back doing her thing with the rest of her people. One thing about her was she would move on if she felt she was being played.

Sasha had her head down, completely into her dancing, when she felt hands wrap around her waist. She looked over her shoulder to see the guy that Candice was dancing had been dancing with was now on her. She smiled and hit the bottle once. He danced, grinding behind her for a few songs, then whispered into her ear, "What's yo name, shawtee?"

"I'm Tasty."

"I bet you is!"

She laughed lustfully. "That's my name," she said, laying her head back on his chest.

Yuri was looking on thinking, *Bitch, damn you, done got fresh like that - Damn! Just get his information, and come on!*

Sasha had gotten so into the guy that she forgot about Yuri and what she was supposed to do, until she accidentally caught eyes with a steaming Yuri, which instantly snapped her out of her flirting. She breathed into his ear as she asked him, "What's your name?"

"I'm Jay, shawtee, an' I wanna take you home."

"What will your girl say about that?"

"She ain't my girl, I jus' met 'er tonight - she jus' wuz on a nigga dick."

"Well, now I'm on it, and I don't want to get off," Sasha said seductively.

As Sasha spoke, he got a hard-on. Sasha felt his impressive muscle grow even bigger against her back. She really started moving her body to turn him and herself on.

"So, Jay, what are you doing after the club?"

"I hope you, shawtee," he breathed a minty breath into her ear.

"I'm with my sister, and she won't let me leave with someone I just met."

"Well, tell 'er she kin come, too," he insisted, as he relit his blunt and hit his bottle, passing the bomb to Sasha. She took a super pull. When she popped pills, she could smoke, drink, and fuck all night. "So shawtee, put ma numba in yo' phone, an' call me when ya git outta here. I'm gone go back ova here with ma folks."

"Okay, boo, and let me put mine in yours, in case I miss you, so you can call me, and we can hang out. I hope it's tonight," she flirted.

"Okay, I holla atcha, shawtee."

"See ya later," Sasha said, moving away slowly, like liquid sex. She knew he'd be watching, and wanting more.

Sasha made her way out of VIP, through the busy crowd, and found Yuri.

"What did he say, Sasha?" she asked, as they were pressed together, face-to-face, by the throng of gyrating bodies.

"Well, his name is Jay, and he just met that chick tonight. He wants me to call him later, so we can hang out, but I told him my sister won't let me leave with a new guy, so he said you could come, too," she laughed, now high on the weed, "and his smoke taste good as hell!"

Yuri said, "I need one more drink, bitch, let me hit the Rosé" she reached for the bottle and continued, "You drank damn near all of it!"

Sasha looked at her, hands on hips. "Bitch, you know how I go on a thizz pill! Order another one, I got us."

Once they left the club, Yuri told Sasha to text Jay and ask him, "What's up?"

Five minutes later, the text came back through.

"What it do, shawtee? Who dis?"

"It's Tasty, the chick from the club."

"Didja git away from yo sista?"

"No, she with me, but it's all good."

"What's all good, shawtee, me an' you, or you me an her?"

Sasha let Yuri see the text.

"Tell him: Us three." Yuri said.

She texted back, "All three of us."

Jay's response was quick.

"Meet me at the Biltmore on West Peachtree in 30 minutes, room 919."

"Okay, see you then," she texted back, then told Yuri, "he wants us to meet him at the hotel downtown at 3:45."

Yuri opened her bag, took the last pill out the plastic, broke it in half, swallowed hers, and handed the other to Sasha. They took it, knowing by the next thirty minutes, they would be super hyped up.

Sasha said, "Girl, Jay's sexy as Hell, and his waves are bangin' in his hair. There's nothin' like a man with a sexy haircut and a perfect line! And when he was grinding on me, I could tell that his dick was good and big." Yuri remained silent. "So, how much we gonna hit him for, Angel?"

"I got this, Sasha. I'll handle all of that. Just follow my lead, like you always do."

"Okay, Sis, whatever you say," she responded, obediently, thinking nothing of it.

Yuri and Sasha entered the hotel. Sasha had never been inside the Biltmore. She was impressed by everything she saw. "Wow, I could get used to this shit!"

Yuri shrugged. "This is nothing, you'll see much better."

They got on the elevator, and didn't speak all the way up to the ninth floor, where they got off and headed down the ornately decorated, plush-carpeted hall.

When they reached 919, Yuri stood to the side, while Sasha knocked. Jay asked, "Who is it?"

"It's me, Tasty, and my sister, Sassy."

Jay opened the door with his shirt off, looking sexy as Hell, with a blunt between his full lips, his jeans partially unzipped, and his Gucci belt hanging.

"Come in shawtee, wuz up?" his jaw dropped open, "Wha-da-fuck, Yuri? Wuz up, shawtee, where da fuck ya bin?"

"Uno, I thought I'd seen a fucking ghost at the club! I thought you were dead!"

"Wha da fuck ya thought dat foe?"

"Because last time I saw you, Shane was trying to get you killed, and the cop said someone had got murdered in the car!"

"Ma boy, Marcus, got kilt. I jump ma ass out da car."

Sasha was confused. She took the blunt out of Uno's hand while they talked, thinking 'Yuri' was another of Angel's made up names for their many tricks, but making a mental note to ask her about the backstory later, as she puffed.

Uno grabbed Yuri tenderly by her slim shoulders, holding her at arm's length, and looking her over from head to toe.

"Damn, shawtee, ya look good! I wuz wunderin' wha' happin' ta ya. I din't haf no numbas fo family or nuthin' ta holla atcha. But I been getting' leads on dat fuck nigga, Shane, an I'm gone kill his ass, ya feel me? Ya still wit dat soft-ass nigga?"

"No. Remember my best friend, Chanel?"

"Yeah, shawtee from DC, the smart one."

"Yup, can we sit down and talk?"

"Sho, come in 'ere."

They walked to the couch.

"Less go in da bedroom an' talk," Uno said, then called out to Sasha, "We be back in a few, shawtee."

She nodded her head in their direction and kept his blunt. She grabbed a drink from the mini-bar and sprawled across the loveseat, trying to relax on the pill.

Behind the closed door, Uno's first words were, "Shawtee, I thought ya wuz tryin' ta git me kilt!"

Yuri thought a moment before speaking. She chose her words wisely - as dumb as Uno sounded, she knew he was no dummy. She knew that she had actually been trying to help Detective Wallace send him to jail, before Shane would have him murdered, but it wouldn't help anything to disclose that now, considering Shane's boys had got on his trail first. Yuri shook her head and began, "I loved you then, and I still love you now, and I would never have done anything to hurt you Uno!"

"So, where ya bin, shawtee?"

"To make a long story short, Shane found out that I had set him up then some shit went down between me and Chanel, about her brother. I was pregnant with your child…"

Uno stood up, interrupting her. "What you say?"

She looked into his sexy bloodshot eyes, sadly, as a stream of real tears escaped from her eyes. "Yes, Uno, and that bitch tied me up and tortured me. She shot me and made me lose our baby, at seven months."

Uno's heart broke for Yuri, and the child he hadn't even known existed, that may or may not have been his.

"Damn shawtee, dat pretty bitch flipped like dat? Wha' da fuck ya do ta hu?"

"Nothing but now she's with Shane and they have a son. She went so far, that she had me put in a crazy hospital after she found out I'd survived. Uno, this last year and a half has been hell."

She broke down completely, sobbing for ten minutes in his arms.

"Well baby, it abou' ta git betta! Da ya know where dat bitch-ass nigga is?"

"Actually, I do. Did you know the chick you were dancing on tonight at the club?"

"Not really, but I got 'er numba, why?"

"Did she say her name is Candice?"

"She said 'Candy' I think," Uno said, while thinking.

"Yeah, that's her name, and she's one of Shane's best friends."

"So ya wuz watchin' a nigga da whole time he lit his blunt?"

"Yes, I was," she smiled.

"So, who is shawtee in da nex' room, dat you sicced on me?"

"She's my new soldier. She's down with whatever I say."

"Well tell 'er ta git 'er ass in 'ere, and y'all git naked, so we kin 'ave some butt naked fun! I want'cha ta show me jus' how much ya miss ya Daddy!"

Yuri came out of the mini dress in less than two seconds. She called out to Sasha.

Uno admired her nudity saying, "Tha' body lookin' good! Even betta, tha' ass done spreaded some! Bend ova pen it up an' shake it!"

As she bent over, Sasha walked in. She glanced at Yuri's provocative position, then at Uno, sitting on the bed, holding his prized possession. She knew what was about to go down.

"Come in, shawtee. Instedda makin' dis good, let's make it great! Come out dat dress!" Uno said.

Sasha looked at Yuri for her approval. Once Yuri gave her the green light, Sasha was naked within seconds, as well.

Yuri walked over to Uno and immediately got down on her knees in front of him, as if she were about to perform a religious ritual. She cuffed his shaft with the palm of her right hand, and gave a few introductory sucks, which caused him to lean back and roll his eyes into the back of his skull. She stroked his dick gently with the other hand, causing him to moan like he was remembering a favorite dream. She switched gears, wrapping all her fingers around his ample girth, and turned her head to run her mouth up and down the length of his pole, like she was playing a large, fleshy harmonica, back and forth along his dick, making Uno stand tall.

As Sasha watched, she ran her fingers playfully over her own pussy, feeling the wetness that the scene before her had created.

Once she couldn't stand it anymore, she crawled under Yuri, to taste her juicy tasty treat, while Yuri sucked Uno's dick affectionately. Uno leaned forward to watch them for a minute or two, before lying back against the pillows. He held Yuri's face in his hands, loving every moment of her super head techniques. He had missed her, and now she was back. He smiled and stroked her hair.

Sasha licked and sucked Yuri's pussy just the way she liked it. This, added to her joy of having found Uno, with his amazing dick in her mouth, pushed Yuri over the edge. She came convulsively.

Yuri continued to suck Uno like a vacuum cleaner as she came, knowing that he must have taken a pill, or he would surely have cum too from that move.

Uno told them to switch up, and Yuri and Sasha flipped each other over like trained acrobats, Yuri sucking Sasha up, and Sasha sucking on Uno for all she was worth.

As Sasha sucked Uno, he said, "Damn, Girl, you a cold piece! Eat dis dick!"

Yuri pleasured Sasha like she always did, and as Sasha moaned, her throat massaged Uno's hard dick, each of them adding a new dimension to the gratifying experience of the others'.

Uno's last request was to wear Yuri out. He told her, "Git up 'ere an' ride Daddy like only you know how!"

Yuri climbed up on him, rubbing and teasing the tip of his dick with her wet pussy until he pushed every bit of himself inside her. She sat on top of Uno's extra-large pole, bucking like a cowgirl riding a bull, she didn't care how much dick he pushed into her - she wouldn't fall off. She was giving him all she had. Sasha cuddled up next to them while Uno teased her clitoris with his very capable fingers.

Everyone was turned up.

After Sasha came again, Uno flipped Yuri over and started banging her from behind. She yelled and screamed in the full heat of passion, while he filled her up, until they both exploded together, sparks flying like it was the fourth of July.

After two full hours, and two sessions of intense thug loving, everyone was worn out. Uno had fucked Yuri in every hole possible, wishing he could have found more.

"Damn, yawl got a nigga raw!" Uno said.

They all laughed. Yuri told Sasha to go wash up, so she could have a few words, in private, with Uno. She hopped up, kissed Yuri, and was about to kiss Uno before she stepped out of the room, but Yuri shot the whole thing down with one mean look. Uno saw that now the fun was over, Yuri was back running things.

Once Sasha was out of the room, Yuri told Uno, "I want you to kill Chanel for me."

"Fuck dat bitch! I'm gone kill her mane! An' I know you ain't still tryin' ta protec' him!" He replied.

"No, but…"

"But my ass! You kill 'er. I'mma kill him, shawtee, an' das on-ma momma!"

CHAPTER 17

Yuri had not spoken with Uno in a few days. He didn't answer or return any of her calls. She was right back in love with him, but realized that now he had money, he was untamable. The kilos he had robbed Spida for had set him straight. He was sitting on half a million, or better, when the most he had ever come up on in the past was about fifteen thousand. Yuri was sitting on forty thousand, which wasn't too bad, for not selling drugs, and having everything paid off, from tricking off her goodies.

Yuri got comfortable on her bed with her laptop, and signed into Facebook. She went to Chanel's page, and what she saw really pissed her off. There was a picture of Shane and her, with the caption, 'WORLD TOUR'. She clicked on it and the first photo read 'BRAZIL'. They had gone to Carnival. Chanel looked happy as she could be. Her Missoni mini-dress was perfect for the occasion. The next shots said, 'DINING AT OUR HOTEL', 'AT THE MINI BAR', and 'EATING FRESH HEARTS OF PALM'. Chanel was feeding Shane in that last one.

This was followed by a picture of Chanel, in Sydney, getting a massage on the beach. She had her over-sized Dolce and Gabbana sunglasses on, looking fantastic, damn her. She went to the next series which read, 'TWO WEEKS OF TRAVELING AND WE'RE LIVING IT UP!' She hated the both of them, and their amazing life.

The last group of pictures were taken in Paris. Chanel and Shane were at an art gallery. She posted, 'JUST SPENT $15,000.00 ON A BEAUTIFUL PAINTING FOR OUR BEDROOM'. Another post read, 'HEADED TO HERROD'S TO TEAR DOWN THE STORE'. Then there were a few of just Chanel: 'GUCCI THIS', 'FENDI THAT' and 'OOOOH, RED BOTTOMS!!!'

Yuri hated Chanel, now more than ever. Chanel was living out *her* life. Reebok broad, Chanel was now a designer bitch. Even though Yuri knew how much she had crossed

Shane, she never expected Chanel to be the one to take her place.

As she stared at the computer, Sasha came up behind her and interrupted her angered musings. "Angel?"

"Yes?" Yuri responded, closing the computer down.

"I think it's about time you told me what was going on with you and Jay. He called you 'Yuri' several times. I've opened up and told you my real name from the jump. With all we've been through together, I think it's time you do the same."

Yuri set the laptop on her night stand and patted the bed beside her, inviting Sasha to sit down.

Slowly, she told Sasha everything, even the part with Chanel that she had never discussed with anyone. It was painful, but afterwards, she realized she felt much better, getting it off her chest. When she told Sasha about the baby, Sasha felt remorseful for her.

"Wow, Angel, she made you lose your baby at seven months? That's fucked up, and that bitch is gonna pay!"

As tears rolled down her cheeks, Yuri thought, *Chanel doesn't have a chance now.*

Yuri was looking at Chanel's Facebook page daily now, stalking her prey. After a month of being out of the country, they returned to Atlanta. She had seen in the pictures that Chanel had brought the little boy back all kinds of gear; he stayed just as fly as his parents. To be truthful, she didn't think he looked much like Shane. Her son had a fat head, and his hair wasn't at all like Shane's. Maybe he just looked more like Chanel; she did see her father in him.

She knew that the time had come to make her move, now that she had studied her routine. Yes, it was time.

CHAPTER 18

Uno had started messing around with Candice. He said he wanted to get next to her, to get at Shane, but Yuri noticed that Uno was sprung, and tricking off on Candice. She was pissed about it, especially when she thought about all the money and things that she had laced him with. If it had not been for her, he would not even be sitting on the half-mill that he had. And now, he was buying Candice five and ten thousand dollar bags, and paying her mortgage, without even being able to go to her spot. All while he was only throwing five hundred to a thousand dollars at Yuri! It had even gotten to the point that the only time he wanted sex with Yuri was when Sasha was involved.

They were all going to feel her wrath.

As much as he liked Yuri, he played her like a slut, on the strength that she had turned against her man for a bum who had nothing. Even though that bum was him, he knew what she was capable of. Candice was, on the other hand, down with her team, and loyal as ever. He had started liking her, and promised himself that when he killed Shane, he would make sure that Candice was neither involved, nor find out that he was. Candice was a keeper, in his book.

After a while, Candice told Uno that she wanted him to meet her best friend. She described him as a cool dude from California who loved smoking on that bomb, like him.

Uno shook his head.

"Look shawtee, I ain' comftable with meetin' too many niggas right' now, cuz its crazy out hea. Ma folks' jus' got kilt ova some fuck shit, dealin' wit peoples, an' I'm jus' not wit it."

"Okay Jay," Candice responded. "But if we continue this little relationship we have, trust me, we will bump into him."

Uno thought, *He gone bump right inta deez nines!*

Over the course of the next four months, Candice stopped sleeping with a few of her regular clients. Candice didn't have tricks. She had a range of clientele, some of whom paid ten thousand dollars, just to be with her for a weekend. Candice pulled in a healthy six-figure income from her job. Uno hadn't known about the clients, but Yuri made sure to inform him.

There was something about Uno that she couldn't get enough of. Yuri knew more than anyone that Uno's sex game was serious. Yuri made sure to put salt in her game, hoping this would sour his view of her. His response was that Yuri should have taken better notes.

Each time Yuri dirty-macked Candice, it made Uno fall for her more. He was most impressed by the fact that no matter how late she hung out to party, she still got up and went to work on time, fresh as a flower. Hardly any of his other chicks worked at all. Aside from Yuri, and the females that he got once he had money, he'd only had hood rats that wanted nothing more out of life than being screwed, and getting their hair, nails, and feet done. Yup, Candice was a keeper.

Uno got Shane's number and other info out of Candice's phone. She showed him pictures of them in California and Hawaii. She also did a lot of pillow talking with Uno, telling him how Shane would buy and sell real estate properties, and about his being a multimillionaire. She said that with all the money he spent on his condo, he should really think about meeting Shane, so he could show him the real estate game. Then he could wash any money that he had, clean it up, and invest it legit. She didn't know that Shane was, and had always been, in the drug game - and once you were in, it was nearly impossible to get out.

Uno told her he didn't want to keep hearing about ole Boy. To make her stop talking he would say, "Damn shawtee, it soun' like ya like dat nigga, fuckin' him, or wanna fuck him summin."

Candice would get defensive and argue, but never win. Once Uno found out Shane's schedule, it was time for him to make a move.

CHAPTER 19

Yuri and Sasha had not been vibing like they were before. Now that Uno was back around, it seemed like everything set her off. Yuri would get mad when Uno moaned while Sasha sucked on him, or when she felt Uno was more into Sasha when they all had sex. It was a no-win situation all around.

One day, when Uno was over, he had drunk a fifth of Hennessey while waiting on Yuri to get home. Once Yuri had not shown up by the time she'd said, he wandered into Sasha's room. Sasha was lying across the bed, in her True Religion bootie shorts and tank top, without a bra.

"Damn shawtee, ya gettin' thicka an' thicka!" Uno said. He walked over to the side of the bed and slid his fingers up the inside of her left thigh, and under her shorts. As he expertly tingled her clitoris, Sasha leaned back, totally aroused, enjoying it.

After a few minutes, Uno told her to get naked, which took no time to do, complying with his wishes, just as she and Yuri always did. Uno unzipped his pants, not even trying to take them off, and slipped on a condom, telling Sasha to come sit on his hard dick. By now, Sasha was dripping wet. She climbed on top of Uno and worked him out like a true porn star. As the thrusts got faster and deeper, Sasha screamed and moaned passionately. Yuri had made it home in the interim, and could hear Sasha having wild sex. She was horny and was thinking she just may join in.

Curiosity got the better of her as she wondered, *who's taming that bitch?*

The door to Sasha's room was open, so she looked in. When she saw Uno fucking Sasha from the back, doggie-style, she was heated.

The only time Sasha was supposed to sleep with Uno was if it was all three of them.

Yuri stood there watching for a minute, while Uno smacked Sasha on her ass while talking to her dirty. Uno was really giving Sasha the business, banging and bashing her while the head board banged into the wall.

Suddenly, Yuri had a flashback of when her mother had caught her with her husband Eugene. They had been in the exact same position; the only difference was that Gene was telling her that he loved her.

Yuri finally cleared her throat. They both looked back, but continued what they were doing, not missing a beat. Uno smiled.

"Hey shawtee, get undressed and join us."

Yuri put her hands on her hips and looked him in the eye.

"Fuck you, Uno," she spat, then turned toward Sasha. "And you, what the fuck do you think you're doing, fucking my man?" Sasha tried to make Uno pull out of her, because she heard the anger in Yuri's voice.

Uno held onto Sasha firmly, saying, "I ain't ya man, and ya gone wait 'til I bust dis nut. Yuri, bitch, ya disturbin' ma groove!"

He started really plowing into Sasha, causing her to cry out in pain as he slapped her ass as hard as he could. "Take this dick, throwback that pussy!"

Sasha felt provocative and gave him all she had.

Yuri walked out, went to her room, slamming the door behind her. After Uno came, he took off the condom and headed to Yuri's room with his soft dick still out.

He banged on the door.

"Bitch, ya betta open dis door now, fo' I kick it open!"

Yuri finally relented, pulling the door open, with a definite attitude. Uno's nasty ass walked in, and grabbed her clean, dry towel, wiping himself off. "Wha da hell is wrong with ya, shawtee?"

Yuri couldn't believe how dense he was.

"Our understanding was that you would only sleep with Sasha if we were both involved."

She shook her head, hurt and still angry.

"Well, ya took too long, an' a nigga was horny as tha' thang."

"As what 'thang'?" She thought that he had picked it up from Sasha.

"Das jus' some slang tha' my St. Louis patna say. Anyway, you started dis, shawtee, puttin' her on me, an' now ya mad."

"You're damn right, and I'm done sleeping with you, with her!"

"Come on now, shawtee."

"I mean it, Uno! And that bitch knows she was straight out of pocket for that shit!"

Sasha heard Yuri, but knew not to say anything, because they had already discussed the way that it would go, but that had been over six months ago, and Uno had been screwing them whenever he wanted to. Yuri continued, "You're already wifein' that bitch Candice, now you want to play me with my bitch."

"Shawtee, ya played yo 'self," Uno responded, with his finger in her face, his hot breath smelling of Sasha's pussy. "Bitch, ya mus' don' ramembah ya tried to set me up fo' dat nigga ta kill me!"

"I didn't, Uno."

"Ya wuz settin' me up fo' somebody." Uno gathered his things and concluded, "I ain' gone argue wit ya. I'm outta here!"

Once Uno left, Yuri told Sasha how she was wrong, and that maybe it was time for them to live apart. Sasha was actually glad, because Kevin had already gotten her a spot in Buckhead for her to go to when she didn't want to drive all the way home. "Fine, I'll move out next week."

"I'm not saying you have to rush." Yuri tried to soothe the situation.

She was surprised at how quickly Sasha had agreed, and that she hadn't been the least bit upset.

"Oh, it's cool. I'm all good. Kevin got me."

Yuri hated that Sasha had cuffed the white boy, and that he had to be as wealthy as he was. She couldn't believe the ingratitude. She could not fathom Sasha thinking she didn't need her anymore.

Yuri's mind raced manically, *I gave this bitch some game, and now she thinks she's the shit! I'll make her do everything I need her to do, or I'll tell that she killed that nigga.* Now she was thinking scandalous, and was about to make Sasha her hostage. Yuri began, "Sorry, Sasha, it's just-"

Sasha interrupted, "It's just that whenever you want things your way, you're cool, but if I do what I want, you have a problem. When Uno wants to fuck us, and you're around, I must join in, even when I don't want to. Well, today he caught me off guard, and it went down, and really, you should be mad at him not me!"

"Damn, Sasha, I said I'm sorry. Now, just chill out."

Sasha folded her arms across her chest and walked out. Uno had Sasha and Yuri becoming enemies, while he was running around giving Candice everything she wanted. Yuri wasn't happy with how things were playing out.

CHAPTER 20

It was a cool, rainy night. Although it was May, it had already rained more than it had during the entire month of April. Yuri was riding down Peachtree, when she spotted Uno pushing Candice's S-550. Candice rode shotgun, laid back in the seat. Yuri followed them in a jealous rage. She wanted to roll up, on the side, and tell Uno to pull over, but she knew he wouldn't. She was tired of hiding, and not letting her presence be known.

After twenty minutes, they pulled up to a building, off 34th and Lenox Road, behind the Houston's Restaurant. The spot was low-key. Uno's new Escalade sat in the driveway. Yuri pulled over, down the street, watching their every move. Candice stepped out of the car with bags of food from the Atlanta Fish Market. Her outfit and hair was on fleek, Yuri knew that Candice had too much sauce, swinging her twenty-inch Indian Weave. They walked to the door, Uno pulling a set of keys from his pocket and holding the door open for her to go first, like a true gentleman.

Two hours had passed and the sun was long gone. Yuri wondered if or when Candice was going to leave. After another hour, there was still no movement. Yuri looked in her back seat and saw a bottle of Grey Goose that still had a few shots left in it. She picked it up, looked around, drinking the whole thing down in one big gulp. Even though she didn't smoke weed, the doobie that Sasha had left in the ash tray was now being fired up. She lit it pulling hard, exhaling choppily, as she coughed uncontrollably from the roach.

Although she almost threw up, Yuri was high within minutes. She started searching around in her bag for anything sweet to eat. The munchies had kicked in - damn she was hungry!

Yuri thought, *I'll just run around the corner to Chick-Fil-A, then come back and sit here until that bitch comes out, so I can follow her, and fuck her up bad!*

158

As she started the car, an inner voice said, *if you leave, you'll miss her.*

She thought about it then cut off the engine. She then turned the key on again, then off. She was loaded from the liquor and weed roach, the combination making her very confused. She turned the car on, put it in gear thought again, put it back in park, and cut it off. She opened the door, her mind playing tricks on her she grabbed her bag, and headed for the condominium door. The liquor had made her bold and aggressive.

Once she got to the door, she beat on it with both fists, yelling, "Uno, open this fucking door right now!"

She banged once more, as hard as she could.

Uno opened the door with no shirt on asking, "Wha' da fuck ya doin' here?"

Yuri's words slurred, "I'm a-coming for my man Uno!"

"Hoe, you's trippin'." Yuri swung on Uno, missing and losing her balance. He grabbed her just before she fell. "Look, bitch, ya can' be ova here makin' no sense and shit."

Candice came out from behind the half-closed door, looking confused, at the sound of Yuri's voice. She stared at her for a few seconds then turned to Uno saying, "Where do you know this snake-bitch from? What the hell is going on, Jay?"

Yuri hollered, "I'm his snake-bitch! And his name is Uno dumb bitch!"

Candice raised an eyebrow at Uno. "So, you've been knowing this bitch all along? What the *fuck* is going on?! I'm calling Shane!"

Uno ran behind her, back into the apartment saying, "Wait baby."

"Wait? Wait for *what*?!" She yelled. "You must not know about her, but you're about to find out!"

Candice ran straight for her bag, pulling out her cell phone, but before she could dial the number, Uno grabbed her by the throat trying to calm her down. She tried to pull away from his stranglehold by clawing at his arms and hands, but her feeble scratching was no match for his strength.

"You ain' callin' 'em," Uno stated coldly.

As she continued to struggle, Yuri stood watching, laughing, with no conscience.

As he choked her, Uno shook his head, "Damn, I liked ya, shawtee." She looked into his evil eyes, as one last tear slipped from her right eye, and down her cheek. Her body went limp Uno took his hands from around her neck, as her lifeless body fell to the ground. Uno stared into Candice's still open eyes, reached down, and tenderly shut them. He turned to Yuri, who was still laughing, with fire in his own eyes.

"Bitch, is ya crazy? Wuz funny? Ya jus' made me strangle 'er, an' ya laughin'?" He rushed over to where Yuri stood, and grabbed her by the neck before continuing, "Bitch, I's gone kill yo' punk ass, too!"

He threw her to the ground choking her, it seemed like she was getting a thrill out of it. Uno squeezed harder, while Yuri looked him square in the eyes, as he did, with a bit of a twisted smile. He couldn't take her staring at him, after what he'd just done to Candice. He let her go. She slumped over, massaging her neck, while gasping for air, as she fell. Once she caught her breath, she ran her hands under her dress, with a spaced-out possessed look, rubbing on her clitoris. Her voice was gravelly, as she said, "Damn, Daddy, you made me cum."

Uno couldn't believe what he was seeing and hearing, "Yo' lil bitch! Yo ass is psycho, shawtee!" Yuri lifted her skirt, which displayed a well-manicured landing strip with no panties under, so he could watch as she swiveled her hips, and licked her juice from her fingers.

"Maybe I am. Now get over here and fuck me. I want to cum again!"

Just then, Candice's phone rang, Uno tore his glance from Yuri, looking back at Candice's lifeless body. He began pacing the floor, wondering what he should do now. He walked to the ash tray and lit the blunt he had left there, inhaling deeply, then exhaled, sitting down on the couch to think. He jumped back up after a minute, and headed over to where Yuri was, still on the floor, pleasuring herself with two fingers. Uno backhanded her ass, as hard as he could, but she didn't budge. If anything, it seemed to intensify her enjoyment as she moaned seductively. Uno saw how wet she was, and instantly became erect. He unzipped his pants, dropped to his knees, and fucked Yuri - fast, hard, and reckless, causing her to moan, laugh, and scream pleasurably.

He climaxed within five minutes, collapsing on top of her, saying, "I hate you," with a tear in his eye.

Breathing heavily, completely satisfied, Yuri responded, "I love you, too!"

Uno got up to clean himself off and then went back to the couch to make some decisions. He figured he'd have his Mexican partner dispose of the car and body, remembering that he could never trust Tow Truck Mike again. He cringed at the memory of how he'd paid him all that money to bury Spida ten feet under, only to find out that Hassan had also paid him, to keep the very same body! Mike would get his, he mused, because as far as Uno was concerned, his days were numbered, as well. He expected to get what he paid for - one way or another. He rolled a second blunt. After smoking it half way down, he walked to his closet, grabbed the navy blue satin sheet, covered Candice's body with it, and after a minute, he decided to roll her up in it.

Yuri asked, "So, what are you going to do with her?"

Uno cocked an eyebrow and corrected her, "Ya mean, wha' ah *we* gonna do? Ya got me in dis shit, so ya accessory ta murda!"

He walked through the apartment, gathering anything he thought may have been Candice's. He told Yuri to take the bleach from the laundry room and wipe down any surfaces that Candice may have touched. He wanted to be cautious, even though he had never met any of her friends. He hadn't even given her his nickname. She only knew him as "Jay," so even if she'd spoken about him, they wouldn't have had much to go on. Candice had been pushing for Uno to meet Shane and Chanel constantly. Now he knew he wouldn't have to. The only time Uno wanted to be face to face with Shane was when he killed him.

Uno waited until midnight, then had Yuri back Candice's Benz up to the door. She popped the trunk, and he laid her body inside. After fixing it a few times, he closed it, telling Yuri to follow him. He took Yuri's keys, and got into her car, not wanting to chance driving his truck. Yuri pulled out, following behind Uno. She liked how Candice's car drove, and decided she was going to have to cop one just like it. She turned up the CD currently playing.

It was "Never Want to Live Without You," by Mary J. Blige, and she thought, *No, this bitch wasn't playing that, riding with my man.*

Her conscience kicked in. Yuri heard, from inside her own head, *Bitch, he is not your man! And if he had been smart, he would have stayed away from your crazy, sick ass!*

Yuri looked around, as if it had been someone in the car that had spoken, she screamed out, to herself, "Bitch, don't worry about it! Here your ass come popping back up, bitch, I have this under control!"

Her conscience responded, *Bitch, you don't have shit under control, that's why you're talking to yourself.*

Yuri accelerated, screaming, "Stop it! Leave me alone!"

She almost crashed into the back of Uno, just as they went past a cop. The officer hit his breaks, looking at Yuri. Her heart was beating double-time, as she said, "I have to pull myself together!" She took a deep breath of relief as the cop kept going.

Uno was wondering what the Hell was wrong with Yuri, thinking that now he would be stuck with her, or maybe she should come up missing also. He pulled into a tow yard. He rolled to a stop, got out, and walked over to a big Hispanic guy with a long black ponytail. After speaking quietly for several minutes, Uno handed him an envelope, backed out of the driveway, and pulled up beside Yuri. He motioned for her to get in and when she opened the door to step out, he instructed her to take off the gloves she still had on and leave them in the car. Yuri had stolen Candice's Hermes scarf and perfume from out of the console, and had also taken the Louboutin pumps from back seat, and put them straight into her bag. She did as he told her to then got into the passenger seat of her car. Uno put the car in gear, and drove off. They rode in silence, until they pulled up at Uno's spot.

He parked, leaving the engine running.

"Can I stay with you tonight?" Yuri asked.

Uno looked at her, knowing she was crazy, answering nicely, "Not tonight. I'm gone go ova ma momma house an' chill. I hit ya up tomarra."

He exited the car without another word.

Yuri drove in the direction of home, not wanting to be alone. She dialled Sasha's phone, hoping she would be there, so they could cuddle.

"Hello," Sasha answered.

"Hey boo, what are you doing?"

"I'm in Augusta with Kevin," Sasha lied. She was at her new condo relaxing. She had become a great liar, easy as breathing. After all, she had learned from the best.

Yuri tried not to sound disappointed, as she asked, "When are you coming home?"

"Kevin has a few meetings this week, so it will be at least a couple of days."

"Oh, that long? Okay."

"Okay Yuri, talk to you later."

"Okay Sasha" Yuri hung up. Her conscience decided to add her two cents again: *Unh, unh, unh, not even Sasha wants to deal with your scandalous, snake-ass.*

Yuri swerved, tears blinding her view as she screamed, "Just shut the fuck up!"

Make me! Make me! Make me! The voice, her own voice, kept taunting her.

She sped up, trying to make it home, knowing that was a no-no in Gwinnett County. She didn't care. Within seconds, she saw the flashing lights in her rear-view mirror. The cops had gotten right up on her. Tears were streaming from her eyes, she did something that she had not been doing; she started praying. She asked God to forgive her for all her sins, wondering why she only thought to pray when she was in trouble.

The officer walked up to her window, asking for Yuri's license and registration. Yuri's heart beating rapidly, feeling like it might leap right out of her chest, as she searched around the inside of her bag.

He watched her frantic motions, and tears, and asked, "Did you know you were going 95 an hour in a 65 mile per hour zone?"

"No, sir, I'm sorry, I'm a little bothered. My mother just had a heart attack back in Missouri." That's where the woman on her license was from.

"Sorry to hear that, ma'am. I'll be right back." He walked back to his car, lights still throwing obscene color all over the street. Yuri was very nervous. She knew that she wasn't the person whose license she was using, but her picture was on it. She thought about Chanel's family from Missouri, while she waited. Once he returned, he put his flashlight on Yuri, scanning the back seat and floors, with the bright beam. He then walked completely around the car. Yuri knew it was over.

He came back to her window and asked, "Have you been drinking, ma'am?"

She shook her head from side to side, unable to speak.

He nodded, and continued, "I just wanted to check for alcohol bottles. Here are your things back, and a nice ticket. Make sure you pay this, or you'll be in more trouble, and it could cause you to lose your license, Mrs. Bradford and slow down."

"I will, sorry, sir."

"I hope your mom pulls through, just keep the faith."

"Thank you, Officer -" she looked at the name on his badge, "Lopez."

"Have a good evening," he said, as he walked away.

Yuri exhaled, not realizing she had been holding her breath for a long while.

She thought about Bliss, whispering to herself, "I owe you one!"

CHAPTER 21

A lot happened in the month that passed. Uno was giving Yuri the cold shoulder, Sasha had been gradually moving her belongings out, Yuri decided that she no longer wanted to live so far out of the city. She had called Bliss and asked her to check on an apartment in midtown. She was lonely way out in Lawrenceville, by herself. Bliss found her a two-bedroom loft, on the east side of Atlanta, off Highway 20 and Boulevard. When Sasha came to pick up her bedroom set, and the last few outfits in her closet, she was proudly displaying a five-carat pink diamond ring.

She giggled, blushing, saying, "Kevin asked me to marry him! He said if I except the ring that he plans to replace this one with is to die for and I won't regret it!" Yuri smiled, congratulating Sasha, who continued, "Yuri, I really like him. No, I love him! I even took him to meet my family, they love him too!"

Yuri knew it was serious. She hadn't allowed Yuri to meet her parents in all this time.

"So, you spoke with them?" she asked, surprised.

"Yes, and they're so happy that I'm getting my life back together, thanks to Kevin. I'm getting back in school and everything."

Yuri thought, *I'm the one who took you out of that rotten, flea-bag motel, from fucking that rapist,* but she didn't say it aloud. "I'm happy for you, Sasha, but you know I need you to help me do one last thing, before you settle down."

"What is it, Yuri?"

"I need you to help me set Chanel up, and get her alone."

"Yuri, I really don't want to be about that life anymore I don't want any bad karma catching up with me."

"You're the one who killed Bilal, so you are this life," Yuri countered.

Sasha was beginning to tear up. "I did it for you, though," she whimpered, feeling like a mouse trapped by a cat with dangerous sharp claws and teeth.

"Well, you'll do this, and your secret will always be safe with me. If not, I have a detective friend who would love to hear all about how you killed someone?"

Sasha hung her head, and shook it, tears streaming from her eyes.

"Okay, Yuri, you got me, but that's it. After this, I'm cutting all ties with you. I just can't believe you're doing this to me."

"I can't believe you," Yuri said, "We're sisters and lovers. You could just walk away from me, just like that?"

Sasha looked straight into Yuri's eyes responding, "Neither real friends, nor caring lovers, can blackmail someone they truly love."

She stormed out of the door to where the men in the moving truck were waiting for her. She thought, *I'm so glad that bitch doesn't know where I live!*

What Sasha didn't know, was that Yuri had installed a GPS tracker in her new car, the last time she had borrowed it. She knew when Sasha had said she was in Augusta, the night of Candice's murder she had really been in Buckhead, at her condominium. Even though it was gated, Yuri had followed a car in, and saw Sasha's 2016 Infiniti SUV, sitting in its parking spot. While Sasha thought she was being secretive, Yuri was always a few steps ahead of her.

Yuri grabbed her laptop, and got comfortable. She signed into Facebook, and pulled up Chanel's page. The first picture was a flyer of Candice, asking if anyone had seen her. Yuri was sure that if they were distributing flyers, they were probably also speaking to the media. She never watched television, but figured there might be something on the news.

She Googled "Candice Coleman." There was a missing person's report on Fox-5, Channel 9, and Channel 4. She clicked on Fox-5 Atlanta, which was the news she watched, whenever she did.

As it came on, the reporter was making an appeal, "We are asking for any information on Candice Coleman. She is twenty-eight years of age, from Chicago, Illinois, and has lived in Metro-Atlanta for the past six years. She was last seen at work. Her mother had spoken with her the night before she disappeared, and her good friend had heard from her that morning." The camera went to Chanel, "Ma'am, can you tell us about the conversation, the last time you spoke to your friend?"

Chanel sniffled, dabbing at her eyes. "We went out to dinner the night before she disappeared: Candice, my Fiancé and Me. She told us that she was going out with a new guy, and that she'd be going on a date with him the next day and she wanted us to meet up with them." She sobbed and Shane appeared at her side, for support, as she continued, "She'd only been seeing him for a short time. I don't know if we'll ever get to meet him now." She dissolved into tears again, and the camera panned back to the reporter.

Looking concerned, the reporter announced, "The only lead we currently have to follow is that the man she was dating is named 'Jay.' If anyone knows him, or has seen this woman since, her disappearance, please contact the Tips Hot-Line at 404-555-4499. A $100,000.00 reward is being offered for any information leading to an arrest, or aiding in the locating of Candice Coleman."

Yuri was sure that Shane had put up the reward money, but after all, it was Candice. She had men like Q who could and would put up that much without a problem. She smirked in a self-satisfied way, as she finished the thought. Not anymore.

Yuri grabbed her phone and pushed the speed-dial.

"What up?" the voice asked.

"What up, Jay?" Uno knew she was being funny, calling him 'Jay', since it wasn't his name.

"Wuzzup, shawtee?"

"Why aren't you returning my calls, Uno?"

"I'ma talkin' ta ya nah, ain' ah?"

"Yeah, but we need to meet and talk or do you want me to just say what I need to say?"

"Shawtee, ya knows ah don' move like dat! Where ya wanna meet at?"

"We can meet at Justin's."

"Gurl, I's not meetin' ya at Justin's. It's too much goin' on."

"Well then, meet me at J.R. Crickets on Cascade."

"Aight, gimme a couple of hours. I gotta handle som'n firs' shawtee."

"Okay. See you then."

Yuri disconnected the call, leaned back, and thought about how she would kill Chanel. She looked at the computer screen, with the picture of Candice and Chanel.

"One down, two to go," she said, out loud.

She was ecstatic that Candice was dead. She remembered the day that Candice and Passion had laughed hysterically, after throwing the chocolate milkshake into her car, when they had seen her on 17th Street. She remembered the night Candice slapped her at the club, when they had gone to the Jay Z Party. Chanel hadn't known what was going on. Every time Candice saw Yuri, she taunted her.

What Yuri didn't think about, was how Candice took her in after she had screwed her mother's husband, Eugene. She didn't give a second's thought to when, as soon as Candice left for the Bahamas, Yuri had seduced her man. She did remember Q beating the hell out of her after she tried to stick her finger up his ass. He had blackened her eye then sodomized her with no lubricant, only the glob of spit he hacked up. Yuri didn't want to think of all the pain she had caused. She thought and acted as though everyone had done her wrong.

Then her mind landed on Chance, her memory flooded with what she had done to him. Chance hadn't wanted to deal with Yuri anymore. He was totally in love with his fiancée, Shannon. They also had had a child on the way. Chance told Yuri that he was cutting ties with her, because he was going to be a good husband, and father, and wouldn't cheat on his wife. He wanted to follow in his father's footsteps who had never cheated on his wife of thirty-one years. Even though Yuri only wanted Chance for sex, she did not want to see him happy. She was getting everything she wanted, including Shane, but she wanted Chance to be alone.

The last time Chance had finally agreed to see Yuri, she had purchased a camera with a built-in video recorder. She set it up in the hotel room, put on her sexy black latex cat-suit, turned off the volume, and prepared for his arrival. Just before he walked through the door, she crushed two powerful ecstasy pills into his glass of champagne, which she had just poured. They bubbled up - but once dissolved, they had the regular look of champagne bubbles. When Chance knocked on the door, Yuri let him in.

He had tried to avoid looking at her, and got straight to the point. She could hear his voice as she replayed the scene in her mind.

"Hey, Yuri, I have to hurry and get back to work, but I wanted to say…"

Yuri had placed a cool finger over his lips, and said, "Slow down. You're acting so nervous." She had gently wiped the sweat from his brow, and picked up the champagne glasses. "Let's drink, and then talk. Here, let's make a toast to our last time fucking."

He shook his head, "I don't want to do this anymore -" he began.

She interrupted, "Okay, then let's make a toast to our final meeting, and your new life."

He took his glass, they clinked the two together, Yuri took a sip, and Chance devoured his entire glass in one long swallow.

Yuri had said, "Let's have a seat, so I can say what I needed to tell you, then it will be your turn." He'd agreed. Yuri told Chance how much she would miss him, and that he'd been her first sex partner, even though she lied. She was rambling in circles, and Chance knew it.

She'd been waiting for the pills to kick in. After thirty minutes, she'd noticed how Chance's eyes were moving. He'd asked for more champagne, drank it down quickly, and then wanted water. She'd known it was time for her to make her move. She'd gone into the bathroom and put the latex mask and suit on. When she walked out, Chance had just stared at her. She told him that she'd purchased the outfit, feeling like Cat Woman. She'd bent over for him, to give him a fully erotic view, the latex clinging to every crevice. He'd continued to stare, looking confused. He hadn't had any desire for her, at first, but he couldn't fight it for long, and Yuri saw she had his nature rising.

She'd pushed him back, on the couch, and said, "I want one last taste, Daddy."

He'd tried to resist, but the erection growing in his pants had won out.

Yuri unzipped his jeans and pulled his big dick out. She'd taken a second to admire the look and feel of his manhood, gently tracing her fingers over each bulging vein. She'd dropped to her knees and ran her tongue around the head, tugging teasingly on his balls. His eyes had begun to glaze over when she sucked him, as if her life had depended on it. Her technique was second to none, and as she'd sucked, so good, and so hard.

He'd tried to push her away, saying, "Stop! I have to pee! I'm about to pee!"

She'd rocked back on her heels, allowing him to get up and stumble to the bathroom, affording her the perfect amount of time to turn on the camera. Chance had come out of the bathroom, stark naked, his eyes big as light bulbs, and his dick, hard as a rock, standing out in front of him. She was so turned on. He'd picked up the bottle of champagne, gulped down quite a bit then pushed Yuri down on the couch, pouring some in the opening of her crotch-less cat-suit. He'd then sucked and licked on Yuri's clitoris like he'd never done before.

Enjoying all the unfamiliar explorations, Yuri thought, *Damn! I should have been giving him pills all along!*

She'd enjoyed how roughly he handled her. After sucking her clit, like a delectable piece of hard candy, he'd thrust his tongue deep inside her pussy, stroking it in and out. It had felt so amazing, Yuri couldn't control herself, or hold back any longer, and came right on his tongue. He had slurped up all her juices, not missing a single drop.

Still licking and sucking, he'd said, "Damn, you taste good, Mama!"

Yuri had wondered whether it was the pill emboldening him to try new things, or if he'd learned a few tricks, since they'd been together last. She knew he was a freak, because she had been screwing him for years, but it was different. She assumed she'd found the reason that Shannon loved him. Yuri had always enjoyed sex with Chance.

As she put it, he was strapped up with an eight-and-a-half-inch sausage, so why wouldn't Shannon appreciate it, too?

Chance had grabbed Yuri forcefully, and commanded "Suck this dick!"

He'd shoved it in her face, she performed spectacularly, for the camera, capturing all the action. He ploughed every inch down her throat, savagely. As well-trained as her gag reflex was, she'd felt as if she might throw up.

He yelled, "Eat this dick, bitch!"

She knew it was the pill talking, because Chance never spoke to her like that, but it had turned the heat up a notch for her.

After she'd sucked for twenty minutes, her jaws began to tire. She'd always been able to make him cum on ten minutes, tops. He pulled her up by the arm and led her to the bed.

As he entered her, he said, "Damn! This shit is wet like the ocean!"

He thrust into her repeatedly, holding up both of her legs, so they pointed to the ceiling. He glided slickly along the length of the latex suit, ignoring the sticky wetness, pounding Yuri as hard as he could. At one point, Yuri had screamed out in pain, her legs all the way up against the headboard, like an uncomfortable yoga exercise, but he'd continued to push without ceasing.

Yuri cried out, "Oh! Oh! You're in my stomach, baby, it hurts!"

Chance paid her no mind. Sweat had poured down his face, as he kept his eyes closed; trying to find that nut that he yearned for. Still, he hadn't been able to cum, so he'd flipped her over, and gone in doggy-style. Yuri remembered thinking, *Damn, he trying' to kill me,* but she'd kept giving it to him.

She knew that his sex drive was strong, but the pills made him go into Gorilla mode.

He announced, in an irritated voice, "Baby, I can't cum."

His eyes had wandered over to the KY Gel on the nightstand. He'd pulled out of her pussy, greased down his hard meat, and jammed it into her butt.

That had made Yuri sweat. She exclaimed, "Damn, Chance! Your dick is big - you can't just go in all fast and hard like that!"

He pushed her back into the doggy position, his eyes gleaming, and determination written all over his face.

After four slow, partial pumps, he went all the way in, he screamed, "Ahhh, yes! Yes! Yes, this ass is good!"

Yuri begged, "Be gentle Chance!"

He'd slapped her on the ass, not very gently, and growled, "Take this dick," but he still wasn't unable to cum.

Yuri knew, from experience, that when Chance went into her butt, that he couldn't even last five minutes, however, ten minutes more had passed, and he wasn't there yet. They'd been at it for over an hour, and Yuri knew what would bring him to a climax before the recorder went dead. It only recorded for ninety minutes. She had only fifteen minutes left.

She turned to him, flirtatiously, and said, "I want to do our special thing."

His eyes lit up as he responded, "Bring it!"

Yuri pulled a dildo out of the nightstand drawer, smoothed KY Jelly all over it, and had Chance lay down, on his back. She swirled the dildo, teasingly, all around his hole, playing near it, until he was ready for entrance. She stuck it in and fucked Chance with it, like she'd done so many times before. He liked it, and had only ever played the butt game with Yuri.

Although he was a freak, Chance had never been with a man, nor had he ever played with dildos, aside from with her or with anyone else, and not by himself, so he didn't consider himself gay. After Yuri fucked him, moving the dildo in and out of his asshole, rhythmically for about eight minutes, he had finally climaxed. He'd come all over the bed, and then collapsed. Yuri' snatched the dildo out quickly, so it could be seen at the end of the recording; the video tape had everything she needed.

Yuri sprawled out next to him, stretching triumphantly.

He'd rolled over and asked, "What did you do to me? I feel so strange."

His cock was still at half-mast, still impressive.

She didn't really answer the question he'd been asking. "I just gave you what you wanted "

After relaxing quietly together for a few minutes, Shannon called, and reality had crashed back in on him. When he answered, Yuri began sucking him back to life. He grasped her hair, telling Shannon he was really busy at work, but that he'd be home on time.

As he told her he loved her, Yuri deep-throated him, he choked out, "Ahhh!" Shannon asked him if he was okay, and he'd responded, "Yes, dear, it's just this report at work."

Yuri smiled, and thought, *Piece of work, you mean!*

Tape in hand, Yuri had gone to Atlanta, and gift-wrapped it into a nice box. She'd asked Candice, who thought it was a wedding present, to mail it to Shannon. When she received it in D.C, Shannon had opened the gift, watched the edited version of the tape Yuri had sent, and saw her fiancé, and soon-to-be child's father, eat a very sexy woman out like he was at a an all-you-can-eat buffet at a seafood fest. She then watched him take more dick up his ass, than she ever had. She didn't even believe in anal sex, but the man she loved was taking at least ten inches in his ass. She'd cried hysterically, as she watched it over and over, then packed a bag and hid out at her cousins' home in Virginia. She got an abortion, and never showed up for the wedding. She was disgraced, after seeing her man get sodomized. The worst part was that he'd seemed to enjoy it; he was like a wild beast! She had to wonder if he was gay.

Yuri then remembered how Chanel had called and told her that Shannon had been found, but when she'd gone to Virginia to speak with her, she'd found out that Shannon had aborted the baby. Chance was already a train-wreck, being so worried about Shannon and the baby. Once Chanel drove back from Virginia with the tape, what he saw destroyed him. He'd cried, just moments before, when Chanel told him Shannon had aborted the baby, but was totally unprepared to deal with sitting with his sister to watch a sex tape of himself getting hammered up the ass.

Chanel had taken the remote, and cut it off. He appeared to be in a catatonic state, as she'd asked him what he was thinking about, and who the dominatrix was. He never revealed that it was Yuri.

Chanel had asked him if he was gay or bisexual and he'd screamed, "No, neither! I don't really know what happened, I think I was drugged!"

He and Chanel had sat and cried together. She told him that it would be okay, but it never would be. His first child was gone forever. His fiancée no longer wanted him. On top of everything else, his pride had been shattered by the tape. He drank and drank for the rest of the day. The next morning, he could not stand the guilt that kept replaying through his mind. He'd prayed, pleading with God to help him through it, and when he reached the conclusion that it hadn't worked, he'd brought a barstool into his bedroom, where the ceiling was high, tied a sheet to the ceiling fan, and slipped his head through the self-made noose. Standing on the barstool naked, he'd started jacking off, and when he'd begun to feel a rush, he'd lifted his body and kicked the stool out from under him. As he swung, suffocating, he pulled and pulled on his meat, came, and died. Yuri felt bad, but she couldn't bring him back.

Now it was time to kill his sister and his nephew.

Yuri arrived at the tavern before Uno. She ordered lemon-pepper wings and fried scallops. While she waited for the food, she sipped on an apple martini. Uno walked through the door, looking his own special brand of sexy. His whole demeanor had changed since he had come up. Just the sight of him made Yuri's hot spot tingle. Uno had the Robin Jeans on, with the Louis belt, and the Louis shades and shoes. His haircut was faded to perfection, and he still wore the silver mountain water Creed cologne she had introduced him to. He sauntered up to the table, looking and smelling like a million bucks. He sat down as the food was being delivered. The waitress checked him out and asked if she could get him anything. He ordered a shot of Remy Martin and a Corona; she smiled and disappeared.

"Damn, she is on your tip." Yuri commented.

Uno smiled. "Can ya blame 'er, shawtee?" He paused looking her deep in the eyes. "Now wazzup, Yuri?"

Uno never called her by her given name, unless he was tripping, because of her bullshit.

"I just wanted to talk to you about Shane, and discuss how we were going to handle him."

"We, shawtee? I got dis. An' I'm all' ready on his trail."

"But I want in!" she cried.

"Ya do wha' ya gone do, but' real men move in silence. Ya already got one murda on me, shawtee."

"Well, I need you to help me get Chanel," She begged.

"I tol' ya ta do wha' ya do. Ya on yo' own shawtee. I kin tell ya one thing, she go to da Whole Foods on Old Milton Pkwy sto' almos' every otha day, ta buy dem salads at lunch time, an' she pick up 'er son aroun' six, at dis day-care off exit 'leven,"

"I already know where the daycare is," Yuri volunteered.

He grinned. "It look like ya cool den, shawtee."

The waitress came back with Uno's drinks, smiling and switching her ass as another waitress watched from across the room.

She gave him her best toothy grin and asked him, "Can I get you anything else?"

Yuri interrupted her flirtation, "No! You may not!" Uno smiled, shrugging his shoulders, apologetically. The waitress looked at Yuri and rolled her eyes. Yuri knew Uno wasn't going to make any moves with her.

She turned to him, whispering, "I've been so horny, can you please give me some lovin?"

"Shawtee, I bin bizzy tryin' ta git dis paypa."

"And you can't make even a little bit of time for me? The last time we fucked was over a month ago!"

"Please don' remind me!" He said with a cringe.

Yuri smiled, knowing that he was remembering that the last time they'd sexed each other was the night he'd killed Candice, just a few feet away from her lifeless body. He told her to wait until the weekend.

Knowing that he'd then conveniently not answer the phone, she negotiated, "No. Tomorrow night. Wednesday is a perfect night. It always used to be our night anyway, plus I can't wait 'until the weekend!"

Uno thought a moment, then came back with, "I'm nah drivin' way out ta Gwinnett County."

Yuri was gaining ground, "You don't have to. I live right off 20th now, over by the Zoo."

"You win, shawtee, but I have to make a move. I'll be there."

She rephrased her question, getting annoyed. "So I can't get a kiss?"

"Man, naw! Ya know I ain' inta all dat mushy in public shit."

She was pissed. The waitress came back with the check, and had been bold enough to write her number on the back of it.

"Bitch, no you didn't!" Yuri exclaimed.

Uno chuckled. He left a twenty-dollar tip, grabbing Yuri's hand, and the check, as they left out. Yuri mumbled, "I should go back in and smack that bum bitch."

Uno shook his head. "Gurl, she a straigh' up hood rat. She be done whupped yo' ass!"

Yuri knew Uno liked hood rats. Well, he used to.

She walked toward her car saying, "I'll text you my address."

He nodded. "I'll see ya tamarra." Uno jumped into his new 2017 Audi pickup truck and sped off.

Yuri thought, *He got a new truck? He's going to put me up in something new, or else!*

CHAPTER 22

Shane flew down 400N, on his grown man stuff, bumping Bobby Womack. He told Hassan that he was almost to Hwy 85, and that they'd meet at the Toys 'R' Us on Lennox Road. Hassan informed him that he'd be there, waiting. Shane dipped through the early evening traffic in his convertible continental GT Bentley. He had just left the car wash. The gleaming white car stood out, with the red leather interior seats with twenty inch Asanti custom chrome rims, like no other. Bentleys were like Hondas in Atlanta, but Shane's made heads turn, especially when his smooth, sexy, chocolate self was behind the wheel. Shane was a head-turner, even without the automobile. He commanded attention without trying. He had the kind of personality that fit in with every and anyone - he was down to earth, well-spoken, and had a gift for putting people at ease. He was a perfect salesman, and a typical, though extraordinary, real estate buyer.

He pulled up to where Hassan was parked. Hassan was also easy on the eyes. He had down-sized from his Phantom, and now drove the four door GT Bentley coupe model, of course. Shane and Hassan always made sure their cars were no more than two years old. Hassan always stuck with the basic black, with no special rims; he was good on all the bling on the tires. They got out of their cars, exchanged dap and got straight to business.

"What up, my brotha?" Hassan asked.

"You got it, bro."

"So, what's going on with Candice? You heard anything new?"

Shane responded it with an even tone, "Man, it's crazy! No one has heard from her in two months now, not even her family. She hasn't called me or Chanel, plus, you know that her friend Passion is paralyzed from the waist down?"

"No shit?"

"Yeah, man, she was drunk and ran off the road, leaving Magic City. I thought I told you bro, she's lucky to be alive, but she got to go home from the rehab last month, and Candice would definitely have been there for her. Man, I don't want to wish the worst, but I think one of those rich ass tricks that she be fucking with didn't fall in love an' done did something to her!"

"I see you've put up a lot of money, man." Hassan said.

"I only gave forty thousand. A couple of the Cats she was dating had already put the initial sixty in. But I'm tempted to throw in another hundred thousand, and see who we can get to talk, because somebody knows something, Dawg."

"So, who is this 'Jay' cat she was hollering at?"

"All I know is that he's from here, because we were supposed to hook up the following day, when she disappeared. She made me promise not to laugh at him when we met, because he was straight up a mush mouth."

Hassan looked lost. "What the hell is a mush mouth, bro?"

Shane chuckled. "We call A.T. Aliens mush mouths, when they talk this 'Hubba-Bubba-Shubba' shit."

They laughed and eased the tension.

"And what else did she say?"

"She said he was fly, but not as fly as me. You know that's hard to do,"

Shane posed, like a model, on the cover of Esquire magazine.

Hassan shook his head as Shane continued, "She also said that what was crazy, she said that we wear the same cologne."

"The Creed?"

"Yeah, so he's getting a little paper, if he'll go spending two-fifty on a bottle of cologne."

Hassan corrected him, "You know he has paper, because your girl Candice, is about her money, and if you ain't spending five thousand, or better, she ain't dealing with you! I'm glad I don't cheat on Sonya, because I would have had to hit that ass, and I would have had my stacks ready when she asked."

Shane laughed, responding, "Trick! Oh, and she also said he drove a brand-new Escalade."

Hassan shrugged and looked unimpressed. "Everybody here drives an Escalade. That's not a good lead, but we'll use all the info we have, and get to asking questions. Now we need to talk about that shipment that's supposed to come in next Thursday. You've been distracted, but we still must pay the bills."

Shane responded, "You're right, as usual."

Hassan didn't miss a beat, "I spoke with Fernando. He said that there would be twenty-five kilos of heroin in the truck, and twenty-five keys of that white. They'll drop it off in Miami, and we can get a better price, because they have some other business down there."

Shane asked, "How much if we go down there and get it? And what's the ticket if they bring it?"

"It's one million, three hundred thousand, which is a break, down to thirty-five thousand a kilo for the China White, and ten thousand dollars a kilo for the coke."

"So how much more do they want to bring it straight to the door?"

"Being that the mule has to roll with the heroin, he wants twenty-five thousand."

"That's all?" Shane mused, "Tell them to run it. I'd rather they came all the way, Hassan."

"You got it, bro. I'll hit him up, and give him the green light. Shane, you know this is a huge shipment, so get your mind right, bro."

"I'm good."

"So, which house are we going to stash it at?"

"I just bought a property off 138, in Union City. I think we can put it over there, because whoever lived in the house must have been from California, or something."

Hassan was curious. "Why do you think that?"

"Because they had bars all around that bitch! People in Cali are the only ones who live like that and the good part is, it was a rich older couple, who moved out of the country, and there are only six houses on the block."

"That's cool."

"So, we'll meet Fernando over by that truck stop on 74, the Peachtree City exit. We can hitch the trailer onto our truck, and be gone. Once we get the truck attached, I'll transfer the funds into his Swiss account."

Hassan nodded, "Well, that's settled."

Shane got serious, and leaned in, saying to Hassan, "Bro, after this run, I really will be ready to give this life up. It's hard living two lives. Chanel means a lot to me, and if she knew I was selling drugs, she would be so upset! She always talks about how she can't stand drug dealers, and how glad she is that I'm a real estate broker. Before we get married, I want to be done with this, so I can be honest with her. I owe her that much, and myself. I mean I have everything I want and more. Greed will tear a nigga down."

Hassan said, "Shane, you could have been out of the game after Spida shot you and took our money. You said that you were done, but you were right back at it, dawg. You're already sitting on several million; the real estate is going well, so all you have to do is, not talk about it, be about it. If you stop, Shane, so will I. My money's right, the whole family has homes with no mortgages. Sonya knows what I do on the side she just doesn't know I got it like this."

Shane raised an eyebrow.

Hassan continued, "Sonya knows she's not rocking that eight carat Marquis, and pushing that new 550 for nothing."

They laughed. "Look man, I have to go get Chanel and Little C. We're taking him to see the Lion King on Broadway at the Fox tonight, so let me get going."

Shane and Hassan did their brotherly handshake, which only the two of them knew, and went their separate ways.

CHAPTER 23

It was a beautiful Saturday.

Yuri decided that she'd spend the day relaxing. Uno had shown up, on Wednesday, high as Cuda Brown. He had screwed her from Wednesday night through Thursday evening. She had swallowed more cum in a night, than she had consumed in her entire life. Uno had given her the roughest, toughest fucking he'd ever done. Yuri had taken it all, but was sore. Her butt had bruises all over it. She had love marks from her neck to her face, and she had a ring around her throat from him choking her. He tried to explode but couldn't, because of the drugs. Instead of having sex, it looked like someone had beaten the hell out of her.

She lay around, thinking of a plan to get Chanel and her son. First, she thought she would follow them and shoot into the car, but she knew her shot was off, and she had to make sure that whatever she did was guaranteed to kill them both. Her next idea was to have Sasha become Chanel's friend then decided that probably wouldn't work, since Chanel didn't talk to too many women.

She rearranged her battered and bruised up body among the pillows on her bed, and closed her eyes.

"I'll figure it out," she said, as if to reassure herself. "I'll come up with something that will get the job done."

CHAPTER 24

Chanel had been passing out flyers all day at the Vigil
for Candice. All the ballers, strippers, and businessmen had
shown up on Peachtree. The reward had gone up to a quarter
of a million. It had been five months since she'd gone missing,
and they had not gotten a single lead, not even about Jay.

Uno had driven by in his Audi truck, watching Shane
and Hassan. He wanted both of their heads, because of the
contract they had out on him. He also remembered how
Hassan had gone around him, and paid Tow Truck Mike not
to get rid of Spida's body.

He'd already taken care of Tow Truck Mike. When he
brought Candice's body to get cremated, Mike had been there,
doing a job for some New York folks. He knew once Mike
saw the hundred thousand reward he just might say
something, but as soon as it got to a quarter mill, Mike was a
done deal.

Uno told Mike that he had a job for him to do. Once
they met up, Uno had him get into the stolen car he was
driving, and pumped him full of lead. He had one problem
less for him to worry about.

As he drove past, Chanel handed him a flyer, and
thanked him. Uno accepted it, and nodded. Chanel
remembered his face; she just couldn't place from where,
especially now that he was bald. There was a circle of people
in Atlanta that you always saw, if you did the club scene.
Even though she hadn't been out for a long time, she never
forgot him.

Chanel went over to where Shane was giving out
bottles of water.

"Baby, you look tired." He said.

"I am," she responded, "I have fifty more flyers to
hand out, and then I'll be ready to call it a day. Maybe we can
ask the Nanny to stay at the house, with Little C, and you and
I can stay in a suite downtown and get massages? I feel that I

have been neglecting my wifely duties, baby." She winked at Shane.

"That sounds good, baby."

"I'm going to go back to the light and give these out. Hopefully someone will know something."

"We are going to find her, lil' momma, I promise."

"I hope so." Shane kissed Chanel on her head, and they both went back to work. Chanel had five flyers left when the Infiniti truck came past. As Sasha rolled her window down, she recognized Chanel's face. Chanel handed her a flyer saying, in a sweet, sincere voice, "We're looking for my Sister. Please take this flyer, and if you've seen her, you can call the number on the bottom. There's a very nice reward being offered."

Sasha looked at the flyer like she'd seen a ghost. Chanel asked, "Do you know her?"

"No, but it seems like I've seen her before. Was she a dancer?"

"Years ago, but she is missing, and we have to find her."

Sasha took the flyer.

As she Sasha drove off, Chanel said, "Thank you and God bless you." She watched as Sasha drove off, curious about her reaction.

Chanel distributed her last few flyers, and was ready to leave. She headed for where Shane was waiting for her.

CHAPTER 25

Yuri got Uno to cash out on a new car for her. She traded in her old one for six thousand dollars, and he had dropped fifteen thousand more at the police auction. He got Yuri a 2012 Porsche truck that was a seizure and foreclosure. She took Bliss with her to get all the paperwork straight. She didn't care if Uno didn't love her anymore. She had something on him, and now he had money. She used it to her advantage, and he hated it. The thought crossed her mind more than once that he might try to bump her off for blackmailing him. She was prepared.

Yuri called Sasha. She told her to meet her at Atlantic Station, so she could show her the new truck. Sasha really didn't want to go, but she had something she wanted to share with Yuri, as well.

Sasha got dressed and headed to Midtown. When she arrived, Yuri was waiting in front of Rosa Mexicano. Sasha got out, and had the valet guy park her truck. They were escorted to their seats. The waiter asked if they wanted anything while they looked at the menus. Yuri ordered the homemade guacamole, prepared at the table, and two Texas Margaritas, their usual.

"Juan, I'll have a red wine," Sasha said to the waiter, and then to Yuri, "Not today, Angel, I mean Yuri. It's hard to call you Yuri, but after all, you're no Angel!"

Yuri giggled. Sasha meant what she said.

They started talking after their guacamole was made, and the chips and dip were brought out.

"So, Sasha, how's everything going with you and Kevin?"

"It's great. We've been going out of the country a lot, and now that I'm pregnant, he has even-"

Yuri interrupted her. "You're *pregnant?!*"

Sasha sighed at her stupidity. "It wasn't supposed to come out like that, but that's what I was coming to tell you."

Sasha's eyes were lit up with excitement.

"So, that's why you ordered the red wine?"

"I'm drug free. I'm eight and a half weeks, and Kevin is no longer seeing that chick in Japan."

"That explains why you're getting married."

"Somewhat, but he proposed before we knew about the baby."

The waiter came back, and Sasha ordered all kinds of things, just like a pregnant woman would do.

Yuri watched in amazement. "Damn, girl!"

Sasha laughed, kindly responding, "I have a hearty appetite."

Yuri was a bit jealous. She had been letting Uno bust nuts up in her, the times that he would give her some play, but wouldn't get pregnant. Now she envied Sasha.

"Are you still messing with Uno?" Sasha asked, as if reading her mind.

"Not really, but he did buy me a truck. I'll show it to you after we eat."

Sasha smiled at her and said, "Kevin just purchased us a home in Sandy Springs, off Northside Drive. It's got five bedrooms and three and a half bathrooms, with a huge playroom, and an open floor plan. I absolutely love it!"

Yuri was now irritated because of all the bragging that Sasha was doing, about Kevin, and her new life.

"Sasha, you know we have one last job to do, before you get too big."

Sasha looked at her, in a patronizing manner, and softly suggested, "Yuri, why don't you move on, and let whatever it is you guys have going on go? Put it into God's hands."

"God? My ass!" Yuri exclaimed, "She did me wrong, and you promised to help me!"

"But I'm pregnant."

"That's even better. I have a plan."

"Yuri, I'm not with it."

"Okay, Sasha, then I will call Kevin and Detective Wallace, and tell them about our - no, *your* 'little accident' in Tennessee."

"Damn, Yuri, you always on some blackmail shit! Speaking of blackmail, I saw Chanel a couple of weeks ago she was handing out flyers, with that chick, Candice's picture on them. Isn't she the one we saw at the Phipps Plaza? And by any chance, the same one that was all over Uno the first night I met him?" Sasha narrowed her eyes. "Would you happen to know where she is?"

Yuri tried staying relaxed about the conversation, playing Sasha's sarcasm off, but Sasha knew when she was about to lie.

"Save it! I bet you had something to do with her disappearance! Am I right?" Sasha said, crossing her arms. "She's probably dead if you had anything to do with it."

"No, you're not right, and I don't have anything to do with her."

"Well, if you didn't do it yourself, you surely know who did! And as far as what I did in Tennessee, you go right ahead and tell, because you're the one who set everything up, so you'll be an accessory to murder, you'll get just as much time as me! And when I finish telling them how I was turned out on drugs, and met you, and was blinded and brainwashed, your scandalous ass will do just as much time as me!" Sasha pulled a one hundred dollar bill out of her Louis bag as the waiter arrived at their table with the food. She slammed it down on the table, storming out. Yuri told him she would be back, and chased after her.

"Stop, wait Sasha!"

"What for, Yuri? I'm so sick of your threats! Don't you realize that I have just as much shit on you, as you have on me? Have you forgotten about Doctor Snider? I know about you being in that nut house, and what he did to you, but you cut his dick off!"

By this point, everyone was looking at the spectacle they were creating, shocked and enthralled.

Sasha continued, "I won't help you hurt anyone else, I mean it!"

"I'm sorry, Sasha."

"No, you're not. You have no heart, nor conscience!" Sasha ranted, "You are the most fucked up, self-centered, nut case that I have ever met! Fuck you, Yuri! Do what you must do. I'll pay for what I've done. I'll go to prison before I do anything else wrong to another soul. Besides, when I looked into Chanel's pained eyes, I saw a grieving, kind, loving Mother and concerned Friend, unlike your scandalous snake ass!"

She jumped into her car and sped away.

Yuri was fuming. What really hurt was Sasha calling her a scandalous snake. She thought about how Chanel had called her phone on several occasions, with those awful, exact words and Candice had used them as well. Her appetite was spoiled. Sasha had left a hundred dollars on the table, which more than covered the food, and a generous tip.

She turned toward her truck. She hadn't even gotten the opportunity to show it off. She was bitter and angry.

She thought, *Fuck Sasha. I'll handle Chanel's girly ass on my own!*

CHAPTER 26

Yuri began following Chanel again, but it was harder than it had been, because Shane was with her practically all the time. It was getting close to their wedding date and he was on her like white on rice.

Yuri wished she had never done Shane wrong. She'd had a good man, who didn't cheat on her, and she chose Uno's broke butt, who had nothing at the time. Shane had money, looks, class, style, and integrity. Uno had nothing; bad choice. Now he was up, and wanted nothing to do with her. He had another baby on the way, by some singer chick who was blowing up on YouTube and World Star.

Yuri pushed Uno out of her mind, and focused on Chanel. She'd started following Chanel every morning, as she dropped her son at daycare, and waited for her to come pick him up, each afternoon - but lately, the Nanny had been doing it.

She thought, *I'll kill the nanny and the baby, then I'll get Chanel.*

But then she rationalized that the nanny really had nothing to do with this, so she didn't need to die. Yuri wanted to kill only Chanel and the baby. She formulated a plan, and hoped it would work.

She called Tony, the guy she had met when she escaped from the hospital. He was happy to hear from her. When she asked how he was doing.

His response was, "Good, now that I've heard from you!"

Yuri told him that she'd missed him, and wanted to hook up.

He was thrilled, and said, "Anytime!"

Yuri told him that she was free for the evening, but he said it wasn't a good night for him, as he had just made his car payment that day, and his funds were low. He wanted to take her to Red Lobster, or something, so their date would be special. Yuri told him that everything would be on her, and they could meet at the Red Lobster on Tara Boulevard at nine o'clock for dinner.

Tony eagerly accepted. "I won't be late."

Yuri got her things together, reserved a hotel room, dressed in her sexiest outfit, and then popped an ecstasy pill, so by the time she got with Tony, her attitude would be right for what she had in mind.

When Tony arrived, Yuri was already at the bar. She was on her third apple martini when she saw him standing at the door. She waved him over. He was in a trance. Yuri was cute the day he met her, and the second time she looked classy, and nice.

Now? *As they say, 'Third time's a charm,' and she looks hot! Really hot!*

Yuri stood up and kissed him on the cheek. He looked at her small frame and fat ass as she turned to sit back down, and couldn't help the bulge that was coming up in his pants, so he sat down really quickly. Yuri asked him what he was drinking tonight.

"Hennessey," he responded.

Yuri called the bartender over and ordered a double shot of Hennessey. When his drink arrived, she made a toast to 'Friendship.' Tony was nervous, and intimidated as Hell; he almost took down both shots in one gulp.

Seeing how nervous he was, Yuri commented, "Relax, what's wrong?"

Embarrassed, he responded bashfully, "I haven't been in a beautiful lady's presence since the last time I saw you."

"So whatever happened with what's-her-name?" Yuri asked.

"You mean La'Quenisha?"

Yuri burst out laughing. "Yeah, her."

"It's been over; we didn't work out."

"So, you're single, Tony?"

"Yes, I am."

"So, we'll change that, hopefully." She smiled at him, invitingly.

When Yuri said that, Tony started sweating. He blurted out, "Sounds good to me!"

They moved to a corner booth and ordered their food. Yuri wanted only salad and stuffed mushrooms. Her appetite was suppressed, because of the pill. Tony ordered a lobster, with shrimp scampi, baked potato, and had five or six cheddar biscuits, while waiting for his meal. He showed no shyness in eating his food.

Afterwards, Yuri ordered Tony another double shot of Hennessey, after which he was a little tipsy. Yuri was on her sixth martini. Once they finished them, they headed out.

Yuri walked in front of Tony, swinging her ample ass. Tony almost tripped he was so mesmerized by the view, not watching where he was stepping. When they got outside, Yuri asked him what his plans were for the rest of the evening.

He leaned against his truck, answering, "I guess I was jus' gonna take it in."

Yuri planted herself right in front of him, about twelve inches away, with one hand on her hip, whispering seductively, "Do you want to go with me?"

He didn't hesitate to say, "Yes."

Yuri left her car in the parking lot and jumped into his truck.

Once they pulled up to the low-key hotel, he parked and they went in. Upon entering the room, Yuri immediately got naked. Tony almost lost his mind he was overjoyed. He pulled out a magnum and came out his clothes. In seconds, he was ready.

Yuri thought, "Yuck," when she saw his sloppy body. She liked men that were toned, but she had to do what she had to do.

She leaned back on the bed, spread her legs open, and purred like an exotic kitten, "Want to taste it?"

Tony's tongue hung out like a dog's. He dove straight in, face first, eating Yuri up. He was nothing to look at, but he had a mean head game. He did things to Yuri that no man had ever done.

Yuri thought, *Damn, he is cold! No at ease.*

At least his head turned her on. She grabbed on his head, as he satisfied her with his extra-long, thick tongue. Twenty minutes in, Yuri exploded in his mouth. Tony licked all her sweetness up, then put his condom on his still throbbing dick, and started making love to her.

She thought, *Damn, his ugly, fat ass has a good tongue and dick?*

Yuri hadn't had anyone who made love to her in a long time. Larry used to, but they had not been sexing. Everyone she had sex with fucked her, like the hoe she was, then sent her on her way, or the other way around. She just knew going into the evening that she would hate Tony's sex, but she found herself moaning. She wondered if it was the pill.

No, Tony was on Hennessey, giving Yuri the business, filling her up with ecstasy literally.

After another twenty-five minutes of lovemaking, Tony got his off, but he wasn't finished pleasuring Yuri. He started at the bottom, and began by sucking on Yuri's toes. He sucked them one-by-one, then licked the soles of her feet. It tickled like crazy, but felt so delicious that Yuri had another orgasm. It took a lot to make Yuri orgasm, especially on a pill, but Tony was doing it over and over again.

He wasn't done, either. He worked his way back up to her vagina, teasing her pearl tongue then proceeded to lick up every drop of juice that she had just produced from between her legs. Not once did he wipe off his mouth; he savored her taste. Yuri didn't like him, but she was drawn towards him, and loved the way he made her feel. Tony finally finished, and sprawled out on his back.

"I'm not done," Yuri said.

"Well show me what you got," he replied, his second wind kicking in.

Yuri climbed on top, riding Tony, sitting all the way down on his nice size package, as he pumped upwards like a bull trying to throw off its prey. Most men would tell Yuri that she was trying break their dick, sliding that hard, and so far down - but Tony didn't say a word, he just put all that he had back into it. Tony's fat ass was a beast in bed.

He lifted Yuri off his still-stiff womb broom, tipped her over, breathing hard and saying, "I been nice. I see you want me to beat this pussy up!"

He started fucking Yuri doggy-style. She screamed and moaned as Tony ploughed his two hundred seventy-seven-pound body into her. Yuri talked dirty to Tony as he had his way with her, encouraging him to do what he did. She didn't stop praising him, empowering him.

Before he came, he screamed out, "Ah ah, ah. I love you, Angel!"

Yuri knew, at that moment that she had him.

She had planned on screwing Tony for a half an hour or less then going back for her car. She looked at the clock and realized that they had played around, and screwed for over four hours. The pill had even worn off, and Tony had worn her out.

Yuri fell asleep safely in Tony's arms.

The next morning, Yuri woke up looking at Tony's ugly fat ass. He was still knocked out. She went to the bathroom and took a leisurely shower. When she came back, Tony was up. He looked at her wrapped in a towel, saying, "I have to be at work by ten, but come here and let me leave you with a little something."

Yuri walked over to the bed. In one swift motion, he grabbed her around the waist, leaned back, and sat her on his face. His tongue stretched all the way up, deep into her vagina. Yuri was mesmerized by that tongue; she wondered how someone's tongue could be so fat, and make her feel so amazing he held her up and sucked until Yuri shuddered, repeatedly, giving his face a shower. He was satisfied and so was she.

Tony drove Yuri to her car.

She kissed him on the cheek and whispered, "Last night was spectacular, and so was this morning."

Tony responded "I love you, Angel, and I would do anything for you."

That's what Yuri was hoping to hear. She smiled "Anything?"

"Yes, anything."

Yuri ran her fingertip down the side of his face, "I'll hold you to that."

Tony looked thrilled, "So when will I see you again?"

Yuri baited him. "I have a lot of problems going on in my life right now, and I really don't want to involve you in them, but once I get myself together, I want to be with you."

Tony responded quickly, "But I need you now."

She got right to the point.

"Well, Tony, do you remember the guy that I was with when we met?"

"Yea I do. What about him?"

"I told him that I've been dating you, even though I lied, because he's still stalking me, and since then, he has raped me." She started crying, as she continued, "He follows me, jumps out on me, and beats me! I'm scared, and don't want to involve you."

"If you say you'll be mine, I'll kill that nigga, if he ever touches you again!" He was enraged.

Yuri hugged Tony, as she looked up into his eyes, with appreciation and said, "Well, I'm yours."

Tony wiped a tear from her cheek with his beefy thumb, assuring her, "I will keep you safe, Angel."

He opened his glove compartment, handed Yuri a small .38 Special, and continued, "It's not registered, but it's clean. If he comes around, when I'm not with you, pop his ass in the heart!"

Yuri took the gun and thanked Tony. They made plans to meet up on the weekend, which gave her time to get the rest of her plan together. She kissed Tony, saying, "Baby, I love you, too."

Tony was sprung. He didn't have a clue what he'd just gotten himself into, or what his future would be like with this woman.

CHAPTER 27

Uno followed Shane as he dropped three kilos of cocaine off, right in his Mechanicsville neighborhood. He wanted to rob and kill him right then, but there were too many children and people outside who could identify him. Shane went into Little Junie's house with the bag. After twenty minutes, Shane came out without the bag his hand by his waist, ready to shoot if something went wrong. Uno knew that Junie had come up on some change, but if he was dealing with Shane, he knew that he was getting a lot of dope, because word on the block was, the only way Shane would come around and deal was if it were a kilo or better. Then, he handled his own business, just in case the Feds were in on something, he would rather be caught alone, instead of being involved in a big conspiracy.

Uno decided to let him go, this time. He knew he would catch him out, one night, slipping, and lay him down, like he had his boys try to do to Uno.

After Shane left, Uno drove down the block. He parked and walked to Brenda's house. She lived next door to Little Junie. Brenda was happy to see Uno. He always gave her dope fiend ass dope. He also threw each of her six kids twenty dollars. He told the older ones to take their younger siblings to the Checkers down the street, and let them spend their money before their mother took it and bought herself a rock.

Uno sat on the porch, and rolled up a stogie, then fired it up. As he smoked, Little Junie came walking out of the spot, with the duffle bag that Shane had just dropped off. He'd grown up, Uno thought. He also knew not to keep dope on the block too long; it was a 'Get and Go' zone.

"What up, Junie?" Uno called out.

"Wuzzup, Uno?" Junie asked.

"I can't call it. I heard you been doin' yo' thang, Lil June."

"I'm doin' me, mane."

"I needa holla atcha." Uno said.

Junie put the bag in the trunk before he said another word, taking his 45 Glock out of the bag, tucked it in his pants, and walked over to the porch. He and Uno gave each other some dap.

Uno began, "Man, I been lookin' for some work. My folks are out, and the homies said you got da plug."

"Mane, my peeps don' like dealin' with niggas. I jus' got to da point a gaining their trust."

"Well, maybe you have what I need?"

"All I'm tryin' ta get is a bird, until ma folks get back, right!"

"When ya want it big homie?"

"Now if I can. Wuz da ticket?"

"Twenny eight fifty is what I got it for, but shit, man, I'm gone hafta at leas' make a small profit."

"Wha' ya want?"

"Gimme two nine fifty, and you kin git it now."

That was enough for Junie to make and re cop in the morning.

Even though Uno had been paying twenty-four thousand a kilo, he told Little Junie to bring it on. He wanted to know what kind of dope Shane was dealing with anyway.

Junie asked, "Ya ridin' aroun' wit thirty stacks in ya whip dog?"

"I'm ridin' wit fawty; I wuz on na mission; I done lucked up!" Uno went to his car, pulled out thirty thousand dollars from a bag in his backseat, and walked into Brenda's house. He told him, "This shit betta be righ', Bro, an' not no bullshit."

Junie assured him, "Man, this is da best plug I evva had. Deez niggas from da West Coast, an' da dope be comin' in from Columbia or some-damn-where. Mane, deez niggas don' evva run outta dope! Day got dat boy and dat white girl-"

Junie had started running his mouth, just like Uno wanted him to. Uno passed Junie the blunt. He hit it hard, choking, as he counted the hundreds that were in thousand dollar stacks.

He told Uno, "Mane, dis shit is serious, you got dat loud pack fo real, but my boy got some shit from Cali called Hurricane Katrina. Dat shit so bomb! I wuz ova dare in da house, trippin' mane. I wuz so high, it took me a minute ta go take da shit out ta da car!"

They laughed, and Uno made the switch.

He gave Little Junie another bag of weed to roll. His phone rang, and he excused himself, to take the call.

Uno stepped outside on the porch. After a couple of minutes, he came back in. Junie had fired up the new blunt, they talked a little more.

Uno tried to get more information about Shane, but now Junie was high, and gave Uno a funny look, "Nigga, ya askin' questions now, like you dem folks."

He laughed at his own joke, but was as serious as a heart attack.

Uno told him, "Boy, if I wuz dem folks, I woulda hemmed yo' ass up comin' out da doe wit that duffle bag!"

They laughed again.

Junie tucked the money under his shirt, and handed Uno the kilo of cocaine.

He said, "Man, it wuz good doin' binness witcha, but I gotta get little an' go handle dis."

Uno nodded, "A 'righ' lil homie, if dis shit is cool, I'm gone git witchya again."

"Fo' sho' fam," Junie replied.

Junie left Uno smoking on his weed. Thirty minutes later, one of Uno's little home boys who worked for him arrived, to pick up the dope he had just acquired. Uno wanted to chill on the block a bit longer. After smoking, a few more blunts, he received the call he was waiting for.

He smiled mischievously. "Nice. You my nigga, if you don' get no bigga!"

He hung up, chilled for a little while longer. He broke the seal on the brick and rocked up a gratified piece of dope for Brenda, noticing she was already high when he gave it to her. He chatted with her, telling her to let him know how the dope was, and rolled out. He had gotten information on Shane, and knew what kind of product he was working with. Brenda was spooked on it.

Later that evening, as Uno counted the thirty-three thousand dollars, a phone call came in.

"Wuzzup, Brenda?"

"I jus' wanna tell ya, don' come ova on da block, because it's hot as fish grease ova here!"

Uno asked, "What? They kickin' in houses, or som'n?"

"Na, man, somebody done killt Lil Junie earlier, ova by Sampson Road."

"What? No shit!" Uno reacted.

"Yeah, they said it wuz a hit, cause the niggas drove up on da side a him, while he wuz gittin' out da car, and domed him. Then they popped his trunk, took a bag an' some money off him. The lil' rat he be fuckin' was 'bout ta come outside, but da niggas start bussin'!" she reported.

"Did she see who da fuck day wuz?" he asked, pissed off.

"Naw, she wuz too scared. She hit da ground!"

"Awrigh' Brenda, I'm chillin'. When ya git an update, lemme know."

"Gotcha, Uno."

Uno went back to counting his stack of cash, which included the extra thirty-five hundred, that Little Junie'd had in his pockets. He felt no remorse. He had paid his henchmen fifteen thousand for the hit, thirty-five hundred of that was Junie's; he had paid his own money for his life. Uno had three free kilos, and would soon have much more.

CHAPTER 28

Yuri had been following just Chanel for the past few days. She knew Shane was doing other things because a couple of times, she had tried to tail him, when she could keep up, without Shane dipping on her. He moved swiftly, and would turn, block after block; some days it was impossible to keep up.

Today, Yuri followed Chanel out 75 South, to Eagle's Landing. She wondered where she was going. To her surprise, she pulled right into the parking area for the hospital that Yuri had been in. She got out of her car, strutting sassy, in her velour sweat suit and Air Max sneakers. Yuri was puzzled over what she was doing here at the crazy hospital she'd had Yuri admitted to, after she'd shot her.

The only thing she remembered was that once she woke up out of the coma, she was partially paralyzed on the left side of her body, and her baby was gone. She'd screamed and fought every day, and was sedated. When she finally calmed down from the tantrums, all she could remember was an endless cycle of being in the crazy hospital, raped almost daily by Doctor Snider.

After thirty minutes, Chanel came out, looking mad and walking fast. Yuri wished she knew what they had told Chanel. She was even more determined that she needed to get rid of Chanel quickly. She didn't care if she got caught; she was going to kill Chanel and her son.

Yuri jumped in her ride, and called Tony, crying and sobbing, uncontrollably.

He was alarmed, and asked, "What's wrong, Angel?"

"I need to see you, Tony, things are not good. My ex is still following me, and he just tried to run me off the road!" She broke down to the point that he could barely understand her. Tony told Yuri he would be off in an hour, and she could meet him at his house in Jonesboro. He gave her the address.

On her way, there, Yuri stopped at a gas station, and pulled up to a pump that another female was waiting for. The hood chick told her to move. When she refused, she jumped out her car, and slapped the shit out of Yuri, bruising her cheek. *Perfect*, Yuri thought.

When Tony arrived home, Yuri had already been sitting there for a while. She jumped out the car and ran to hug him.

Tony patted her back saying, "I'm here," then held her away looking at her face, "Did he hit you?"

Yuri nodded, and cried against his shoulder. Tony's blood boiled.

He put his arm protectively around her, soothingly. "It's gone be a 'right," he crooned as he led her into his small house.

As Yuri walked in, all she could think about was going over her friend Marie's grandmother's house back in D.C. Tony had a burgundy velour sectional, with a gold, five-finger floor lamp that arched up from the corner, and over the couch. He still had the big black and gold picture with the panther that was from 1988.

Yuri thought, *He's got some shit in here that's as old as me! Someone had to have given him this shit, or maybe it came with the house!*

To top it off, it smelled like moth balls.

Tony saw the look on Yuri's face, and said, "I know, I need to clean up."

Yuri's thoughts were going more toward his needing to upgrade. She told him not to worry about it, and to sit down, as she went through her sob story. She told him the guy's name, and how he was giving her hell, because she had told him that she no longer wanted a drug dealer, and now she was with a legit man. She told him, in graphic detail, how he had smacked her, and choked her, and referred to Tony as a low-life, for working a nine-to-five.

"He also said that if he ever sees us together in public, that he's going to kill you, and bae, I know he will." She trailed off, and turning up the tears a notch, she went on, "So I think we should break it off, because I don't want to see you hurt."

Yuri broke down again, as if she couldn't bear the thought of losing Tony, and it was breaking her heart.

"I already told you that he can't run me off, and I will kill him, before he gets me."

Yuri looked up at him, through her tears, and whispered, "It's a terrible thing to have to say, but I'm afraid that's the only way we'll be able to be together. I love you, Tony."

She reached for his belt, and unbuckled it.

Tony said, "Baby, I have to shower."

Yuri took his meat out, and started licking on his salty balls. Tony gave up, leaned back on the couch, and allowed himself to be pleasured. He was in love, like he had never been before, and he was ready to do whatever he had to for Yuri's love.

CHAPTER 29

Yuri had continued to seduce Tony for weeks. She had seen Uno once or twice, but without Sasha, he didn't want to have sex with her. He would come to Yuri's only because of her blackmailing him, and then the sex was missionary-style, boring, unfulfilling, and way too quick.

Yuri decided to call Sasha. When she finally answered the phone, she asked her how she was doing.

"I'm okay, Yuri, how are you?" Sasha replied.

"I'm okay; just trying to get my life in order."

"So, that means you've changed, and you're not following that Chanel girl around anymore?"

"Well, I've slacked up, but if the chance comes, her ass is grass! So, how is the pregnancy going?"

"It's great! I'm thirteen and a half weeks, and next month, on Kevin's birthday, we have an appointment for an ultrasound to find out the baby's sex. We're also planning to get married that weekend."

"Congratulations, Sasha!"

"Thank you."

"So, am I invited to the wedding?"

Sasha hesitated, "Well, it's really for immediate family only, but I'll send you an invite. Are you still in Gwinnett?"

Yuri lied, "Yes, I am. Sasha, I have one last favor to ask, before your life totally changes."

"What is it, Yuri?"

"I want you to sleep with me and Uno, one last time. What do you say?"

"I say, bitch, you are one crazy hoe! I don't even know why I answered this phone! I'm happy with my fiancé, and I'm pregnant! I can't believe that even your fucked-up, crazy ass would ask me some bullshit like that! Let me tell you something, Yuri. You almost destroyed my life, once you turned me into a dyke, and you think you did something for me? Stay the fuck away from me, and don't ever contact me again! I've seen that chick, Candice, is missing. Fuck with me? I'll tell them you had something to do with it, because I'm sure you did, and I will send them straight to your apartment! You are a horrible person, and a psychotic bitch! And my number will be changed as soon as we hang up!" With that, Sasha hung up.

Yuri was humiliated and pissed. She thought about getting in the car, driving to Sasha's new house, or the condo that she still had, and beating the shit out of her, for a few minutes. But the feeling passed, and she focused back on Chanel.

She started writing ransom notes, for when it came time to kill Chanel and Little Chandler. She hated his name. She knew Chanel had named him that because that's the name Chance and Shannon had intended for their child.

Two weeks passed. Yuri sat at home, fantasizing about how she would kill Chanel and the baby. She didn't want Shane to be around when she did it. She wanted Chanel to feel the pain that she herself had gone through, and to die a slow, tortured death.

After sexing Tony for months, he was mesmerized and hypnotized. He was in the habit of always watching his back, because of all the stories Yuri told him, about how he was being followed. Yuri had put so many kinds of drugs in his water, juice, and anything else he drank, so that he was getting crazier, with each passing day. Tony had been randomly selected to be drug tested at his job, and when the results came back saying his urine was dirty, he didn't understand how that could be possible, and swore that the UA must have been faulty, as he knew he was drug-free.

He was fired immediately, and fell into deep depression. But, at least, he still had Yuri - Angel, as he knew her. Yuri encouraged Tony to start smoking weed. It helped his depression. Then she began lacing it with PCP, which was angel dust. Tony turned into a monster. Even his family didn't recognize, or know what was happening to him. Within a month of being on the PCP, Tony was hooked.

One night, Yuri got Tony high, and then told him that the guy was coming to kill them. Tony was hallucinating. He asked her to drive him to the gas station. She put on her shoes, got the keys to Tony's truck, and they were at the gas station in ten minutes. Tony went inside and paid, then filled up his gas can, spilling more gasoline than he was getting in the can.

When Yuri pointed out that he was getting gas everywhere, telling him that he was going to blow them both up, Tony yelled, "Shut up! I got this!"

Yuri knew he was high, because when he was sober, he would never say something like that to her.

She giggled, "What are you going to do?"

Tony told her to pull around to the park. He started drinking the six-pack of beer he had just purchased, then once he'd downed each bottles' contents, started filling them with gas.

He stepped outside the truck to relieve himself, after peeing out all the beer, then got back in the truck, and asked Yuri to drive him where he needed to go, so he could take care of their problem.

Yuri jumped on 75 North, then onto 85 North. Before they arrived, Tony lit up the sherm stick.

Yuri yelped, "You're going to burn us up!"

He paid her no mind. Once they got to their destination, Yuri followed someone in, through the gate. She told Tony to get out, like he was walking and lived there, so he got out carrying the six-pack, as she stayed with the car and waited outside the gate. She told him which number condo to burn up. He was on his way.

Yuri waited twenty-seven minutes before she saw a blaze of fire erupt high into the sky above the condos. She smiled, and got down on the floor of the truck. Tony was among at least a dozen people who came running through the gate. He jumped into the truck, hesitating to take a moment to watch the blaze, which snapped him back to reality, and instantly sobered him.

Back to his senses, he thought, *what have I done?* Yuri looked up at him from the floor, and instructed him to drive away.

In front of Tony's house, Yuri told Tony that she wanted to sleep at her place, alone, for the first time in months, since she was sure her ex-boyfriend wouldn't be bothering her anymore.

He kissed Yuri, and was about to walk into his house, when she suggested, "Baby, why don't you give me those clothes, so I can get rid of them, as soon as possible?"

Tony came out of his clothing, right there, on the doorstep, and handed the whole pile over to Yuri. She went home, smiling.

The next morning, Yuri woke up and turned on the TV. The breaking news was about the Lennox Park Condominiums fire. The news anchor announced that there were two dead in the fire, and rattled off their names: Kevin Choice and Jerry McGregor.

Yuri thought, *What about Sarah?*

They added that five more people were injured. Yuri wondered if Sasha was one of them.

Tony hadn't finished the job properly if she was still alive.

CHAPTER 30

Sasha had been with her parents all night, celebrating her good news. She and Kevin were expecting a baby girl, and they would be married on Saturday. Sasha had eaten everything in sight, and was starting to feel tired, so told her mother that she was going to head home. Her mother begged her to stay and play one more game of Scrabble with her.

She didn't want to because of the long drive back to Buckhead, but finally gave in, saying, "Okay, Mom, but you know you can't beat me!"

Her mother laughed, and said, with tears in her eyes, "I'm just happy to be sitting here, with my beautiful daughter, with my beautiful granddaughter growing inside of you. I love you, Sarah, and I am so grateful that everything has turned around in your favor! You found a wonderful man, and I can't wait until he's my son-in-law. Just know you're my baby and will always be!"

"I love you, too, Momma!"

A half hour into the game, Sasha's mother announced that she was also getting tired. Sasha was glad. "Good! I'm going home to my soon-to-be husband."

Although she was happy to be reunited with her family, she missed Kevin. Her mother kissed her on the head, and as she walked out, Sasha felt admiration and comfort. She couldn't wait to tell Kevin how very happy she was. Her world felt complete for the first time, since she couldn't even remember when.

She sang and hummed as she drove. Before she even got close to her condo, she saw the flames. She prayed that it wasn't her building that was on fire. As she crept closer, the police would not let her come down her street. She was alarmed.

"But that's where I live!"

When they wouldn't let her through, she parked, and ran down the block as fast as she could, holding her stomach. There were a lot of people outside the gate. As she tried pushing her way past the crowd, her neighbor, Pamela grabbed her, and told her that she couldn't go in the building.

Sasha screamed, "But I have to! Please let me go! Kevin's not out here!"

Pam looked at her, apologetically, and told her, "Your apartment is the one burning. I don't think Kevin or your neighbor, Mr. McGregor, made it out."

Sasha let out a heart-wrenching scream and begged, "No! Don't say that!"

Pam grabbed Sasha, hugging her tight, trying to calm her.

Pam asked one of the officers if he would speak with Sasha. He was not the least bit comforting. On the contrary, he was so cut and dry, that Pam wished she hadn't sought him out at all. He told her that she may need to come down to the morgue with Kevin's parents to identify the body if she wasn't his wife, and verify that it was her fiancé. Sasha was devastated. She cried as she called Kevin's parents, then hers, to tell them about the fire.

She thought, *And I wanted to stay at our house tonight.*

Sasha went to the coroner's, and identified Kevin's burned body. She didn't remember ever crying so long, or so hard. She prayed, and told God that even though Kevin was gone, she was grateful, that Kevin had changed her life and thanked him for saving her, and their baby's lives.

She thought, *A mother's instincts, and God's will, had saved us.*

Her mother wanted her to stay and play one last game of Scrabble. The timing of that game saved her, and her child.

She asked the police what had started the fire. They told her they wouldn't know all the facts until an investigation was performed, but they had found glass bottles that may have had gasoline in them, and that they had likely been set deliberately. Sasha's thoughts immediately went to Yuri, but Yuri didn't know where they lived. Even though she knew how devious and conniving Yuri could be, she decided to let the police do their job.

Sasha cried, knowing their child would never be able to meet her father; that she would never know the best man that Sasha had ever been blessed to be with. She would tell her all about him. She'd make sure their baby knew and loved him too.

CHAPTER 31

The months had flown by, and the hype about Candice's disappearance had died down, even though her friends never gave up hope. Sasha had moved back in with her parents, but only until she delivered the baby and got back on her feet. They thought she had been through quite enough during her pregnancy, wanting her to have less stress for a while.

Yuri had been dissing Tony. Now that he had killed Kevin, she played him like the fool he was. Tony stopped smoking and drinking all the drugs that she had fed him, and tried to get himself back together. Even though he thought he loved Yuri, he realized how she had manipulated him, and put him up to kill, and now showed no interest in him. She had keys to his house, his truck, and didn't use any of them. He felt bitter, but also knew that he was better off without her. He could feel that her spirit wasn't right.

He came from a very spiritual family, and felt like God was sending him a simple message: *Stay away!*

CHAPTER 32

Yuri followed the nanny all week. She knew the times she picked Little C up and how long they stayed at the park. There wasn't a detail of their schedule that Yuri hadn't observed and analyzed. She was studying her prey. She was getting closer to the time when she'd be ready to make her move.

Chanel was still focused on the preparations for her upcoming wedding. Even though she had stopped putting all the details on her Facebook page, Yuri had overheard the nanny telling one of Chanel's friends at the park, that she would be married in a couple of months, and she thought she'd seen an invitation that would be coming to her soon.

Many times, Yuri had sat on the park bench, reading her magazine, like a normal person enjoying the park. The nanny paid no mind to the fact that she was being followed. She was of Hispanic descent, spoke fluent Spanish and good English, but never watched her surroundings.

Yuri's plan was about to unfold, just as she'd planned it.

CHAPTER 33

Chanel was sitting in her living room, going through the bills, when she came across the twenty-eight hundred dollar bill for the hospital. She called for Shane.

When he came downstairs, he sat next to Chanel, looked at the bill in her hand, and remarked, "So, I have a say-so in the bills today? You must have gone over your shopping limit."

He smiled at her playfully.

Chanel pouted. "I don't spend that much, and besides, my pay-checks cover my shopping; you just pay the bills."

"Well then, what is it, baby girl?"

"Like a month and a half ago, I stopped by the hospital, to check up on Yuri, and to my surprise, she had escaped. Not once did they call to let us know, and we're still receiving monthly bills, to pay for her room."

"She escaped?!"

"That's what I was told when I went there. It had slipped my mind. They said that she had drugged the male nurse who was attending to her, and vanished."

"I'll contact my attorney to stop them from billing us, and probably start a lawsuit to get back the money we've paid for an empty room! Did they say how long she's been gone?"

"Well over eight months."

"Eight fucking months? They owe us over twenty stacks!"

"I don't want to sound crazy, but Candice came up missing five months ago, you don't think-" Chanel curiously asked, but he cut her off.

"She's not that damn crazy!"

"Yes, the hell she is Shane! Look what she did to my brother! Look how she treated her own mother! Look what she did to you, baby!"

"Calm down, baby girl. I'll have someone start investigating. Come here."

Chanel curled into Shane's waiting arms. "Baby, I won't let anything happen to you, or my little man." Chanel felt safe in her fiancé's arms. The door opened, and in burst Little C, followed by Jocelyn. He ran over to his parents. Shane scooped him up and swung him high into the air. When he brought him down, they both laughed. Chanel gathered him into a tender, motherly love hug, and planted a big kiss on his cheek. They told Jocelyn that she could have the evening off. She was very grateful. Shane pressed three appreciation one hundred dollar bills into her palm, telling her to go treat herself.

Jocelyn was very grateful - she loved her boss. She knew that Shane sold drugs, as one day she had walked into the garage while he was taking a bundle of cocaine out of the trunk of a car that had a stash spot. When he looked up and saw her, he apologized, because he never brought his illegal work home, but had no choice. On that day he asked her to never say anything to Chanel. She promised him that she wouldn't, and had never breathed a word about it since, to anyone. She was a live-in nanny, making two thousand dollars a month, which was twice as much as she had been making at her last job.

Jocelyn came from a family in Honduras, who had tried to get out of their country for years. Luckily, her mama and brother had made it, but the rest of the family had gotten caught at the border. She now had her green card. She was a kind, thirty-two year old, Hispanic lady, with long, wavy black hair, hanging past her behind. She was very smart, and loved Chandler, Chanel and Shane, whom all loved her just as much.

She packed an overnight bag, and told them she'd be back in the morning, long before it was time for them to leave for work.

Little C ran over to her when she picked up her car keys, he asked, "I go?"

They laughed. She hugged him, telling him that he wouldn't be coming along this time, but that she'd be there when he woke up. He started to cry as she left. Chanel picked him up and asked him if he wanted cookies.

He shook his head vigorously and said, "With chocolate milk, Mommy."

He was really beginning to speak well, especially when it concerned something he wanted. Chanel gave him a few cookies, and a cup of warm chocolate milk, bathed him, and carried him to bed. He was asleep before his head hit the pillow.

Chanel got into the shower, and after a couple of minutes, Shane stepped in behind her. She turned around to admire her soon to be husband. They stared, deeply into each other's eyes. Their hands found themselves wandering, and they began kissing, passionately. One thing led to another, and they made love, without a spoken word, from the shower to the bedroom floor. He was the first man Chanel had ever made love to, and he would be the last if she could help it. She would make sure that she did everything right to satisfy and make her soon-to-be husband happy.

CHAPTER 34

Yuri finally had her plan worked out. After writing over twenty-five different ransom notes, she settled on the one she felt was best. She tried as hard as she could to get Uno involved, but he told her that he had his own vengeance to handle.

What she didn't know was that he planned to kill her as soon as he took care of Shane. He'd never been blackmailed so much in his entire life, and he was sick of it. There had been several nights he'd wanted to kill her, but Yuri was smart. She made sure her neighbors knew that he was the only man that came to her house. They also heard them argue a lot, and when Uno would storm out, Yuri made sure to run after him, and cause a big scene.

She knew he was not feeling her vibe anymore, especially since he'd told her she was a treacherous, conniving bitch, and needed to get a life, to which she responded, "You are my life, Uno!"

His money was right, and he wanted nothing to do with Yuri; he was totally over her. To be honest, she had always been a jump off, even when he was broke.

It was time to implement the plan. Yuri called Tony. Even though he had gotten his life back on track, Yuri still had the power to make him weak. She told him she wanted to come over and make love to him. He tried to say 'no,' but couldn't; the wrong head had won. She told him she was on her way.

She then called Uno telling him, "I don't know what you're going to do, but tomorrow, my problems will be over."

He growled into the phone, "Mane, don' be hittin' me wit dat shit ya gone do!" He hung up, annoyed at how crazy and ignorant Yuri was to keep calling him on his phone with her assault plans.

Thank goodness it was a burn out phone, he thought.

Now it was time for him to plot his scheme, as well.

Yuri drove out to Tony's. She stopped along the way, and bought a bottle of Perrier-Jouet rose champagne. Tonight, would be a night that Tony would never forget. She pulled up. Excitedly, Tony opened the door. His Angel was in an all-white linen coat, looking just like an angel sent to him from Heaven. She seductively untied her trench coat, revealing that she had nothing on under it. Tony was instantly erect. He reached for her, but she stopped him with a gentle reproach, instructing him to go get two glasses, so they could share a drink.

Tony hesitated, and said, "I haven't drunk in a couple of months."

She told him they were drinking to their future together as she ran her tongue over her lips while trailing a well-manicured finger down his oversized abdomen. He ran, like the fool he was, to get the glasses.

When he returned, he popped the cork on the champagne. Yuri asked him to get the can of whipped cream she'd brought. He really ran, knowing that he was about to get a treat or be the one doing the treating. Once he was out of the room, Yuri dropped the pills into his champagne.

Tony came back, his throbbing dick leading the way. He squirted some of the whipped cream on Yuri's right breast, and licked it off. She moaned for effect, and he moaned in response, trying not to cum before anything had happened; he was so excited. Yuri handed him his glass. It was deja vu for her. Tony drank it down in one gulp, and started back, working on Yuri. He pulled her down to the edge of the bed, spread her legs, and sprayed her clitoris with the whipped cream, then went to work. Yuri enjoyed how he had her for dessert. She thought about how Uno would only pleasure himself, and then be done, but now all the attention was on her. After she let out all her juices in his face as usual, they had sex.

Tony was deep inside her, and Yuri was wondering why the pills hadn't taken effect on him. Tony's adrenaline was going. He had not had sex since his last time with Yuri, so nothing got in his way. She started meeting his thrusts, which really excited him.

He yelled out, "Throw that pussy, Angel. Aww, aww, I love you!"

Yuri tightened her vaginal muscles, as hard as she could, and Tony couldn't take it any longer. She licked in and around his ear, then proceeded to spit on his nipples and bite them. He was sweating profusely, and she had won. Tony exploded, and collapsed on top of Yuri.

He could barely raise his head, as he panted. "Damn, Angel, you got me with that move!"

He was breathing extra hard, he started wheezing, as he told Yuri that he needed water. She dragged herself out from under him, walked to the kitchen, and came back with a bottle of water.

Tony drank it down, then slurred, "I'm too tired ta git a towel, kin ya jus' lay wi' me?"

Yuri curled up next to him. Within seconds, he was completely knocked out, still with the condom on.

With practiced expertise, she removed the condom and bagged it, cleaned him up, wiped every surface down, for prints, and left. She drove her car to the Red Lobster on Camp Creek Pkwy., then called a taxi.

Yuri went home, and tried to go to sleep. When she couldn't, she called Uno. He answered on the third ring, she automatically started lying, telling him that she'd seen Shane, and wanted to tell him about it. Within the hour, Uno showed up. He let himself in with the key that he never used, unless she'd conned him into coming over.

"So, wuzzup, shawtee? Where ya see dat sucka at?"

"I was over at the Red Lobster on Camp Creek, and he pulled up. It looked like he was making a drug transaction."

Uno knew that Yuri was lying. He had followed Shane enough to know that he wasn't that careless, with handling drugs in public.

He glared at her and tensed his jaw, as he responded, "Ah wuz busy. Tha's all ya called me fo'?"

Yuri was disappointed. "I wanted to see you, Uno."

"Gurl, ya gots problems."

"Not for long," she chirped, as she wrote out her last ransom note.

Uno looked at the letter and could only shake his head, as he read it.

Walking toward the door he said, "I'm outta here."

"But, Uno…"

"I wa holla, shawtee," and he was gone.

Yuri was hot. She ran into the kitchen and grabbed her wine. She was so mad. She caught sight of herself in the mirror, which was hanging on the wall, and threw the wine glass at her angry reflection. Both the glass and the mirror shattered, wine splattering in all directions. She went to her bedroom. She didn't think she could sleep with all the aggravation running through her veins like acid, but she desperately wanted tomorrow to come.

It was five o'clock in the morning, when Yuri finally dozed off. At 6:30a.m. she was right back up. She jumped on 85 North, to the 400. She was glad that the traffic would be going in the opposite direction. She needed to make it to the Chick-Fil-A that Jocelyn took Little C to before she dropped him at daycare. Yuri was familiar with their routine, and every morning, she brought him there, for breakfast.

Yuri pulled up at exactly 7:45a.m. She parked at the entrance. As soon as she saw the nanny drive into the lot, she drove around to the side, where she had parked. The space beside Jocelyn's was occupied. Yuri watched as she got out of the car, went to the backseat, unbuckled Little C, and led him inside by the hand. After what seemed to be a fifteen-minute wait, the car parked beside Jocelyn's left. Yuri pulled into the spot, with her shades and blonde wig on, covered up in a hijab like a Muslim woman.

Jocelyn and Chandler finished their meal and walked out; laughing happily about some silly sing-song game they were playing. As she approached the passenger side of the car to put Chandler in his car seat, Yuri rolled down her window asking, "Excuse me ma'am, would you happen to know how I get to John's Creek? I'm lost."

Jocelyn picked Little C up.

She said, "Yes," as she walked to Yuri's window. Yuri stuck her with the tranquilizer, and Jocelyn instantly went weak at the knees, slumping to the ground like a sack of potatoes. She couldn't move.

Yuri jumped out of the car, looking and sounding concerned, "Are you okay?"

She was down for the count. Yuri scooped Little C up and sat him in the driver's seat until she could lift Jocelyn and roll her into the backseat. Little C started crying, knowing that something was going wrong with his nanny.

Yuri tried to reassure him, "She's okay," as she moved him from the front to the back, and buckled him into the car seat that she had brought. Once Chandler was next to Jocelyn, he stopped crying. Yuri gave him a lollipop and drove off.

She drove to an empty warehouse that she'd purchased from a man Bliss had told her about. Bliss didn't know that Yuri had purchased it, totally under a false name. Yuri wrestled the unconscious Jocelyn inside, and handcuffed her to the door. She then drove back out, with Little C fast asleep in the backseat, to deliver the ransom note to Chanel. She drove to Chanel's job, leaving the sleeping baby in the truck, as she walked through the parking lot, searching for Chanel's work car. To Yuri, it was a woman's everyday car, but Chanel referred to the 2012, fully-loaded, Toyota Avalon as a 'work' car. There was one man, looking for a parking space. Once he pulled out of her view, Yuri stuck the piece of paper under her wind shield wiper blade.

As Yuri approached her truck, Little C began to stir. She opened the door and slid inside.

He glanced at Yuri, then looked around and started whimpering, "I want my mommy."

"She's coming to get you," Yuri responded. He started crying, which was already driving Yuri nuts. As she pulled out of the lot, he screamed louder.

Yuri glared at him, in the rear-view mirror, and yelled, "Shut the fuck up! Now!" Little C stopped crying, but gulped for air and hissed, like he was going to hyperventilate, staring wide-eyed at Yuri, more scared than he'd ever been in his entire short, little life.

Yuri said, "I'm sorry, but you have to stop screeching and carrying on like this. Do you want McDonalds?" He shook his head, 'No,' which meant, 'Yes,' something else that Chanel had posted on her Facebook page, luckily.

Yuri found the nearest McDonalds, and pulled into the drive-through.

Little Chandler clapped his hands and sang, "Happy Meal," as his eyes lit up with excitement. Yuri shook her head and thought about how smart he seemed for such a small child, and what a shame it was that she was going to kill him. It almost made her sad. Almost.

She paid for his food and handed him the bag.

"Tank you," he said. She looked into his eyes and felt a twinge of guilt and unease for what she was going to do to this polite and innocent child. That was an unfamiliar emotion for Yuri, one that even she couldn't figure where it came from. She pondered it for a moment, then shrugged her shoulders before driving off.

CHAPTER 35

Uno had remembered everything that Yuri's ransom note had said. He knew that Chanel was supposed to meet Yuri at the warehouse, at two o'clock sharp. He was familiar with the area, where the warehouse was located, and knew it was secluded, and that he could have a hell of a shoot-out, without anyone but the mark getting struck.

He thought, *Yuri will be in for a s'prise when she see me! Ah'll kill Shane firs, den dat bitch, for threatenin' a nigga!*

He worked himself into a state, thinking about all the bullshit Yuri had put him through, and could almost taste how sweet his revenge would be once he killed her. He called Shane.

When he answered, Uno said, "Wuzzup dare, fuckboy?"

Shane didn't recognize the voice. "Who is this?"

"Dis da nigga ya tried ta kill a-couple-a years ago."

"What? Who?"

"Ya heard me, nigga! Dis Uno, an' I got yo' son, an' if ya wan' 'im back, ya'll meet me at 1:30 p.m., on Bankhead Road, at dis warehouse, wit a million dallas, an' if ya brings anybody wit ya, ah'm gone kill dem, an' den yo' big head ass son!"

Shane spoke in a hostile, even tone, "You bitch-ass nigga, if you hurt my son, I swear I'm gone kill you, and your whole muthafucking family!"

"Yo' phone is bein' monitah'd, so don' call yo' gurl or' no buddy, or' like ah said, a lotta folks gone git hurt! So, come alone. Take Bankhead Road second block, make a lef and come scrait ta da dead end."

Uno hung up.

Shane had to pull over, he was so inflamed. He didn't want to call Chanel and get her upset. He pulled back onto the road and continued driving. He was going to meet Hassan. Together they'd figure this out.

He didn't have far to go, and was driving like a bat out of hell, but it seemed to take forever to get there. As soon as he saw Hassan, he screeched to a stop, jumped out of his car, beating his fists on the roof. Hassan immediately sensed trouble. The anger was emanating from every pore in Shane's body. His brown face was red, his eyes bulging, and the hairs on the back of Hassan's neck prickled to attention.

"What's up, my brotha?" He asked while scratching his head. "What's gotten into you?"

Shane spat the words out, "That nigga, Uno, is alive, and he got Little C man!"

"He what? Hold up! What happened?"

"That nigga just called me and said to meet him at a warehouse off Bankhead with a million dollars, at 1:30, or he gone kill Little C, and he said to be alone!"

"Man, I'm going' with you!"

"Man, I'm gonna kill him if he hurts my son."

A tear fell from Shane's eye, as he wondered how could he have let something happen like this. Hassan knew it was time for war.

He told Shane, "Look, Bro, I'm going to grab the change, just in case we need it, and I'm going to get the guns."

"Hassan, I need to do this alone."

"Well, you're not! It's eleven o'clock. We have two and a half hours, so I'll meet you back here in an hour."

Shane shook his head, with his head hanging down.

Hassan said, "Pick your head up. We're going to get Little C!"

CHAPTER 36

When Chanel went to her car to head out for her daily organic salad at the wholefood store, she spotted the note on her windshield. She looked around, as if she was being watched, grabbed the note and proceeded to get into her car.

She started reading the letter:

'Hey, BFF, I am pretty sure you know who this is, since you put me in a crazy house, after shooting me and killing my baby. Now I'm about to kill yours!

If you would like to exchange your life for his, meet me today at 2:00p.m., off Bankhead Road, at the warehouse that sits at the end of the road. I will have 'Chandler' or 'Little C,' as you call him. Oh, and he's not as funny-looking as I thought. If you bring any police, or tell Shane, I will dome the little bastard, before you can call his name!'

Chanel screamed.

She sat in the parking lot crying, praying, and wondering what she should do. She knew Yuri was crazy, and was sure she could hurt Little C. She had to act, and quickly. She was about to put the address in her GPS, but then reconsidered. She reached into her glove box, and took out the .38 Special she'd purchased as soon as she found out that Yuri had left the hospital. Although Chanel thought she had been prepared for anything, she had underestimated that Yuri would go this far.

Chanel didn't call Shane. She planned to get her baby back all by herself, and if that meant she would die in the process, so be it.

CHAPTER 37

Hassan returned. He had two bullet-proof vests, two nine-millimeter hand guns, and a couple of Colt 44 Desert Eagles.

He told Shane, "Let's go get my nephew, and if something happens, Bro, our families are taken care of. We gone get Little C back, and kill Uno's fool ass!" They dapped each other up, hugged, and jumped into the do-dirty car that was registered to a dead man. Their vests were on, and they were on their way to get Little C.

Yuri had gotten there at 1:15p.m., so she could spot Chanel beforehand. As she pulled around to the back of the building, she spotted a blue Honda on the far side of the warehouse. No one appeared to be in it, but it had definitely not been there when she had dropped the nanny off earlier.

Whoever the car belonged to never saw Yuri pull in, because she had entered from the rear gate, the short cut way that the owner had shown her to go for less traffic. At exactly 1:30p.m., another car drove in. Yuri couldn't see who it was through the dark tinted windows. She wondered if Chanel was early, drawing the small slimline subcompact Glock 42 from under her leg, ready to take Chanel out.

The car came closer, and rolled to a stop. The door opened, and out came Shane, carrying a gym bag. Yuri was confused. Questions were fighting for attention inside her head.

What's he doing here? What's going on? Where the fuck is Chanel? Didn't I tell that bitch not to get him involved? As she tried to sort her thoughts, and decide on her next move, she saw Uno on the roof of an adjacent building with what appeared to be a machine gun that looked to have a silencer on it.

She hissed under her breath, "Oh my God!"

Uno started letting off rounds, and Shane began running, because he didn't know where the shots were coming from. Hassan jumped out busting both Desert Eagles in the direction he'd seen and heard the shots fired from. Shane followed Hassan's lead, shooting the same way. Uno ducked, counting their shots, letting Hassan and Shane unload. Once he knew they were empty, Uno came up, shooting once again. Shane ran to the car for cover, reloaded, letting off nineteen straight shots, with both of his nine millimeter Berettas, holding things down as Hassan reloaded.

Yuri couldn't believe what she was witnessing. Both sides had been firing shots for quite a while, but no one had been struck. She hoped they would kill Uno. Her thoughts ricocheted to Jocelyn, and the fact that she had left her handcuffed right by the door, where the gunfire was striking the building.

Uno jumped off the roof, behind a tree, letting the fully automatic machine gun rip. He had come for war, and they knew they couldn't compete with what Uno had going on.

'Sppiiidat dat dat dat!' was the sound they heard.

As they attempted to run to the car. Shane fell to the ground, fast and hard. He was hit. Hassan watched him go down he went crazy, unloading both Desert Eagle forty-fours towards Uno.

Chanel was driving down the block in silence, praying. Once she got close to the warehouse, she heard all the gunfire that sounded like a firework display. She saw a car sitting in the entrance of the warehouse, but there was so much chaos and commotion that she backed away, not knowing that Shane was the one in a gun fight.

As Yuri saw Shane go down, she gasped, and was even more shocked when Uno shot him once more, before Hassan could get to him. She also saw Chanel put her car in reverse, and retreat down the block. Hassan helped Shane into the car and drove away fast.

Yuri was distraught - she remembered how Uno had studied her ransom note; she'd led him straight to Shane!

Uno was also upset, but for different reasons.

He was talking to himself and kicking things. First, because Hassan had put the bag of money back in the car, and second, that he hadn't killed Shane. He knew he had done damage, but the fucker was still alive. Add to that, the fact that Yuri hadn't shown up so he could kill the snake bitch.

Yuri called Chanel, so she wouldn't panic. She said she didn't know what had happened at the warehouse that she'd heard shots fired, as she'd pulled up, so she left. When Chanel heard, Chandler crying in the background, she was flooded with relief.

She quickly blurted, "I didn't call Shane or anyone, Yuri. Just don't hurt him, please!"

Yuri told her to get her panties out of a bunch, stop whining, and meet her at four o'clock, at Welcome All Park, off Camp Creek Parkway. She said she had something to handle, instructing Chanel to go sit by the swings, and she'd exchange Little C for her, knowing that she just planned to kill them both.

Chandler cried out, "I want my Daddy! I want Mommy!" breaking Chanel's heart.

CHAPTER 38

Yuri called Uno. He acted as if what she'd just witnessed had never happened. She told him that she had seen the whole thing, and then followed Hassan. She got him to stop, killed him, then finished Shane off, and got the bag, which contained a lot of money in it. He said, "Thas mine, an' I wan' it!"

"No, it's mine, because I have it! But I'll tell you what, meet me off Welcome All Road, over by the train tracks, and maybe we can talk, and split it, plus I want to fuck," she teased.

Uno agreed immediately, with no hesitation. "I'm on my way!"

He couldn't wait to kill Yuri, and go on with his life. The hell with anymore talking!

Hassan was flying down the road, trying to get Shane to the hospital, before he bled out. One bullet had pierced him in the neck, and he could see another wound on his shoulder. Shane was spitting blood, as he tried to speak. He pulled his wallet and bloody phone from his pocket, handed them to Hassan, slumped against the seat of the car, and took his last breath.

Hassan was so enraged; he didn't know what to do. He continued to the hospital, pulled up to the emergency room doors, he pulled and hauled Shane's lifeless body from the car. He was devastated about his best friend, and was ready to kill anyone who got in his way.

He stared at the gym bag full of money and yelled, "This shit ain't worth it! Damn, Shane! Why did you have to die?!"

Chanel knew she needed Shane. She started calling his phone, and when he didn't answer, she left message after message.

"Shane, I'm going to meet with Yuri. She has Chandler. I should have told you when I received the letter, but I didn't know what to do! I'll be at Welcome All Park, at 4 p.m.," she burst into tears, "If you get this, I need you, Little C needs you! I love you baby."

She cried, and prayed to God to cover her and Chandler with his blood.

She kept repeating a verse from the Bible that her mother had drilled into her head, "No weapons forged against me will prosper, and you will refute and you will refute every tongue that accuse me." She repeated it over and over, as she cried out to the Lord for His mercy and grace.

The time had come; Yuri sat by the train tracks. On her way there, she had run into TJ Maxx and purchased a bag similar to the one she'd seen Shane with. Uno pulled up, faster than ever. He was no longer in the car that he'd driven earlier; this one looked like a rental car.

Uno got out, smoking his blunt, as if nothing had happened, and like nothing was going to happen, in his eyes, the message was clear: *It was time for Yuri to meet her maker!*

Uno got into her vehicle, glancing into the back seat and exclaiming, "Ya still ridin' roun' wit dis lil' nigga? Bitch, ya crazy fo sho! Where da money at, so we kin split it?"

She cut him off, saying sexually, "We can't get together tonight?"

"Hoe is you crazy! Lemme get dat bag!"

"It's back there, on the floor, baby."

As Uno leaned over the seat, simultaneously reaching for the money bag and his gun, Yuri put two slugs into his side with a G 42 Glock. He grabbed his side, not knowing what had just hit him.

Yuri yelled, "That's for messing with my plans fuck nigga! You didn't want to help me with Chanel, but you used my ransom note to lure Shane! That's for me and Shane, you pussy-ass-hoe!"

The bullets had ripped through Uno, his body jerking twice. He never had a chance to get back up. Little C cried frantically as Uno's body slumped over the seat, right in front of him. The loud noises he had heard all day had him holding his hands over his little ears.

Yuri looked at Uno's lifeless body and continued her rant, "I know you were going to try to kill me, but I beat you to it!"

Yuri drove back to the Red Lobster. She grabbed Chandler and his car seat out of the truck. As she exited, she grabbed Tony's clothes out of her car, and put them in side of the truck.

She looked in Uno's direction spitefully saying, "Go to Hell, bitch!"

She got into her car, which she had left the night before. Now it was time to meet with Chanel.

Hassan went back to the trap spot. He had his nephew, Donnie, get rid of the guns and the car. He called his South American cartel connection, and immediately put a two-million-dollar contract out on Uno. His next call was to Chanel, so he could meet up with her, to keep her safe and give her the devastating news. When she didn't answer the call from his phone, he called from Shane's.

CHAPTER 39

The couple walked out of Red Lobster hand in hand. They giggled and kissed like a pair of young love birds. He was tall and stocky, she was slim and petite. He walked her to the passenger door, and happened to glance at the truck parked too close for his liking. It appeared that someone was slumped over in the truck, and it looked strange to him, so he suggested his girlfriend go tell the hostess that there was a man who seemed to be passed out drunk in a truck, and maybe they should check on him. She went in to let them know. They got in their car knowing that the manager in Red Lobster would handle things, then they drove away.

The manager came out eight minutes later, to see if everything was okay. Hoping that one of the customers hadn't drunk too much, he tapped on the window a few times. Hearing nothing, he then put his face up to the light tinted window, looking inside. When he saw that there was blood spattered on the seat, he ran inside to the counter phone, and quickly dialed 9-1-1.

Once the police arrived, they roped off the crime scene, and ran the tag number of the truck. Dispatch told them that it was registered to a Tony Greene, and that the plate was almost the same as the one that the caller had given them back when Sasha's fiancé, Kevin, was killed in the fire. It was off by one number, but the vehicle description was a match. The police automatically put out an APB for Tony Greene, labelling him 'armed and very dangerous'.

While the police were investigating Uno's death, another call came in on their radios. A man collecting cans, off Bankhead Road called in about a shooting he partially witnessed earlier that day, behind a warehouse. He identified the exact same truck, parked along the back side of the building. He had hidden in a hole while all the shooting was going on. When it stopped for a few minutes, he had been afraid to be seen, so he ran into the warehouse for cover. When he pulled the door open, he found a woman, shot several times, in her back and torso. They reported that she was dead, handcuffed to the door. She was like a sitting duck; she never had a chance.

Tony would not only be charged for the murders of Kevin, the next-door neighbor and Uno, but also for Shane and the nanny - a grand total of five.

The police sent a task force squad to Tony's home address. He had just stepped out of the shower, getting ready for a new job, when the door was knocked down.

The officer screamed at Tony as he caught sight of him, "Get on the ground, motherfucker, or I'll put a bullet in the center of your forehead!"

Tony dropped to the floor, not knowing what had happened. Once he was cuffed, the two detectives walked in, read him his rights, and informed him that he was being taken in for several murders. Tony was shocked and confused, asking if he could at least call his mother. The cop told him he would get a call, after he was booked in.

He stared blankly and repeated, "Booked?"

"Yes, you're under arrest. Anything you say can and will be used against you..."

Tony didn't hear much else.

Once at the station, they sat Tony down in a small, cold room. The detectives introduced themselves as Detective Reginald Wallace, and Detective Bobby Ramos. They asked Tony where he had been in the last forty-eight hours, and Tony told them that he had slept the entire last day away.

Detective Wallace asked him, "If you were asleep, then who had your truck?"

Tony didn't know his truck had been gone, he had never even looked. He told the detective that someone must have stolen his truck, because he didn't lend it out to anyone.

Detective Ramos started hollering, "You say that someone stole your truck, but the column was not tampered with! Tell me something else, Mr. Greene. Where were you on the evening of March second?"

Tony tried to think back. "That was a few months ago, I really don't recall."

"Your truck was spotted in Buckhead, at the Lennox Park Condominiums. There was a fire that killed two people that night. Now there are bodies spread all over town! One at the hospital, which was dropped off after your truck was spotted leaving the scene of the crime, one at the warehouse at Bankhead, and one in your truck! You had better start talking, Mr. Greene, because from the way it looks, you'll be facing the fucking death penalty! Now start talking!"

Tony stared from one stone-faced detective to the other, and asked to speak with an attorney.

CHAPTER 40

Chanel drove to Welcome All Park. She prayed the whole way, repeating, "No weapons formed against me shall prosper."

At this point, she didn't care if she lived or died. She would gladly give her life, to keep Chandler alive. When she pulled up, she saw the Lexus sitting on the other side of the park. She jumped out, with her gun in her bag, hoping she wouldn't have to kill Yuri. Once she was halfway through the park, Yuri approached, from behind a tree. She told Chanel to keep walking to the swings.

Chanel stopped. "I won't move another step until I see Chandler." She could barely keep her composure. "What do you want from me, Yuri? I'll give you money, or anything, just tell me!"

"I don't want money, bitch! I want your life! You shot me and caused my baby to die!"

"Yuri, please understand. After I found out what you'd done to Chance, I was devastated, and I lost it! Now I'm pregnant with Shane's child. Please give it the opportunity to make it in this world; to meet his father."

Yuri was pissed.

"You dumb bitch," she screamed. "It looks like your baby will meet Shane in Heaven or Hell, depending on whether he repented before he died."

Chanel felt faint. "Before he what? Did you kill Shane, Yuri?" She whispered, feeling sick.

They both reached for their guns, at the same time, but before either of them could get off a shot, bullets came ringing out at Yuri.

"Bitch, where is Little C?"

Yuri dropped to the ground, dodging the bullets, and started shooting at her car.

She screamed, "If I'm going to die, so is he!"

Chanel looked at the Lexus and shrieked, "Don't do it, Yuri!"

Hassan was shooting, aiming straight for Yuri's head.

CHAPTER 41

The attorney went into the interrogation room to speak with Tony. He explained to him that he was looking at no bond if he didn't confess to all the murders. He also said he'd most definitely be facing the death penalty. Tony took a deep breath, like a man approaching the gallows, and told Mr. Summer that he had set the fire at the condominium complex. He explained how he'd met Angel, and how she had some sort of spell over him; that she'd laced his weed with PCP, and dissolved pills in his drinks.

Tony told Mr. Summer that he had fallen deeply in love with Angel, and that when she told him about how her ex-boyfriend was threatening to kill the two of them, he lost it. High on LSD, liquor and pills, and tired of living with the constant threats, he went to where she told him the boyfriend lived and threw the cocktails into the condo.

Mr. Summer sighed and shook his head. "Well, one of the guys was a software genius, and the other was a retired firefighter. Both were white men, well-respected, and pillars of the community. Sorry to say, but you'd have done better to have copped to killing the two black men, and the Spanish woman, who died earlier today. The ones you said you had nothing to do with. You know how it goes when you kill a Caucasian, and you killed two."

"A white guy? She said he was a thug, and a gangsta! She neva said he was white. Ah'm sorry. Angel had me brainwashed an' in love. She fucked up my mind."

"That's her name? Angel?"

"Yup."

"What's her last name?"

"I don' know."

Mr. Summer hammered, "You don't know? Holy shit, Mr. Greene! She had your nose that wide open? Where does she live?"

"I dunno tha' eitha. We always useta meet at the motel, or ma house. Actually, she was the las' person aroun' b'foe ah pass't out."

The lawyer couldn't believe anyone could be such a sucker! "Do you have a picture of her, at least?"

"I gats one in ma phone. It's not a good one. She wuz comin' out da store, an' ah snapt it.

The detective thought, *he's as dumb as he sounds.*

"I'm going to go try to get your phone out of your property, to look at it, if they'll give me permission ..."

"Tha's fine, it's ma screen saver, so as soon as ya turn it on, Angel will pop up."

"Is that the only picture you have of her, on your phone?"

"Yup. It's da only one I gots. But I still wonta see my lawyer."

Mr. Summer had been in the room for what seemed like forever. When he exited, he saw his buddy, Detective Wallace.

They shook hands. "How's it going, Reggie?"

"Man, it's been a crazy day, Sam!"

"I see; you missed our morning workout."

"I had a ton of work last night, and then all these murders popped up."

"Look, I need my client's phone, out of his property. Can you sneak it out, for just a couple of minutes?"

"Sam, you always want me to do something illegal for you."

Sam laughed and patted his friend on the back, "Look Reggie, this Tony guy says that his girlfriend, whose last name he doesn't even know, or her address, for that matter, had him kill the people at the condos a few months back."

"So, what about all these bodies from today?"

"I really don't think he had anything to do with those, and that's off the record, Reggie."

"I know, Sam. So, what does the phone have to do with all of this?"

"Man, he says he has a picture of her on his phone; the only picture. I want to see what this woman looks like, to make him kill for her."

Reggie shook his head, saying, "She must have put it on his big country ass!"

They laughed in agreement.

"Give me a couple of minutes; let me see what I can do."

Once Detective Wallace returned, he handed the phone to Sam.

As he turned it on he exclaimed, "Damn! No wonder she had his head in the clouds. She's sexy as hell! Big Country isn't even in her league. She had to be selling him a dream, Reggie, just to get him to do what she wanted."

"Man, let me see her," Detective Wallace moved closer.

Sam passed the phone to him. He looked the photo over and examined it hard for nearly a minute, looking strange.

Sam commented, "Dang Reg, you're studying it like you know her."

"What's her name again?" Reggie asked.

"It's Angel, but shit, who knows, that may just be what Mr. Greene knows her as."

Reggie couldn't take his eyes off her. "Yeah, she is a looker, Sam."

"Okay Reggie, let me go talk to him some more, and see what else this fool knows."

Detective Wallace looked at Yuri once again. He had not seen her since the day he had driven her to the hospital. Somehow, she had disappeared without a trace. Even being a detective, he couldn't find her. She was like a chameleon, adept at blending in and becoming one with her environment. He rushed to the phone and called the hospital, inquiring as to whether they had a name on the deceased John Doe yet. The doctor told him they didn't, but that the inscription engraved on the inside of his ring read, "Shane and Chanel."

He hung up quickly thinking, *Shane was about to marry Chanel?*

Now he was sure that the picture was definitely Yuri.

He wondered where she had been, and more than anything, what she was up to. He knew how she had deceived Shane. He grabbed his suit coat jacket and jumped in his car, ready to do some investigating of his own. Detective Wallace had never stopped loving Yuri, and now he wanted to find her before something terrible happened to her, once again.

He'd put two and two together. He thought about the news that had been flashing sketches of the alleged woman who had cut off a doctor's penis at a motel, several months back. The doctor reported that he had stopped to eat at a Waffle House, when a lady who had been sitting at a nearby booth came over to talk to him. The story he told was that she drugged his drink, took him to a room, and cut off his prized possession. Reggie knew, now, there must be more to that story; the sketch was definitely of Yuri.

He called in for Doctor Snider's address, turned on his car's siren, and made his way to Love Joy.

When he got to Doctor Snider's home, he finished up on his call. He'd gotten the lowdown on the doctor's background. He found out about all the sexual allegations that he had inflicted upon his patients at the mental hospital. He didn't know where Yuri fit in, but it was time to pick Doctor Snider for everything he knew.

He rang the doorbell once. After a couple of minutes, no one answered. The Benz that was registered to Gary Snider was parked in the driveway. Detective Wallace rang the bell a few more times, losing his patience, he banged on the door. He heard a voice yell out, "Who is it?"

"Dr. Snider, my name is Detective Reginald Wallace. I'm here to ask you a few questions, concerning your issues at the hospital."

Doctor Snider screamed through the closed door, "Talk to my attorney, unless you have a warrant!"

"I don't think you want me to do that, because you're not being honest with him about Yuri Jones." Reggie responded calmly, in a patronizing tone of voice.

The door opened rapidly. "How do you know about Yuri Jones? I never said her name, just gave a sketch."

"Sir, I had a run in with her before, and I told her she looked familiar. She swore to me she didn't, but I was sure of it, and warned her that if I found out why and where I knew her from, I would bust her ass! She told me to fuck off, because she knew I couldn't hold her for the crime she'd committed, due to a lack of evidence. Then she did something even worse, which I can't talk about."

"Detective, if I'm talking to you without my attorney, I want to know what she did, and whatever I tell you, can't be used against me. If you can assure me of that, and not write down or tape record anything, we can speak."

"Doctor, as badly as I want to catch her, and lock her up, you don't have to worry."

"Well, first of all, I assume you've been watching the news, and have read all the papers concerning my case?"

"Yes, about how you were fondling and having sex with all those female patients?"

"I can't say 'all' because they are exaggerating, and anyway, I want to hear your story first."

Without hesitation, Detective Wallace went into a story about how Yuri had cut another man's penis off, but she had him so terrified, that he wouldn't talk.

"The crazy part about it is, he's my cousin, and he won't even talk to me! Any bitch who's crazy enough to run around cutting off dicks, needs to be locked up, killed, or stopped somehow!"

As Detective Wallace spoke, Doctor Snider got angrier and angrier.

He burst out crying. "I want to kill that nigger bitch!"

With an even tone, Reggie responded, "Hold up! Don't you ever say that word again, or we'll have serious problems!"

"I'm sorry, Detective," Doctor Snider apologized, with tears streaming down his face, "It's just that she destroyed my whole life! My wife has left me, and I can't have sex!"

Reggie thought, *that's what you get, asshole, for raping all those unconscious, helpless patients,* but what he actually said was, "So, how did you really meet Yuri, Doctor?"

"Well, it was over a year and a half ago. A woman arrived, and admitted her into the hospital. I believe they paid a large sum of money to keep her identity hidden, as if someone dangerous was looking for her, and that's exactly what the Hospital did. Patient confidentiality. Somehow she ended up on my floor, where the patients may not be all that crazy, but by the time they leave, they're total fruitcakes! Anyway, I'll confess that a couple of times I did touch her."

"You just touched her, Doctor?"

"That's all I'm saying, Detective. However, somehow Ms. Jones had charmed the young male nurse. She had been hiding her pills, and he must have made one wrong move, and she drugged his coffee. The hospital never sent out a Missing Person's Report, or filed an Escape Notification, since they were still being paid, under the table, and probably still are."

"So, the people who admitted her were never notified as well?"

"They just kept collecting the monthly payments, so while I'm going through this, they are, too, because I have a lawsuit against them."

"Go on with the story, Doc."

Doctor Snider lit his third cigarette in fifteen minutes shaking like an old beat up truck.

He pulled on it hard, continuing his story. "So, after a few months of her being gone, I was hooking up at the motel that was by the Waffle House off Eagles Landing, with a young lady named Sasha. She was a meth head who needed a friend. Her parents had thrown her out, so when things were not going well at home, with my wife-"

"Or at the hospital?" Reggie cut in sarcastically.

Doctor Snider put his head down shamefully. He hit the cigarette down to the butt. "So, I would have sex with her, and pay her hotel fees. Ms. Jones must have been following me. Somehow she met and manipulated Sasha to turn against me."

"You must not have treated Sasha right, either, Doc, I mean look at this house. It's immaculate, and it's worth what, a few million, and you were gentleman enough to pay for her to live in a sleazy motel?"

"Hey, she could have gotten more, had she asked. That's all she wanted. A closed mouth doesn't get fed, right Detective?"

Reggie tried to hide his disgust. "Back to the story, Doctor."

"Sasha drugged my coffee. When I woke up, I was handcuffed, with Ms. Jones sitting on my face."

He smiled devilishly, as if remembering a favorite scene in a movie.

"What do you mean, 'sitting on your face'?"

"She had her vagina in my mouth, letting me taste her wet, juicy…"

He stopped smiling when he saw the look on the detective's face. He couldn't read it, but it was a strong emotion. Doctor Snider thought 'revulsion,' when in actuality, it was guarded lust. Detective Wallace was remembering the taste of those same wet juices in his mouth. He realized the doctor had stopped speaking, and snapped out of his lustful reverie.

"Continue," he growled.

"Well, once she got me aroused, she jumped off, grabbed a scalpel, and severed it completely! Detective, she knew what she was doing, and which vein to avoid, so I would suffer all the pain, but not die! I was in so much pain! Can you believe the psycho bitch just laughed and kicked me a few times, as I writhed in agony?!"

Detective Wallace wanted to burst out laughing, but he knew he had to maintain his composure, "Then what?"

She un-cuffed me, threw it at me, and ran out! I chased them, with my penis in my hand, but I was in a lot of pain, once when I ran outside, I tripped over the dog from next door, and dropped it!"

"You dropped what? Your penis?"

"Yes, and the dog grabbed it, and tried to eat it!"

"What? So how did you get it back?"

"We scuffled over it, but he had chewed on it so much, that they couldn't put it right back on! Now I'm paying for numerous surgeries to get it back right."

"Get it right, Doc?"

"Yes, Detective, I'm spending my entire life's savings, trying to get a new one."

Detective Wallace couldn't hold his laughter back any longer; it came pouring out. Doctor Snider was annoyed.

"Detective, I don't think it's funny! I can't make love to anyone, nor do I have anything to jack off but a fucking nub!"

"So, it looks like you have a vagina down there, huh?" The detective knew he had to be professional and pull himself together. "I'm sorry, Doctor. Have you heard anything else from either one of them?"

"I saw Sasha on the news, a few months back. She was pregnant, and talking about how someone had set fire to her condo in Buckhead. Her fiancé was killed, and so was another businessman that lived next door, if I'm not mistaken."

Detective Wallace thought about what Tony's attorney had told him, concerning Tony's confession about setting the Buckhead fires. Now it was time to go. "Thanks, Doctor Snider. All I can say is, you got what you deserved, you sick-ass pervert!"

Doctor Snider looked nervous, feeling uncomfortable.

Detective Wallace leaned in closer and spat, "You're lucky none of those victims were my family members, because I would have cut your dick and balls off, and shoved them up your punk-ass!"

As he was walking out, he looked back, saying, "You're cursed for life."

Doctor Snider lit another cigarette with shaking hands as he watched the car drive away.

Detective Wallace got a call about a shooting that was taking place on the South Side, not far from where Uno's body was recovered. He jumped on 75 North, speeding towards Highway 285.

Yuri had shot the last bullet from her gun. She used three shooting at the car, and the rest at Hassan and Chanel. Once she saw Hassan, Chanel told him not to shoot at Yuri by the car, because Little C was in it. Hassan screamed out, "Yuri, come out from behind the car!"

"No! I'm going to put nine more bullets into this trunk, if you walk over here!" Yuri yelled back. They knew she would. What they didn't know was that she was out of bullets.

Yuri heard Chandler crying like he was hurt, and so she screamed, "Hassan, let me get in the car and check on the kid; he's screaming. You probably shot him."

Hassan hollered, "Bitch, you're the only one who shot that way, and if he's not okay, bitch, I'm gone kill your whole family in D.C.!"

"Fuck my family! My mom hates me anyway, so kill the bitch!"

Hassan yelled, "You're an uncaring, senseless bitch!"

Yuri lifted the gun to the window, where Chandler sat. She called to Hassan again, "Now, let me get in the car, or when you kill me, he'll die, too!"

Sirens sounded like they were coming from all directions. Hassan told Chanel, "Come on, we have to get out of here!"

"I can't leave Little C!" Chanel cried.

"You have to, ma. Shane is dead, and if we don't get out of here, we'll be caught up in a lot of shit!" He grabbed her by the arm and led her to her car, instructing her to follow him through a back way that he knew. She looked back at Yuri, and the Lexus, and did as Hassan told her.

Once Yuri saw them get into their cars and drive away, she jumped into hers. She glanced over her shoulder at Little C, and realized that he was unconscious. She started the car, wondering where she should take him, or what she should do. She wished she'd have given him to Chanel now that she knew he was shot. Just as she was about to drive off, she was surrounded by police cars, blocking every possible escape route.

They told her to put her hands up, and as she did, she screamed, "There's a toddler in the back seat! He's been shot, please help him!"

As the first officer got close enough to the vehicle to see inside, he saw the Glock 42 on the seat, next to Yuri, he yelled, "Keep those hands up, where I can see them or I'll kill you!"

He opened her door and snatched her out of the car, onto the ground, in one swift motion. The paramedics screeched to a stop, took Chandler out of his car seat, and placed him on the ground, to perform CPR on his small body.

"I have a heartbeat! He's been shot in the leg. We need to get him to the hospital as soon as possible, he's losing a lot of blood," she reported.

They hooked him up to oxygen and various other vital sign measuring devices, and drove off, sirens blaring.

Police were everywhere. Detective Wallace had finally pulled up. Since he was the lead homicide and armed robbery detective, he would definitely be assigned to the case.

He asked the responding officers what was going on. They told him that they had a lady in her mid-twenties, who had a fake Missouri ID. She said she wanted to speak to an attorney, so they hadn't gotten anything out of her.

"Did I hear that a child was shot?" He asked.

"Yes, Sir, they just rushed him to Atlanta Children's Medical. It appears that he was shot in the leg, and had lost a fair amount of blood. He was alive when they pulled off. Also, Detective, there are three different kinds of bullet casings around, but all we found was a 42 Glock on the suspect."

"Where is she?"

"She's in the back of squad car 59, waiting for a wagon."

Detective Wallace thanked the young officer. He walked over to the car. There sat Yuri. When she looked up and saw him, she shook her head unapologetically. Detective Wallace felt sorry for the beautiful woman he once loved, but he felt worse for the child, who was fighting for his life. He walked away, knowing he'd have a chance to speak with her at the station.

CHAPTER 42

Once Hassan got Chanel to his home, he took her gun. His nephew was waiting to get rid of both of their weapons. Hassan's wife had already heard about Shane and Chandler. She hugged Chanel and told her everything would be okay.

She cried out vulnerably, "How? How is anything ever going to be okay, when I've lost the love of my life, and she has my son, who I don't know if he's dead or alive?"

"God will take care of Little C. I have some bath water running for you. I need you to soak in it, so we can get all the gun powder off you, and baby, you go get in the shower, also." Dana said.

Hassan had poured himself a double shot of Remy Martin, and downed it.

He poured one more and held the glass up. "This is for you, Shane, my brotha."

Chanel slid way down into the tub and she cried out to God for strength. She reached for her phone and called her parents, telling them everything except that Yuri was the one who caused all the havoc. They said they were on their way, catching the next plane smoking.

Dana had already called Shane's parents. They were also on their way from Los Angeles.

She had called Mr. Mitchell, knowing that Jamille, Shane's mother wouldn't be thinking rationally upon hearing about the death of her only child, whom she loved unconditionally.

Chanel used her toes to add more hot water to the tub then turned on the 23" television, hanging in the corner of the bathroom. The 6:30 p.m. news was on. It was crazy, because she now learned that a Spanish woman in her thirties had been killed, but they couldn't release her name until someone identified her body; a black male was found in a truck, murdered, and a child was shot, and taken to the hospital, in critical condition. Her child! She sniffled, and wrapped her arms around herself, bracing for what she knew was next. A dead man was identified a few hours ago, as Shane Mitchell of Los Angeles, California. She cried out, sobbing uncontrollably. Dana had gone to identify him. She and Hassan were his family, too. Dana came running in the restroom. She hugged Chanel, rocking her, as she sat in the tub. She washed Chanel's back, brought her a bath towel, gave her two pills to take, and sang, 'Precious Lord'.

Nothing would ever be the same. The life Chanel had envisioned for herself would never be.

CHAPTER 43

The first thing they did when Yuri arrived at the station was fingerprint her, since she refused to give her real name. After a few hours of useless interrogation, she asked to call her attorney. They gave her one call, which she used to telephone her father. Mike answered on the second ring. She cried, "Daddy, I've been arrested, and I need you to call Steward Burns, to try to help me get out."

"What have you done, Yuri?"

"Nothing, I was just caught up with the wrong people. Daddy, this is the only phone call I will get, since they found a gun in my possession."

"A gun?" Mike yelled, "Oh my God, angel! I'll call him right now. He'll be there in the morning. Don't you say a word"

"Thank you, Daddy, I love you!"

"I love you, too Angel!"

"Daddy, please don't call Mom, until we see what's going on."

"You got it. Love you."

As they hung up, Detective Wallace walked up to her.

"Can I speak with you?" He asked.

Yuri looked up at him and responded, "When my lawyer arrives."

He whispered, "Your prints are already back, and they know your real name. They also have a guy here, by the name of Tony Greene, who will be identifying you in a line-up, first thing tomorrow morning."

Yuri knew he wasn't lying about Tony, because she had tried to pin all the murders on him, expecting to totally get away.

"Identify me for what?" She asked.

"He said you put him up to killing the two men, back in March at the Lennox Park Condos."

"He's lying. I don't even know him."

"If he didn't have a picture of you, on his phone, coming out of a Kroger grocery store, maybe you could go with that."

Yuri didn't know about the picture.

"Look Reggie, between you and me, I ran away from a crazy hospital, and that guy picked me up. He was running around, killing on his own." She said.

"Yuri, you better come up with some better lies, because they're getting that girl, Sarah, to come in, too. She has already made a statement against you."

"Sarah who?" Yuri feigned innocence.

"The one you had helped you cut off Doctor Snider's penis," Detective Wallace answered while watching her every reaction.

Yuri knew she had to speak with her attorney. From the sound of it, she was up Shit's Creek.

Detective Wallace leaned in close enough for her to smell his cologne, and whispered, "I still love you, but this time I can't help you."

He walked out, feeling no remorse for her. He assigned the new Junior Detective to the case. Yuri was taken to her cell.

She tossed and turned on the uncomfortable metal slab, with no cushion, that smelled of stale urine and body odor, wondering what would happen tomorrow.

CHAPTER 44

Chanel's and Shane's parents had arrived. They had to prepare to take Shane's body back to L.A. Jamille couldn't stop crying. She worked herself into such a state that she suffered a minor stroke, and had to be admitted to the hospital for observation and tests. They expected to release her in a day or two.

Chanel had spoken to the detectives about Chandler and Shane, while both of her attorneys were present. Hassan had discussed everything and gone over and over it with her. He even had her rehearse the lines before she spoke with her lawyers. She explained to them how Yuri had kidnapped Chandler, she didn't actually know from where, she just knew it was sometime before Jocelyn was supposed to drop him at school. She told them what the ransom note had stated and also handed it over to the detective. She didn't have a clue of how Shane had ended up at the warehouse, because Yuri's letter specifically instructed her not to involve Shane, so she'd kept her mouth shut, trying to save her son's life. They told her that Jocelyn's body had been riddled with bullets from several different guns.

Chanel's heart was hurting for Shane, Jocelyn, and Chandler. Even though Little C was still alive, she needed to feel him in her arms. Chanel started crying, wondering what she would tell Jocelyn's family. Even though she was a nanny, she had a wicked family. Chanel knew they would try to avenge her death, just on the strength that she had been killed execution-style. Chanel was already thinking that she would wire a million dollars to them in Honduras, but the money wouldn't matter to them; they'd want blood.

The detectives had asked who killed Shane. Hassan had already told her about the gangster-style shoot-out, and how Uno had gunned Shane down. Chanel told them that she didn't know, and that it was their job to find out. For all she knew, Yuri had set him up, and killed him; but whatever the case might be, Shane was dead, and someone would have to pay.

The detectives told Chanel that they would be contacting her, as soon as they received more leads. Chanel and her attorneys left. Before they parted, the female lawyer, Jessica James, reminded her not to speak one single word to anyone, unless they were present.

Hassan was waiting for Chanel outside. He asked her how she thought it went.

She began to cry as she choked out the words. "Everything is fucked up! They killed my fiancé, and my nanny, and Lord knows if my baby is going to live! I hate that bitch, Yuri! I should have killed her! I want to kill her snake-ass!"

She dissolved into convulsive sobs. Chanel had never felt this much pain. She was frightened for Chandler and bewildered about the whole situation.

Hassan hugged Chanel, saying, "Calm down, sis, your boy is going to be alright."

Chanel tried to control her emotions, but couldn't. She had a pain in her heart that only a mother and a widow could understand and feel. Her phone rang. It was Shane's father. She tried to hide her tearful gasps, but just seeing his name made her cry.

When she answered, Mr. Mitchell said, "Hello, Dear, it's okay, stop crying."

She told him she had just left the detectives, and that she still had to get back to check on Little C.

Mr. Mitchell tried to reassure her. "My grandson will be okay. My wife never liked that Yuri, but I never expected things to play out like this, to confirm what she'd been feeling all along. I should have paid closer attention. My wife's sixth sense is never wrong. If I had listened to her, maybe my son wouldn't be on his way back to California in a body bag, and my grandchild wouldn't be in the hospital, fighting for his life." He paused, as if deep in thought, then continued,

"Chanel, Shane's body will be shipped back on Monday, and the funeral will be on Wednesday."

Only a few days had passed, but the Mitchell's didn't want to waste any time laying their beloved child to rest. As soon as Jamille was released from the hospital, they would be boarding a jet, taking their baby home, the way he liked to travel. Chanel told him that she understood, but she would not attend, if Chandler had not come out of his coma. He also understood her love for her only child. He was all she had left. Even though her parents said they'd stay with Chandler, and Hassan offered to fly her back and forth in one day, in a G-5, so she could at least be in L.A. for the funeral, then back by Little C's hospital bed. She couldn't imagine leaving him lying there alone helplessly.

Hassan and his wife, Dana, would be there. Shane was Hassan's best friend and business partner. Hassan had five million dollars or more of Shane's money. He was not going to keep one dime of it. One million would go into a college trust fund for Chandler, Chanel would get a couple of million, and Shane's parents would get the rest. That didn't include the money from all Shane's properties, which were worth well over another five million dollars.

Hassan had one thing on his mind, to kill Yuri. Then he would give up the drug life, and be with his wife and kids. He wanted to sneak into the police station, and blow her head off right away.

Yuri's attorney, Steward Burns was getting irritated with her. She had already told him three different stories, making him feel that he didn't want to represent a liar. Yuri thought it was a game, but the truth of the matter was, she was facing a lot of time, if not the death penalty.

In the month that had passed, Tony had identified her as the person who gave him the PCP, and led him to the condominiums, the night he killed the two men in Buckhead. He also told them that the night before all the other murders, she had drugged him, and stolen his truck. They knew Tony was telling the truth, but he was still going to prison for killing the two very rich white men. He would be sentenced twenty to life. Yuri tried blaming Tony for everything, but it wasn't working. Her attorney said she may could get self-defense for Uno, since he had reached for his gun first, and that they'd also found the machine gun in his car, which he had murdered Shane with. Jocelyn had been riddled with so many bullets; they didn't know who to charge with her murder. Even though all the shooters were dead, she thought she had it good, sitting in the jail like she was invincible.

The following morning, Yuri was woken up by being charged with first-degree murder and accessory to the two men in Buckhead. She asked her attorney, "How the fuck are they gonna charge me with first-degree murder, when the bitch-nigga was going to smoke me first?"

The lawyer explained that it wasn't for Uno, he explained, "The little boy died, Ms. Jones, and the 42 Glock that the police caught you with? That's the gun that murdered him. I thought I would share that with you before I resign from being your counsel. You are a sick young lady. You've told me so many different stories, that there's no way I could represent you. Good luck, you're going to need it."

He walked out shaking his head.

Yuri went straight into crazy mode, knowing she had fucked up royally. Mike had paid the attorney a twenty-five thousand dollar retainer fee, which he gave straight back to him, warning Mike that the only thing he could tell him was that his psychotic daughter should plead insanity, especially since it was documented that she had escaped from the mental hospital. He said it was the only thing that could save her from losing her life.

CHAPTER 45

Chanel did end up flying out to California to attend Shane's funeral. She couldn't miss it. Her parents and Yuri's mother, Barbra, stayed at the hospital in Atlanta with Chandler. They kept 24-hour vigil at his bedside, praying and praying that he would wake up, but God had other plans. Exactly one month later, Chanel was back in L.A., burying Little C next to Shane and Spida. It was the saddest thing she'd ever experienced, seeing the tiny casket lowered into the ground. The bullet from the Glock had torn his small fragile leg apart, hitting a major blood vessel. He tried to fight, but the battle was the Lord's. He wanted his angle not to suffer.

During the following few months, they had to take Yuri out of general population. A lot of women wanted to hurt her for killing a child. She stayed in a secluded unit, in solitary confinement. When she was able to get an hour out of her cell, she watched the news talk about her high-profile trial coming up, and how crazy she was. She alternated between laughing and screaming at the T.V, "Fuck you! I'm not crazy, bitch!"

Even the other crazy women hated her.

Yuri did all kinds of crazy things, even in court, which proved that she was totally insane. She played with herself, she blurted out nonsensical words that were completely out of context she stared off into space, or picked at her skin.

When the shrink came to evaluate her, she had so many issues, they had no choice but to pack her out of the jail, and send her to a mental institution. She was locked into a padded cell, 24/7. She wasn't allowed out at all.

Chanel finally got up the nerve and guts to confront Yuri. She signed in, and sat down, waiting for them to bring Yuri into the small, monitored, visiting room. When she was led in, Chanel wasn't prepared for what she saw. Yuri was strapped into a white straight-jacket, like something out of a television show. She didn't think those things existed. She was also shackled, like the psychopath she was. Her hair had all been cut off, because she kept pulling it out when her hands were not bound, and her face had broken out terribly, from all times she picked at her skin with unclean hands. They sat down with the table between them.

"Hello, Yuri."

"Why are you here, and what do you want?"

"I just wanted to ask you if it was worth it. Look at you, you're a mess! You killed my brother, you slept with your mother's husband, and then you had a good, no, *great* man, who you never loved or appreciated, who gave you everything, and this is the thanks he gets? The worst part is all the deception, lies, and cover-ups! That guy I saw, that night at the club, twice, was your lover, who got you into all this!"

Yuri said nothing, but smiled when she brought up Uno.

"Yuri, answer one thing, did you kill Candice?"

Yuri looked her right in the eye and answered, "No, Uno did."

Chanel dropped her head into her hands, tears and fury spilling over, "Yuri, you destroyed so many lives! I hope you die here!"

Yuri chuckled, as if from far way and said, "I don't care about dying, and you shouldn't either. We all have to go some time or another and I wouldn't have turned out like this, if you hadn't murdered my baby!" She was escalating. "That's why I killed your son, so you would know how it feels!"

Yuri was shaking, angry, feeling betrayed.

"Yuri," Chanel smiled slightly, but remained calm. "My son, Shane Mitchell Jr will be born in two months. She opened her jacket, displaying a round stomach, which she rubbed as she responded in and angry, but even tone, "Chandler was your son Yuri, and you murdered him. All that time you had him, you didn't look at him? He didn't look anything like Shane. He didn't have any similarities to me, or anyone in my family. Think about it. He looked like Spida, and your Father. That's why I let Mr. Mitchell bury him with Shane and Spida."

Yuri thought about Little C's eyes. She knew that she had seen someone in him, but was too vengeful to recognize it.

Chanel gave her a minute to ponder the possibility then continued. "I was going to give him back to you, once you had got yourself back together, but you broke out of the hospital, and we didn't know, until it was too late. I was going to do the right thing. I loved you, Yuri, you were my best friend, and out of jealousy and envy, look how things turned out."

That was all the composure Chanel could maintain. She stood up, tears streaming down her face, as she backed towards the door.

She gulped air, as she choked the words out, "So now you know. Chandler was your blood! Your son and you killed him! I hope you go crazy, for real thinking about it! I hope he haunts you in your sleep, and that the truth seeps in deep so while you're playing crazy, the reality of what you've done drives you insane. You're a sick snake bitch! Maybe you'll even find a way to kill yourself, but who cares? I thought I would never say this to anyone, but *I hate you*! You're the Devil!"

"No!" Yuri screamed like a wounded animal, foaming at the mouth. The nurse came running in, and as her mouth continued to lather, Chanel pointed at her and repeated the Bible verse, "No weapons formed against me shall prosper!"

As the doctor and nurse tried to calm Yuri, with a shot, Chanel put her Chanel shades on, and walked away, rubbing her stomach, ready to head back to Maryland with her family.

Yuri fought and screamed, until she was fully sedated. When she woke up, sometime the next day, she thought about everything Chanel had told her. She closed her eyes and remembered Little C's eyes and nose, which resembled her Dad's. She struggled to free herself from the arm and leg restraints, so she could kill herself.

She cried out, "I hate you Chanel! You made me kill my baby!"

Her conscience decided to kick in, responding, *Hate yourself! Like she said, you had the perfect life, a great family, and a good man, but you chose evil over goodness. Now you'll pay.*

Yuri screamed, "No! Shut up! I want to die!" The voice was still there, taunting, *Die then, snake bitch.*

Yuri was finally sentenced to life in a mental institution. Had she not plead insanity, she would have been killed by lethal injection, which would have been much easier on her, in the long run. Barbra never showed up at court. After she heard about Yuri on every radio and television station, she turned to she wondered where she went wrong. She'd given Yuri the world, and now her child was on every National television station in the world, breaking her heart. Mike forced himself to show up, no matter how painful the proceedings got. It was difficult, watching his daughter get sentenced, smiling, with no hair, looking nutty as a fruitcake; a tear dripped down his stubbed cheek. He prayed, *Lord, be with my child.*

Yuri looked back at him, as the judge finished up, she called out, "Hey Daddy, I killed my son, but I didn't know he was mine, but don't worry, I'm gone have you another one."

He cried, uncontrollably, as they led her out of the courtroom, happy as she could be.

The End

Epilogue

Yuri's back ... with a vengeance!!!

The girl you loved to hate in *Yearning for Yuri* is crazier than ever, and bent on revenge! Nothing can stop her, until everyone on her list is dealt with - no one is safe from her fury! No matter how old or young, whether she's known them a short time, or for a lifetime! No limits, no feelings, no conscience!

This is a book you won't be able to put down. You'll gasp and cover your eyes, while peeking through your fingers, because you need to know what happens next. When you read it, you'll be shocked, and intrigued! Sex, drugs, murder, sugar daddies, high rollers, and more! Prepare to be entertained, frightened, aroused, and surprised! When you get to the last page, you'll wish there were another hundred! Enjoy!

ABOUT THE AUTHOR

Demetria 'Mimi' Harrison is the mother of three and grandmother to seven lovely grandchildren. Ms. Harrison has written two books, previously, *She's Just Like Me*, and *Yearning for Yuri*. This is the sequel, *Yuri's Vengeance*, with many more to follow. It will certainly not be her last literary endeavor. She plans on delivering a wide selection of books to you, for your reading pleasure.

Mimi is currently a Florida resident. She engages daily in activities to grow and challenge herself. She is taking college classes at Daytona State College for Business Management, as well as a Publishing and Writing course. She engages in anything that helps to keep her focused on her goals. With support from her family, friends, fans, and the Highest, her Father God, on her side, she continues her quest to achieve literary greatness.

While incarcerated, writing and exercising had been very therapeutic activities. Each new novel, with an ever-expanding cast of characters, seeks to draw the reader in, so they feel like part of the book, becoming emotionally involved with the plots and players.

We are quite sure you will enjoy this book, and watch for future novels by Demetria 'Mimi' Harrison.

Write the Author - mimi@bossstatuspublishing.com
Visit www.bossstatuspublishing.com for her latest releases, merchandise, apparel, and where to find Mimi next.

"There's no greater agony than bearing an untold story inside you"

Maya Angelou

Write a book and leave a legacy!

Visit our site @ www.BossStatusPublishing.com and choose one of our affordable packages...today!!